ATOMIC FAMILY

Atomic Family

A Novel

CIERA HORTON McELROY

—BLAIR—

Printed in the United States of America
Cover design by Laura Williams
Interior design by April Leidig

Blair is an imprint of Carolina Wren Press.

The mission of Blair/Carolina Wren Press is to seek out, nurture, and
promote literary work by new and underrepresented writers.

We gratefully acknowledge the ongoing support of general operations by the Durham
Arts Council's United Arts Fund and the North Carolina Arts Council.

This novel is a work of fiction. As in all fiction, the literary perceptions and
insights are based on experience; however, all names, characters, places, and incidents
are either products of the author's imagination or are used fictitiously. No reference
to any real person is intended or should be inferred.

Library of Congress Cataloging-in-Publication Data
Names: McElroy, Ciera Horton, 1995– author.
Title: Atomic family : a novel / Ciera Horton McElroy.
Description: Durham : Blair, [2022]
Identifiers: LCCN 2022025122 (print) | LCCN 2022025123 (ebook) |
ISBN 9781949467949 (hardcover) | ISBN 9781949467956 (ebook)
Subjects: LCGFT: Novels.
Classification: LCC PS3613.C4226 A94 2022 (print) |
LCC PS3613.C4226 (ebook) | DDC 813/.6—dc23/eng/20220525
LC record available at https://lccn.loc.gov/2022025122
LC ebook record available at https://lccn.loc.gov/2022025123

For Mitchell and Foster
And for Dad, of course

PART I

Today, every inhabitant of this planet must contemplate the day
when this planet may no longer be habitable. Every man, woman
and child lives under a nuclear sword of Damocles, hanging by
the slenderest of threads, capable of being cut at any moment
by accident or miscalculation or by madness. The weapons of war
must be abolished before they abolish us.
—John F. Kennedy, Address before the United Nations, 1961

Do I love this world so well
That I have to know how it ends?
—W. H. Auden, *The Age of Anxiety*

FIRST, THERE IS THE PLANE. The boy watches from the water tower, using his binoculars for a closer look. It moves slowly, widens like an ink spill. The sky is gray, the light pale.

This is November 1, 1961. A Wednesday.

Below him, the boy can see the whole town. The houses are brick and uniform. South Carolina flags flap blue and white in the wind. Pumpkins still smile from porches, and paper lanterns lie abandoned on the sidewalks, crumpled now and singed. A procession of women marches down Main Street. They're wearing black and carrying signs.

On the edge of town is the bomb plant, all cement, steel, and smoke, with men in hard hats, men with briefcases, men in army vests with guns strapped to their backs. Past the barbed perimeter, down the snaking river, vapor dissolves over the cypress trees like breath in cold air.

The steam is a steady cloud that cups the town.

When the plane passes, its pewter belly low in the sky, there is a roar, then a cavity of quiet. But what the protesters will remember are the birds: that shock of frightened plovers. The women lower their pickets, pause with their baby carriages. They watch the gray clouds shift above them, see the ruffle of white and brown feathers as the birds lift into the sky. They return their gaze to the courthouse, where a woman in black stands warning about nuclear war.

Just below the boy is a schoolyard, brick and columned. The water tower rises to the sky like a watchman along the school's fenced wall. This is where the children stand screaming, pointing up. They see his little brown head, far above them, barely discernible at the tower's edge. He watches the plane.

It's only a passenger plane, heading to Atlanta. But the boy perched on the water tower does not know this. Their town is the site of a bomb plant, he knows. Their town is a target.

He is a small boy—he is an odd one. And when he falls, his body folds into an impossible shape, like an origami crane. His binoculars, having slipped from his neck, hit the ground first.

NELLIE

The party is not going well.

For one thing, Dean is late—and most of the guests are his friends, not Nellie's. Half the time she opens the door and blanks on the person's name as they bustle past, carrying dishes wrapped in aluminum. They are coworkers, mostly, and plant wives. They are, quite frankly, friends of convenience. Not to mention, no one seems much in a Halloween mood, not when the news this morning spoke of a real terror, the stuff of nightmares. The Soviets launched a test bomb in the Arctic, 1500 times more powerful than Fat Man and Little Boy.

Nellie had no conception of destruction like that, could not imagine 1500 Hiroshimas.

Still, the party guests come with their "spooky" dishes to share. The house is over-warm and overcrowded. Orange light slices through the venetian blinds and catches the dust particles dancing in the air. Nellie plays hostess like it's a game. She throws candy at the trick-or-treaters and suffers through small talk about that Catholic in the White House. She keeps the radio on rockabilly and even compliments frumpy Harriet's checker-print dress.

She is trying her best, she really is. But she nurses a laundry list of complaints, not the least of which is that Dean is late when this was his idea to begin with. There are not enough wine glasses, not enough chairs. The ice is all melting, and they've run out of tea. Dean gave her a tiny, shameful budget, so she had to ask guests to contribute food. (How her mother would be mortified.) Plus, the house is really too small for anyone but three: nine hundred square feet of wallpaper and wood decorated with secondhand furniture. "Good bones," Dean said when they moved years ago, but she hated this image. So skeletal, so ghastly.

Nellie stops by the crowded couch, watches Frank Tuckerman and Sander Preston deal a game of rummy. Allen Conway—a squat man, soft in the stomach, but a loud type—pokes through the bookshelf. *Brighter Than a Thousand Suns: Physics and Human Knowledge.* Hal Sorenson, Dean's boss, examines the cuckoo collection over the mantle. And there by the potluck table is Wilson's teacher—Nellie always forgets her name. Patricia? Pamela? Peggy? Best not to guess and be wrong—and Nellie doesn't remember inviting her. But here she is with her husband, who runs the Civil Defense Agency. Nellie only remembers this because he phoned last spring to say that Wilson cycled over, alone, with questions about fallout, and was she aware of this? She said, "Yes, of course," because any other answer would admit a sort of negligence. She rarely knows where Wilson is.

The men cheer as Frank Tuckerman plays a winning pair.

All day there has been this: the manic rush before the storm of a party. She walked to the grocery store and carried the bags back herself. She dragged an ammonia-dipped rag along the floor. Of course, she consulted her Bible—the Sears catalog—for inspiration, trying to make their Halloween potluck as posh as humanly possible. Still, as she arranged breadsticks—or "wizard wands"—she couldn't help but feel shallow for caring about a party. Especially with the news on the radio: *The Soviets have launched the largest hydrogen test bomb in the nuclear age. Already they're calling it "Tsar Bomba."* Is it wrong that she worries about having placemats that match? That she cringes at the sight of the card table in the makeshift living room space? She wants cocktails in glass. She wants wedding china on arranged runners, table settings with hand-tipped name cards, not borrowed bowls with foil. Her work seems of little consequence beside the hefty weight of Dean's research at the plant. Years from now, scholars and students will remember his name, his contributions. He could win awards. (The Nobel!) He could have his name on a plaque. But her light will fade like dying stars. No one would remember a failed party. Everyone would remember a failed bomb.

It's 6:45. Time for a cigarette. Nellie squeezes past two crewcut men in a quarrel about Checkpoint Charlie. "We were this close, this close to another goddamn fight in Germany."

This is not proper party discussion. Then again, how can one think of anything else these days? The world has gone mad. Sometimes it seems like the war never ended, only evolved into something dark and thick like molasses, something impossible to swallow.

At the coatrack, Nellie fumbles through her purse for a cigarette. She finds one, just as the doorbell chimes. When she swings the door open, a flush of cool air enters the house. A girl stands on the steps, no older than six, wearing a tubular black dress and wide-brimmed hat. She is pale with cinnamon freckles. Pearls collar her neck.

"And what are you, little pumpkin?" says Nellie, cigarette between her teeth. She stoops for the candy bowl.

"I'm not a pumpkin," says the girl. "I'm Holly Golightly." With the child's lisp, Nellie hears "go like me."

That movie. Nellie saw the film at the cinema and immediately, it struck something deep and long-buried inside her. There was a wistfulness she recognized. She saw Audrey Hepburn outside Tiffany's with her Danish, always looking in on a private, secret world, never able to enter, never quite *there*. And she thought, why yes. That's exactly what it's like.

"Caramel or chocolate?" says Nellie. Before the child can answer, Nellie drops a caramel in the pail.

What mother lets her child see *Breakfast at Tiffany's*, anyway? That's what she wants to know.

She watches the girl retreat to the sidewalk. But instead of returning to her guests, Nellie follows and closes the door behind her.

The sun is warm as it sinks behind the trees, but the air is cool. Around her, the neighborhood seethes with life and color. Jack-o'-lanterns grin with candlelit eyes, and the trees gleam with autumn gold. Their street is lined with station wagons parked one behind the other, like a row of Wilson's matchbox cars. Children flit in small bands from house to house, clad in ghost sheets and witch hats. Their laughter is a staccato pitch through the air, headache-inducing. She remembers her cigarette, lights it, and sighs.

The Soviets have launched the largest bomb in history the day before her party. The Soviets have upped the ante. Dean is late.

IT WASN'T JUST THE test bomb that cast a pall over the party. Ever since they arrived with their costumed children and covered plates, the wives stayed clustered by the sink. They busied themselves by opening cans of fruit cocktail or refilling the ice, but they spoke in charged whispers, out of the men's earshot.

When Nellie entered the kitchen to check on the food, she caught the furtive note in their voices. The tension was thick and palpable as pudding.

"I have to bring her with me," Bev said. A baby jiggled on her hip, all rolls. "Got no other option."

"Don't worry about that, it's a good thing. Myra said bring the kids," said Harriet, a small and birdish woman. She poured a glass of wine and sipped it gingerly. "Babies in the stroller is half the image. It softens it, I think."

The women smiled shyly at Nellie, as though surprised to see her in her own home.

"What?" she asked.

Lois Shepherd leaned against the counter and sipped a beer. Her cheekbones looked severe under the harsh kitchen light, like rivets in marble. She nodded at the other women as if to say, *It's fine.*

"I take it you know about tomorrow," she said with significance. When Nellie just blinked, Lois prodded, "The rally? Myra's?"

Nellie had forgotten all about it. Sure, she received a bulletin in the mail: *Are Our Children in Danger? Join the March, Strike for Peace!* It went straight in the trash. She's not the political type. When she votes, she votes like Dean. But then, somehow, she ended up on a call list. Myra Sorenson phoned out of the clear blue asking if she knew about the contamination levels in cow's milk, the danger to children's health, the risk of ingesting strontium 90. She asked if Nellie would attend an antinuclear march. This was a month ago, and Nellie listened, dazed from a morning nap, as Myra went on about *disarmament* and *test bans* and *decontamination.* "If you care about these issues at all, you should join us. It's especially important for women like you to be there," said Myra. And as that conversation surfaced in Nellie's memory, it dawned on her what that meant: wives of the atomic men. It seemed obvious to Nellie that they were not protesting the hydrogen bomb in some moral abstract but the nuclear plant where their husbands worked, the life-blood of this town. Easy enough for Myra. She was a scholar, a former suffragette, a born activist. She lived in Los Alamos during the Manhattan Project and, rumor was, had witnessed that very first bomb as it shuddered over the desert. She became newly incensed about a test ban after Bertrand Russell was arrested for an antinuclear demonstration in Trafalgar Square.

But no, Nellie would not join. Dean would be furious in his simmering way, and she didn't need more trouble with him. Besides, she had no interest in being branded unpatriotic.

"I got the flyers," Nellie said simply. She tried to busy herself with rearranging the tray of jalapeño mummies wrapped in rolls. "Do the men know about all this?"

Nellie glanced at Bev. Her husband, Allen, had a reputation for being volatile. She'd seen him angry before, roused over sporting events of all things, and his face turned a bruised pink, as though punched from the inside.

The wives exchanged glances as Bev reddened and shook her head. "Not yet anyway," she said.

"Hm. Well, good luck with all that. But aren't you worried, even a little? I mean, aren't they calling in people for less all the time, holding them up for questioning?"

Lois looked resigned, as though Nellie was a lost cause.

"That's just the beauty of it," Lois shrugged. "No one cares what housewives do."

"It's not that," said Bev. "Because if they don't care then what's the point?"

"The point is, who wants to arrest some sweet little mother with her baby carriage?" said Harriet. "It's bad publicity."

"Bottom line, they've got more important fish to fry than women like us."

"Honestly, the only reason I'm going is because it gave me a panic, learning about the milk." Bev pinched her baby's cheek. "Strontium 90 can cause leukemia, they say. Now, don't quote me on this, but how I understand it is, the fallout gets onto the grass, then into the cow, then into the milk, just as simple as that. I refuse to buy milk anymore."

Wilson took milk in his cereal that very morning. Nellie poured it herself.

"Anyway, tomorrow's bigger than any one town," said Lois, straightening. "Myra's just our local organizer. This whole thing was put together by that illustrator, what's-her-name. Wrote *The House That Jack Built*. You'd recognize it, I'm sure. But tomorrow's bigger than all of us, so there's safety in numbers. There'll be marches all over the country. L.A., New York, Washington!"

Nellie considered this. Women with baby carriages, leaving their jobs and aprons, leaving to march in the street tomorrow at ten. A gathering of women, dialed through phone books and Christmas lists and rotary clubs and garden clubs and cross-stitch guilds. A secret network of women and their clubs protesting radioactive milk.

But there was more.

According to Lois, the local dentist had started collecting baby teeth. She'd taken in her daughter, Penny, for a cleaning when Dr. Henton noticed a loose molar. He said to phone when it fell out; he said he needed donations.

"He's been asking everyone." Here, Lois finished her beer and dropped the bottle with a *clink!* into the trash.

"Donating them where?" Bev's baby—barely six months, still dewy-eyed—gummed her fist.

"To the plant. For research."

This has grated at Nellie since she excused herself from the conversation. As she moved to the refrigerator and retrieved the remaining deviled eggs, she thought of the smoke (or was it steam?) that always coiled above the canopies of kudzu and Spanish moss in this town. What had kept Dean today? She imagined him in a white coat, holding baby teeth to fluorescent bulbs in a sterile laboratory. Kept late today of all days—the night of grim news; the night of the party.

Fifteen hundred times larger than Hiroshima, the news said.

Nellie ran a fingernail through one of the whipped yolks and licked it clean. The paprika was tart on her tongue. The women's words replayed through her mind.

Baby teeth. What could the plant possibly need with baby teeth?

SHE HAS BEEN TO the Sterling Creek Plant perimeter only twice, dropping off Dean when a ride fell through. The woods are thick there outside town. From the checkpoint, she could see nothing but the rounded curve of country highway that vanished behind the boughs. She will never forget how Dean clipped the clearance badge to his blazer and closed the passenger door. A guard in military gray opened the gate as Dean walked alone down the throughway, hands firmly in his coat. She thought fleetingly—childishly—of trying to follow, pushing her car through the rail just to see what was there. But she simply turned around and left, Dean in her rearview mirror.

The plant has always been more than a physical barrier. It is the fourth member of their family, a silent and dangerous presence. It is the horror that haunts the town.

When they first moved to Oakleigh, Nellie pressed Dean for answers: "Your PhD is in dirt. Why do they need a soil scientist to study bombs?"

He gave a sardonic smile. "Who said I study bombs?"

WHEN HER CIGARETTE BURNS to a nub, Nellie sits on the brick steps and rifles through the candy bowl. She unwraps a caramel for herself. It's amazing how danger can seem so innocuous. A blink in the sky, a satellite. Fresh cow's milk. Sweets. A few years ago, news broke about an ornery old man, arrested for giving out candy laced with laxatives. Is anything safe in this world?

Supposedly, the Soviet's radioactive cloud has already stretched over the Atlantic. Even now, fallout rains on their houses like secret ash. In the words of the morning radio announcer, "Armageddon steadily approaches." To which Nellie laughed out loud: "What's new?"

She is about to return to the party when—soft and low, tires on asphalt—Dean's car pulls in the drive.

As his broad shoulders emerge from the driver's side, she sees him just briefly, as she did when they first met, this man locked into himself, tall enough to feel awkward by the length of his own arms. He is a humble sort of handsome. She stands, but he does not notice. He laughs as Jim Shepherd clambers from the passenger seat with a six pack. With them is a woman carrying a straw bag. Has Nellie seen her before? Doubtful. The woman is small and pretty and young (can she be much older than a college graduate?) with dark hair parted down the middle. A secretary, perhaps, or stenographer. Nellie was a secretary once.

At last Dean catches her eye.

When he does, there is a tightening. She notices the lines around his mouth, the slight tension of his shoulders. It vanishes almost instantly, replaced by a tired but true smile.

"Good ol' Nel." He lifts his hat as he climbs the brick steps, then pecks her cheek. He smells of the plant—cigarette smoke and gunmetal and the unmistakable tang of soil. "What're you doing out here?"

He pulls back, and Nellie straightens her windowpane dress.

"Needed some air is all. It's cramped inside, and I've got one of those headaches." She makes herself smile.

"Well, we've practically got half the neighborhood here, don't we? I swear I could hear the music half a block away."

Nellie says nothing.

"Mrs. Porter," nods Jim as he and the woman sidestep them into the house.

"I'll be right behind you." Dean's eyes follow them into the party. When he looks back, Nellie can see the exhaustion in his shoulder slope. She is about to ask about that woman when Dean says, "Are the kids still out? What is Wilson this year?"

It takes her a moment to understand his question. What is Wilson? He is his father in miniature. His hair, an earthen brown, cast gold in certain light, recently cut like a bowl. He is thin, wan. He is strange, otherworldly. Was it just this morning that he asked to read Dean's paper and sat like a grown man, sipping his juice? What is Wilson this year? Wilson this year is the same as Wilson last year: a child with his head craned toward the October sky.

"Oh, he's a GI. Blabbered about it all afternoon. He came straight from school, just biked home and got ready. Apparently, there's a haunted house right by Porky Jones's with fake blood and Dracula teeth and everything. But yes, they're still trick-or-treating. They should be back soon, I think. Not sure."

"I'm starving," Dean says and checks his watch. "I think I forgot lunch."

"Well you are home late, so the food's probably cold." It comes out like an accusation. She hadn't planned to address this now, but something about the distracted shade of his voice kindles her frustration. "Everyone's been waiting."

"I called to warn you. I did the best I could, but some things piled up today. You know how it is."

"I don't, actually." She wishes she had another cigarette. Her hands need something to do. She balls her fists so the nails pinch her palms. "All your friends are here. Your boss is here."

What she doesn't say: *I don't know most of these people. I want my house back, quiet. I want a drink, gin.* How strange that she can spend all day in anticipation for something and then yearn for it to end.

"I know. He left before me. It sounds like everyone's having a swell time." He smiles. He is a man who smiles with his whole face, every wrinkle made happy somehow. "Come now, cheer up. It's just a party."

Nellie darkens.

"Swell time. All everyone wants to talk about are depressing things like that Vietnam business or Berlin. And it's embarrassing to ask people to bring food, like we can't afford to feed our own guests."

He isn't really listening. All he says is, "Were you on budget?"

She nods.

"Good. Just leave everything from today on my desk."

His hand reaches for her elbow and gives the softest nudge. But Nellie stays still, fury rising. Her anger is always like this, quick to strike, a match always ready to light. Usually, she can pinpoint and brood on the exact offense—like the time she caught him rummaging through her medicine cabinet, rearranging every bottle and vial for no reason. But tonight, it's not any one thing: it's this house overfull, this stupid party and Dean running late, the threat of incendiaries claiming the sky at any moment, any day. It's the way he said "just a party" as though assessing a guppy on a fishing line. It's only a little nothing. Too insignificant to matter. She is about to snap something pointed when Dean waves at two children coming up the walk.

"What have we here? A princess and a hobo!" He kneels for the candy bowl and drops big fistfuls into their open pillowcases. The boy, dressed in patched jeans and a fake beard, looks about Wilson's age, with that same mop of hair. Dean rustles the kid's head and wishes them a happy Halloween.

Dean has always been like this, more tender than she is.

Nellie watches the trick-or-treaters march down the driveway.

"Dean," she says as he straightens, "are we in danger?"

"What makes you say that?"

"I don't know, the other wives were saying—never mind, it's just that bomb in the Arctic. I heard about it. You were late because of that news, weren't you? That bomb in Russia."

God, why does she say this? Of course he cannot answer. She knows he cannot answer. *SOVIETS RELEASE 50-MEGATON WEAPON; U.S. JOINS WORLD IN PROTEST.* The world is unraveling like a catch in a sweater, line by line, a cat pawing at yarn, and he—her husband, a good and steady and infuriating man—is connected to the chaos.

She has his attention now. His eyes reflect hers like tinfoil.

"You mean the Soviet Union."

"Whatever." The words come out quick and slippery. "It's just, I heard on the radio this morning that the bomb was bigger than any we've ever dropped. Much bigger, which is downright frightening if you ask me. They say the fallout cloud's already reaching New York, which means we might see it here, right? And with your work at the bomb plant, it just feels awfully dangerous, you know, and close. I just thought—well, hell. It's all gone to hell."

"Nellie." That voice, the hint of warning.

"The radio was all doomsday-this and doomsday-that, great conversation topics for a party, let me say. But of course, that doesn't matter, does it? Because it's just a party."

"Wilson didn't hear any of that, did he? This morning?"

"How should I know what he hears? The news is everywhere. He's bound to hear something."

Dean rubs between his eyebrows.

"Come on, Nel, don't be like this. I'm too tired. Don't be difficult tonight."

"I'm not."

Then. She doesn't miss it: he leans forward ever so softly and studies her face.

"Have you been . . ." He doesn't finish his sentence. He doesn't have to.

Silence hangs heavy and taut between them. Nellie narrows her lips to a tight line. She says nothing as Dean tilts the brim of his hat and steps inside, instantly engulfed by music.

Later, much later—after the day that will wreck her life—she will regard this moment as when she began to break.

THE PARTY HAS SHIFTED to counter the weight of Dean's presence. He is a man magnetic. People warm to him; they shake his hand and call him "Sport" and "Deannie boy" as if they've known him all his life. He is, at once, the most academic and chummy man she's ever known. The instant he's inside, it's like their conversation never happened. He discards his hat and badge on the coatrack and roves the living room in a figure eight, slapping Sander Preston on the back and telling Frank to turn up the music. Jerry Lee Lewis's "Great Balls of Fire" streams from the record player.

Nellie stays by the door. She needs a distraction, a drink. Something. The hostess game is still going, but she can only stand and watch her party as if from a distance. Wilson's teacher and her husband have started to dance in tight rock-steps; older children file through the kitchen and help themselves to sandwiches; Bev's baby has started to cry. Nellie's eyes land on Dean. A laugh ripples through his body, vertebrae by vertebrae, as Jim Shepherd hands him a Coke.

She must busy herself, appear hurried, appear needed. She must rejoin the wives. But there is Dean, his back toward her—as if she's nothing, as if she's forgotten—and by God, she wants to hit something.

Just leave everything from today on my desk.

The receipt, he means, and change from the five-dollar bill he gave her. Dean started counting change after Wilson was born. In his home office, on his pine desk, in a cardboard cigar box, he keeps the neat Hamilton stacks and quarter rolls. Money for gas and groceries, for Nellie's hair appointments, and for paying the milkman. Their—his—full savings are locked in a closet safe. She does not know the code.

The men erupt in roaring laughter as Sander wins the card game. And now Dean says, "We've got horseshoes. Anyone want to take this outside?"

Everyone files behind Dean out the back door, grabbing peanuts and sweating bottles of beer.

The house settles. Only a few have stayed inside—Hal sits on the now-empty couch and turns the radio dial: *Only new Contac gives you twelve-hour relief power, no relief let down! Contac relieves all day. Contac relieves all night.* Bev and Lois still hover in the kitchen. Through the panes in the back door, guests move in and out of sight.

Nellie cuts through the living room. Her steps whisper down the hall. Past the wedding picture in its silver frame. Past Dean's office. She floats into the master bedroom, cluttered with unfolded laundry. And—oddly—the slightest chill. The window is slightly ajar.

Wilson is here. She knows as soon as she enters. Nellie can sense when she is being watched, which happens often. There is that sickly sweet smell of grass, the tingling feeling that something (her robe, perhaps, now draped across the floor) has shifted.

"I know you're in here," she says, struggling to keep her voice level. Nothing.

"How many times do I have to tell you our room is off limits?"

A quick shuffle as Wilson shimmies from under the bed.

"Sorry," he murmurs.

"How'd you get in?"

"Window. Climbed."

Dean's army hat is askew on his head. Now that she thinks of it, did Wilson ever ask Dean's permission about borrowing the outfit from the war trunk? Likely not. Touching the trunk is usually not allowed. Perfect.

"So, you're back already?" Nellie says. "Get any good candy?"

"They had Butterfinger bars at the Morrises'." He rubs a dirty sleeve across his nose. "Whole ones."

"That's generous." The bowl by their own door is a five-and-dime bag.

Wilson says nothing. He gives her that look she can't stand. He watches her like she is a plane in the sky.

"What?" she says. "Aren't you having fun?"

He shrugs. "I don't know."

"Well, go on then, I'm tired."

He doesn't move.

"Well?"

"Can we play in the shelter? Me and Eddie. The others, too."

Ever since Dean built the fallout shelter, Wilson has viewed the subterranean hideaway as his personal playground. (And the shelter isn't much—more cellar than anything, a hatch like driftwood among mulch. Other families have flushing toilets and real flooring, like tiny underground houses.) Wilson claimed the shelter like a pioneer in homestead. He slowly brought in more games and comics. He left action figures on the steps. He turned army-issue blankets into a fort.

"Sure, whatever you want." She bats her hand. "Just run along."

He disappears in an instant. She reclines on the bed and nets herself in the sheets.

The sounds of company continue through the open window. Laughter spikes. There's the swing of the back door, footsteps. The wives start a game of charades in the living room. Nellie should join them. Good hostesses do not retire to their bedrooms. Would Holly Golightly sleep through one of her soirees while friends dance and drink, while debutantes and diplomats cross paths with writers and artists? No, good hostesses laugh and offer more wine and pick up candy wrappers. They do not have their guests bring food or stand in the kitchen opening cans of fruit cocktail. Good hostesses play charades with their friends.

THERE WAS SOMETHING ELSE Nellie loved about *Breakfast at Tiffany's*.

As she sat alone in the Oakleigh cinema, she almost choked at the revelation that the sprightly Holly was a runaway wife. This glamorous woman with the chignon and cigarette holder, with the kitten heels and diamonds, was formerly Lula Mae, a young bride in rural Texas. And her husband wanted her to come home.

"Distasteful," someone said in the row behind her when Holly refused to leave New York. And Nellie understood, in a way. Lula Mae had four children to look after. She'd left her family and escaped to a life of parties and satin and powder room tips. Nellie understood more than most. She was Wilson's age when her father left. No one divorced then—they were the first in the county. In school, Nellie heard that her parents were going to hell, that they separated because they didn't want her. Once, while prowling through her mother's private things, she found the wedding ring, unworn and upright in the jewelry box. Nellie stole it and hid the ring under her pillow. She loved the diamonds, like stars she could hold! At night, she wore the ring and cried and prayed for her father to come back. When Mother found out, she screamed and threw away Nellie's dolls as punishment. But for seven days, Nellie was in possession of a secret, beautiful thing. How could one love and leave? she wondered then. She would wonder that for years.

But that day in the cinema, Nellie only sipped her soda and stared at the screen, enraptured. And when the credits ran, she sat through the film again. She marveled at the clean white walls and the delicate hats trimmed with feathers. She felt a chill of excitement at the shoplifting scene, as Holly slid a cartoonish mask on her face and simply walked onto the streets of Manhattan. Holly had no other mouths to feed, no husband to control her, no worries but finding the mate to her snake-skin shoes. She was no longer Lula Mae, she had become someone else entirely—she'd remade her life, and wasn't that liberation?

As the ushers moved through the rows and the lights dimmed, Nellie stayed still and silent in her seat. She was the last to leave.

NELLIE STRAIGHTENS HER SHOULDERS. She will reenter her party, emerge with all the grace she can muster. She stands, adjusts her dress. Then there are heavy steps.

"I was looking for you," Dean says and closes the door firmly. He hasn't changed from his work shirt, though he's grabbed a sweater from the hall closet. His hair is still neat, combed, economical.

"Must not have been for long." Nellie turns to the vanity, cluttered with face cream and lavender perfume. "I've just been here."

"You okay?"

"Fine. Just needed a few minutes." She tucks a stray curl behind her ear.

He pauses, pockets his hands. Now in the silence, she senses that he is displeased. What now? His demeanor—which made him an ideal army officer, calm under pressure, a rock that cannot be altered except under extreme heat—infuriates her. Nellie read in a magazine once that the Kennedys' marriage is like an iceberg. A small tip is visible to the public, and the rest remains hidden, in obscura. Dean is like this. His public life is a small square window, a pane of light—PTA meetings and restoring clocks and building shelters, sleeves rolled to calloused elbows. His private life skulks beneath the surface.

Dean says, "Look, Wilson brought the other kids to the shelter. They're all down there."

"So?" She takes the face brush and dusts powder on her nose.

"So, he said you said it was okay. I'd already told him no."

She should have assumed this. Wilson never asks permission to play in the shelter, he just does. He arrives home after his pharmacy deliveries—which is really more a hobby than a job, since he does this with his best friend, Eddie Pace—grabs a snack, and clambers down the ladder. What he does there, she has no idea. But the house is left quiet, child-free.

"Well, he didn't tell me that."

"Nel, we've talked about this. He's not supposed to play out there, period."

"Then go and get him," she shrugs.

"That'll make a scene."

"You're the one who cares about this right now." Her voice wavers. "He's quiet and calm and entertaining himself and frankly, I like all those things. It's free babysitting."

"This isn't funny," says Dean in his distant way.

"It kind of is."

She snaps the compact closed and turns to Dean, one hand on the vanity. In the living room, the radio changes to Rodgers and Hammerstein tunes.

The room has darkened visibly. They stare at each other until Dean says, "What do you think this shows him, Nel? That we're not on the same page? I say it's only for drills, not a playhouse. You say he can do whatever he wants. The boy is distressed. It's not good for him, not healthy. How often is he out there?"

How she wants to laugh! Dean must be under the impression that the evening is a success, that the only hiccup thus far is the matter of Wilson in the shelter. Only now, in this moment, are they "not on the same page." *Just a party,* he'd said. *Just leave everything on my desk,* he'd said. Now this is what angers him? What's the problem, really, if Wilson takes his little friends to the shelter? Wilson is a strange child, always running off with Eddie Pace, but boys will be boys. They will play war games. They will turn fallout shelters into clubhouses. If the boy is distressed—and who isn't these days?—then it's the bomb plant to blame, not playing in the shelter. It's the unanswerable questions. The threat of attack here, 50 megatons, 1500 times larger than Hiroshima. The rumor of missiles, whisper of protests. The whole goddamn town has lost its mind. Who wouldn't be distressed?

She drums her fingernails on the vanity and says in a cool voice, "I don't know how often, all right? I don't know."

"I can't be here all the time. Don't you see what's happening?"

"What is strontium 90?"

His shoulders tense.

"Don't change the subject, Nel."

"I didn't. We're talking about the effect of all this madness on our son, aren't we? So what is it?"

"If you're hearing about that from the other wives, don't worry about it. Everything will be fine."

His tone—final, firm.

"They said we shouldn't give our children milk anymore. But a child needs milk. He's small as it is."

"Just keep doing what you're doing."

"Is it true that the plant asks for baby teeth?"

He hesitates briefly, then says, "Yes."

"So, it's theoretically possible that your lab has examined Wilson's teeth?"

"I know we have." He doesn't look at her when he says this.

Her mind spins. Her head aches. She can only say, "What?"

"I took some of his last year. Remember when he lost three in a row?"

"You took his teeth? To be tested?"

He looks at her as if from some far distance. "Yes. We called it Operation Tooth, as a kind of inside thing." His mouth curls into a half smile.

"But why?"

"I can only tell you what's public, you know that." He speaks slowly, choosing his words as carefully as placing a puzzle piece. "But strontium 90? It's an isotope in fallout. We've found it in cow's milk and also in children's teeth. By examining the teeth, we can measure the uptake in radiation."

"Oh my god," she says. She has a sudden sinking feeling, as though the floor will give way. "Oh my god, oh my god." Fear mingles with fury.

Dean steps forward, one hand up. Lecture mode.

"Don't get me wrong. Negligible amounts, Nel, hardly worth noting."

"See, this is why I ask. Is he in danger? Is our son in danger? Am I?"

"No, Nel, don't catastrophize, you always do this. That's partly why

I didn't tell you. My own lab was asking for donations from employees and dentists. I didn't want to frighten you. There's nothing to be worried about."

"Damn you." She's shocked to silence. He's been lying to her, stealing their son's teeth. It feels so barbaric, this secret testing on their boy, treating their family like a private experiment.

Dean's face sags with disappointment.

"Don't look at me like that." He touches her wrist, but she flinches ever so slightly. He pulls back.

"Does Wilson know?" she says.

He shakes his head.

"Look at me, Nel. The real danger is not in the teeth or in the milk—it's his obsession with this whole thing, with him playing down there. Is that what you want?"

"Don't ask me what I want." The rage spikes through her. "This whole thing is not what I want."

She knows he knows what she means. She never envisioned life in the bomb town, their whole existence tainted by the nuclear site. Dropping him off at an armed checkpoint is not what she wants. The fact that they even have to have a shelter in the backyard! And has he even thought of that?

She stares at him. A slow dark cloud has risen inside her, growing like fallout. Poisoning earth and sky and milk. The cloud has gathered power and surged with stormy rage through the party, this night. She says nothing. There's too much to say, where to begin? If she opens her mouth, she might cry or scream.

Laughter comes from the living room, the timbre of Lois impersonating Desi Arnaz.

"What's that supposed to mean?" Dean says softly.

Before she can say anything, the doorbell pings and children cry, "Trick-or-treat!" Dean straightens his shoulders, keeps one hand in his pocket, and leaves the room in two steps. The music is louder now: *Don't try to patch it up, tear it up, tear it up!*

Nellie is numb; she is confused. Her eyes rove the room: walls periwinkle, sprays of rotten irises left too long by the bed. She has lost all resolve to return to this party. Such failure! She moves to the window and watches the guests on the lawn. They clink cups. They laugh. Older girls kneel on the grass over their crafts of lace and pipe cleaner. The naked moon shines through frayed clouds.

She cannot see the shelter entrance from here, but she imagines the children seated on the floor, trading candy. Little Wilson, her strange, strange boy, with his teeth in a jar somewhere. Dean returns to playing horseshoes with Jim Shepherd. They toss the shoes in rainbow arcs. Two women run to fetch them after each round—one is that secretary who arrived with them.

Lightning marbles the sky in fierce bolts. The lightning is in the distance, yet still Nellie has the sense of brooding, dread. A storm is coming. As the veins of light move closer, Nellie watches intently. Dean throws the horseshoe. The woman fetches.

Nellie knows then what she will do.

She moves through the house. The party has thinned. Bev and Allen have left—there's the baby to take home. The ladies in the living room still play charades. "Oh, it's Wilma Flintstone," shrieks Harriet as Lois mimes opening an oven. Nellie slips down the hallway and into Dean's office. The Antony and Cleopatra cigar box sits proud and prominent on his desk. She opens the lid and counts two hundred, which she stashes in her pocket.

And tomorrow, she will march. It will be a small explosion.

WILSON

He wears a green visored cap—Father's during the war—and an oversized men's shirt tucked into his dungarees. To complete the ensemble: rain boots, wool socks, and a white scarf around his neck. In the canvas rucksack are his binoculars and the canteen he rummaged from Father's army trunk. He carries these at all times. Even now. Especially now. Halloween is the type of night that's a perfect excuse for *evil*. Reds can hide out in the open. They can dress as Commies and get away with it. They could say, "I'm just pretending—tricked you!" so someone has to be ready and vigilant. And that someone is him, Wilson Adley Porter.

He prowls through the neighborhood, feeling something close to elation. There's a buzz in his brain. Down the narrow streets, past houses with pumpkins and scarecrows leaning on fences, houses that could hide secret menacings, propaganda tucked beneath magazines and newspapers. He is an officer in Father's uniform. He is hero, soldier, spy. He is an operative. This, his mission. The other kids filter ahead of him and pound on doors. The other kids have weird costumes. Donny Lisle is Felix the Cat. Jo and Jane, twins in his grade, are Tarzan and Jane. One kid built a suit of armor with aluminum foil. Another is Raggedy Ann. Penny Shepherd is "Penny Longstocking" in a chicken feed sack dress. Becky Conway is the youngest in their group, age six. She is quiet and sniffly and carries Patti Playpal everywhere, a doll that looks eerily like her. She screams at the scary houses and walks bowlegged around the neighborhood as if she wet her pants. And then there's Todd Shepherd, Penny's older brother, dressed as Elvis Presley. He gyrates his hips and curls his lip as they walk. Todd is what Father calls a "bad influence."

Eddie Pace—Wilson's best friend—wears a costume that makes no sense at all. He's part cowboy (in riding boots) and part astronaut (in a cardboard helmet). He carries a sign that says, FROM SADDLE TO SATELLITE.

"It's a joke," Eddie explained when Wilson first roared with laughter. "It's called *irony*."

"It's called dumb!" Wilson cried.

Without fail, anytime someone opens the door and asks who everyone "is," Eddie needs a full minute to explain.

But Wilson loves Halloween. He loves the skulking, the stealth. The street at dusk, gray-hazed. He loves the magic of seeing into someone's home. Usually, he has to bear-crawl through the hedge. He has to shimmy up a tree, binoculars bouncing on his chest.

"Geez Louise, all I've got are Brachs," says Eddie as he rifles through his pail. "I hate Brachs. Anyone have Milky Ways?"

"Me." Wilson passes him a shiny wrapper.

"I'm tired," says Penny. A few curls have escaped the haywire braids and cling to her forehead like radio coils. Wilson loves that. Penny is scrappy and wild, but she can turn on a motherly air when she wants to, like Wendy tending to the Lost Boys. Wilson has the prickling sense that Eddie likes her, too.

"It's not even dark yet," says Todd. "Get over it."

They stop at Gracie Collins's house. The lights are off, but Eddie knocks anyway, and Wilson rings the bell. Gracie's face appears in the window. Her mother answers the door as they chime, "Trick-or-treat!"

"Don't you know this is Satan's holiday?" says Mrs. Collins. She shakes her head and passes out licorice sticks. "I should be giving you all prayer books, not candy."

Mrs. Collins is not a prime Communist candidate. She is, instead, quite nunnish.

They skirt away to the next house. Jo and Jane run ahead. Wilson clutches his rucksack with one hand, his pillowcase of candy with the other. He walks gingerly, eyes trained on the ribbon of road. He is alert. All senses tingling. They pass hordes of other children, all costume-clad and brightly colored. Becky trails behind, and there's the scuff sound as Patti Playpal drags along the concrete.

They near Bob Thorman's house, painted a deceptively cheerful color. They do not approach to knock. This house gives Wilson the creeps. Last year, Mrs. Thorman, who was so often seen spraying her vegetables with a tiny blue spritz, died in her car, in this garage. The adults said it was an accident. They whispered about it, the way adults do when they don't want the children to know what's happening. But what the parents don't understand, Wilson thinks as they avert the Thorman house and head straight to the Morrises', is that there's nothing kids love more than a whisper. A whisper means, don't listen. Which of course means that they listen more than normal. Besides, stories have a way of growing arms and legs of their own, walking out closed doors and introducing themselves to anyone willing to listen.

Yes, he is quite knowledgeable about death, though he's never been to a funeral. Father says he's too young; it would be traumatic.

But there are lots of things Wilson is not supposed to know about but does. For example: conspiracy theories. He's heard about the Roswell crash, which may have been a weather balloon, or may have been an alien ship, or may have been equipment detecting ballistic missiles. He knows this, too: how ballistic missiles are guided by gravity. He's heard about the Illuminati and the New World Order, which scare him, frankly, but not as much as other things. Other things he knows: where the bottles are. He's found at least three in the shelter, though he never touches them (never!) and two in the pantry and five under the bathroom sink. He knows how sex works, sadly, because Todd Shepherd told him what fits where. Todd has this girlfriend named Irving, a seventh grader who lets him kiss her if he gives her fifty cents. Todd also showed him how to draw shapes while peeing in dirt and how to start fires with strips of birch. Wilson knows how bodies change—once, he walked in on Father peeing (the door wasn't locked, not his fault!), and Father's penis was wide and plump, nothing like the little nub Wilson has. He also knows how to ride a bicycle with his eyes closed, though Father says *never* do this, he could get hurt—he could fall, hit his head, but he never has. Plus, Wilson knows the truth about Halloween and witches and the devil. He's heard about the Salem witch hunt, which Father talked about a lot years ago, that and Senator McCarthy, who Father says gave Republicans a bad name. What Wilson doesn't understand is, if you had witches in your town, wouldn't you want them gone? What's so wrong with that? He knows that a bomb went off yesterday—the test bomb in the paper, *50 MEGATON BLAST*, and that, frankly, is what scares him.

In addition to all this, he knows what to look for in a Commie. He studies up. He's read important pamphlets like *How to Spot a Communist* or *Red Supporters in Your Neighborhood? No More!* He knows that not all Communists are bearded or carry briefcases that may contain bombs. (That is just something you see in cartoons.) He once found a list of "words that Communists use," and he pasted it in his field guide. The list includes *integrative thinking, vanguard, comrade, hootenanny, books, bourgeois, nationalism, jingoism, colonialism, hooliganism* (lots of -isms), *ruling class, demagogue, witch hunt, oppressive, materialist.* Wilson doesn't know what most of these mean. But if someone so much as says "hootenanny," he will know, "Red Sympathizer Alert!" He's prepared. But the difficulty with scouting for Commies is that they can be sneaky little bastards. They can hide their party identification cards. They can work like everyone else! (Do any work with Father? Just think—the danger of a Commie at the bomb plant!) But here's what Wilson does know: Commies will slip up eventually. And there are the telltale signs. If someone supports a Communist organization, they may be Communist. If they berate the United States and Mr. President, if they read leftist newspapers (*The Daily Worker*, for example), they may be Communist. But others are more discreet, more silent and lurking. These are the ones Wilson must catch.

This is what Wilson thinks about as they go door-to-door, as their pillowcases expand.

Because here's the truth: Communism is a red iceberg. It is Titanic-level bad. It has already sunk Hungary, Czechoslovakia, North Korea, and it might just sink the whole world. This is, unfortunately, the RED MENACE. But if a Commie ever tries to convince him to join the cause, then well, well, well—he'll have picked the wrong American! Because Wilson will be ready. He'll remember what the Civil Defense Agency says: *When a Communist goes to work on you, tell him that you are on to him and his dirty game. Tell him, further, that you think it your patriotic duty to make his activities known to others and to the police. Tell him that you know no tactics are too low for a Communist: lying, cheating, betrayal, ruin, and even murder. But be sure to tell him, too, that America is on the alert and that his scheme for world domination is doomed to fail.*

This preparedness is what makes Wilson a good Watchdog.

It was Eddie's idea to start the Watchdogs. They were walking home from school one day, after a lecture on Geiger counters, when Eddie said, "What do you think would happen if the Soviets actually bombed us?"

"I don't know," shrugged Wilson.

Of course he knew. He was practically an expert. When a blast came—and he'd know by the telltale light, by the blackening mushroom cloud—he knew to hold up his thumb, squint at the sky, and check the horizon.

"I bet the whole town would explode," said Eddie. His voice burned with mischief. "My dad says nuclear bombs aren't real bombs. They pull apart air. I bet they explode you from the inside out like this."

He clapped his hands together with a smack and then slowly pulled them apart.

"Do you think it'd hurt?" Wilson asked. He asked this, though he already knew. He knew it would hurt.

"Geez Louise, sure it would." Eddie sounded matter-of-fact. This was when he suggested they start a secret club. There was safety in numbers. In exchanging preparedness tactics and survival strategies.

Their goal was simple and twofold: (1) seek out Commies in Oakleigh, (2) prepare for imminent attack. To Eddie, the Watchdogs was always more game than mission. Eddie loved the wildness, the staring. He loved to laugh when they spotted someone dressing through a window. But Wilson knew to be serious. He knew what was at stake. And it was Wilson who suggested they establish a headquarters. Home base. The ideal location was obvious: Father's fallout shelter, as it was already stocked for nuclear annihilation. Inside, they found:

Tin barrels of water, to be converted into waste pails after use

Pill canisters lined in neat rows

A first-aid kit

Facial tissues

Dixie cups

A gray cot with a U.S. Army blanket

Cornflakes and Butterscotch Bits

Five candles

Six cans of Spam

Fifty cans of Coca-Cola

A bar of soap and towel

A fire extinguisher

Flashlights and batteries

Father's spare tool kit

Bleach to purify water

Board games

Books and magazines

A stack of clothes, including the patched overalls that barely fit him anymore

An army surplus case filled with magazines and a phone book

A radio, an alarm clock, and a hunting knife

A yellow Geiger counter for checking radiation

Yes, the shelter is the perfect safe zone, and the Watchdogs meet regularly to exchange notes. They rendezvous on the playground during recess. They stake post in the oak tree or by the south fence. They pull binoculars from their backpacks and watch the other kids, scout the pedestrians walking the pavement. On weekends, they convene in the shelter. They turn the radio dial to CONELRAD 640 for emergency broadcasting. The CONtrol of ELectronic RADiation frequency is the official channel for news in case of attack. Wilson tunes in regularly.

They unroll their map of town, circle "hot spots"—potential Red hideouts—and note shelter locations in every vicinity. That way, there is a designated safe zone within five minutes' distance, no matter where they are when the alarm sounds! They are quite thorough. The Watchdogs is serious operative business. It takes intensive training.

The only problem is Father, who doesn't approve of Wilson being in the shelter. (Not a place for games, Father says.) But this isn't a game, Wilson wants to explain. This is *work*. This is *necessary*. This is *training*. At least Mama lets him do what he wants. He's tracking down the outlaws, illegals, spies. He'll find 'em and *Bang, Bang, Bang!* He'll get them before they get him. Ha ha!

Ahead is Annie Yuknavitch's house. He has long suspected that Annie Yuknavitch is a spy because her last name is Yuknavitch, which doesn't sound American. Plus—she speaks three languages, and no fourth grader in America should speak three languages. Her parents are professors at the community college and have suspiciously eastern names, Oleksander and Daria. Father says they're immigrants whose family fled after the first world war. Academics, and nothing to be afraid of. But here's the deal: Communists love to infiltrate schools. They want to bend minds. Brainwash. Shape children into red Commie balloons.

The Yuknavitch house terrifies and fascinates Wilson. Usually, he wouldn't go nearer than the mailbox, a safe distance giving him a head start on the four blocks home. The house is a startling white with a boxed garden on the porch filled with lavender, mint, thyme. When Wilson and Eddie scout here, they climb the tree in the Uttichs' yard next door, hide among the boughs, and peer over. What they see is usually boring: the parents on the patio with cigarettes and glasses, Annie playing the piano or pounding the floor as she practices tap dance. Even Commies can tap dance.

Wilson lingers by the porch steps, whitewashed and decorated with gourds wrapped in checkered flannel. The other kids filter forward, led by Jo and Jane. Mr. Yuknavitch sits in a rocking chair with a bowl of candy in his lap, a book in his hand.

"Ah—here comes the whole crew," says Mr. Yuknavitch. He plops candy in their bags, and everyone threads past Wilson again, back to the sidewalk.

"Suspect alert," Wilson whispers to Eddie, who's busy adjusting his astronaut helmet.

"We can't just not go," says Eddie.

"Can, too."

"Can*not*. He'd know we're onto him."

Wilson considers this. Before he can say anything, Eddie chimes, "It's your turn. And see what he's reading."

"What about the candy? How do you know he hasn't poisoned it?" Wilson remembers a lecture from Mrs. Jenkins's class. The words BIO-LOGICAL WARFARE scrawled on the chalkboard. That candy could most certainly be poisonous.

Eddie's eyes gleam.

"You don't have to eat it, just go."

Wilson climbs the porch steps, trailing Becky and Patti Playpal. These are Communist stairs. The window shutters, red. And Red with a capital "R" is a dangerous thing—Red is the color of blood. Red is war, Red is danger, Red is Russia. And Mr. Yuknavitch is reading *Edgar Allan Poe*, and that sounds downright fishy. The cover has a skull picture. This whole thing is questionable. But Watchdogs can't be scared, Watchdogs can't run at the faintest sign of danger. He needs to discern the danger and report it.

"Trick-or-treat," Wilson croaks.

He holds out his bag, manages a smile. Mr. Yuknavitch smiles back, showing long yellowed teeth. He wears a white button-up shirt. A package of cigarettes shows through the square pocket on his chest. Up close, he is thin. His skin, leathery. He has a faint, wimpy mustache and watery brown eyes. He doesn't look much like Annie, who is thick-boned and muscular, even at ten. There is no turning back now, not as the candy falls into the pillowcase, guided by gravity. (Like a ballistic missile!) The taffy lands with a rustle, and Wilson cries, "Thank you!" in a voice that sounds definitively *girlish*, and he hopes that Penny didn't hear because he thinks he loves that Penny Shepherd—she's not the afraid or quiet type, but the barefoot, overalls-wearing type. He likes that in girls. He likes that a lot.

Feet back on the ground. He's good and safe now on the grass, on the sidewalk. Easier to run. Maybe, he thinks as they move to the next house, maybe there's a basement where the Yuknavitches tap Morse code into a radio. (Morse code is on his list of Things to Learn for Safety.) He once heard that a KGB spy used hollow nickels to transfer microfilm with secret messages. Commies are often clever this way, using pitted shaving brushes and trick film canisters. They transmit messages with shortwave radios. Just think! Oh, the danger. Oh, the things that could happen behind closed doors—especially here, with the bomb plant just miles away.

They walk on, down the street lined with paper lanterns. The lights flicker, threaten to burn the white paper. They walk on. They knock on doors; they pass school friends; wave at neighbors who rock on their porches; they pass the trees and bushes used for scout posts; they walk on and on until Becky cries that Patti Playpal is tired. Above, the sky fades from orange to purple. There is a single talon of moon.

THEY RETURN TO THE Porter home around 7:30, as the hem of night drapes over town.

"Should we go to the clubhouse?" Eddie says, nodding to the shelter.

Wilson leads the way. They're almost to the hatch door when Father's voice booms across the yard. "Wilson Adley Porter!" Wilson turns slowly, hot and fuming. It's downright humiliating to be called by your full name in front of your friends. It's even more humiliating for Father to say next, "What have we talked about, hmm?"

The other kids back away shyly, then run inside to grab sandwiches and colas. Wilson stews behind, watching the lawn, the party, Father in his adult world.

Then: idea! Wilson tiptoes to the window of his parents' room. He lifts the glass and, with great stealth, climbs inside. His mother will say yes to the clubhouse. She always does.

And she does.

"We're a go," Wilson whispers to Eddie, who he finds on the back steps with the others, draining the last drops from their soda bottles. "But we gotta follow the two Q's: Quick and Quiet!"

Wilson waits until Father is hammering a horseshoe stake into the ground before he makes a beeline to the hatch door.

One by one they descend to the shelter that is not a shelter but a headquarters. They go carefully down the ladder. Their unit is a basic model, and Wilson is proud of it. Wilson helped build the shelter, meaning he read the instructions aloud while Father built. There are lots of things to consider when building a fallout shelter. The danger is not just from the blast. One must consider the effect of radiation— the possibility for flash blindness, for heat that could popcorn the skin. Their shelter is not large. Ten by ten. The walls: wooden slats. The floor: cinder blocks over soil. If he stands on the cot and reaches, he can touch the planks overhead. On the far wall, they have a makeshift bookcase filled with board games, Mama's magazines, food and supplies. Near the hatch, a single lightbulb and a hand-crank pump to clean the air in case of fallout. (Though Wilson has his doubts about this. Couldn't fallout still get in? Would specks like sand or pumice slide through?) The kids arrange themselves around the shelter and pour candy into piles like treasure hoards. The girls claim the GI cot. Todd hunkers near the ladder. Wilson and Eddie share the rim of a water barrel. Wilson watches as Penny slips off her boots and sits crosslegged in her bare feet.

While the girls trade candy—"Give you a Sky Bar for Swedish Fish!"—he and Eddie play a game called Who Can Tell the Grossest Joke, and Eddie wins with: "What's green, then red with the press of a button? A frog in a blender." Wilson belches with laughter, and all the girls scream.

They debate what to play. Todd suggests Murder in the Dark. He explains that you write roles on pieces of paper, place them in a hat, and pick one. Someone is a murderer, and someone is a detective. With the lights off—and in the shelter, it's dark as ink—the murderer "kills" whoever he can. He does this by tapping a shoulder or, more excitingly, by groping at the neck. Wilson wants to play, but only if he can be the detective, because being a Watchdog is rather like being a detective. But the girls protest.

"It's Halloween," says Jane. "We should do something really scary."

"Like what?" says Todd. He takes a comb from his back pocket and touches up his Elvis hair flip.

"Like Bloody Mary." Jane's eyes gleam. "Like—we summon her back. Everyone knows spirits come back on Halloween. And Halloween *only*."

Todd snaps to attention, pockets the comb. "Or," he says, "we make a Ouija board."

"What's that?" says Wilson.

"It's like a telephone from here to hell," Todd says, his voice all quiet-like.

Todd says they need a make-shift board. Paper and pen will do; they can write their own letters. Wilson scrabbles through his bin-of-everything (paper clips, abandoned keys, one canteen, wool socks) until he finds crayons and a notebook.

"Red," says Todd, palm out.

Wilson shakes his head and pulls out black.

Todd kneels and builds the board letter by letter. Becky sits back on the cot and whimpers. She has Patti Playpal's ear in her mouth. Wilson watches as the letters grow. It just looks like an alphabet to him—an alphabet with numbers and the words *Yes, No, Hello, Goodbye*.

"That doesn't look like a telephone," says Wilson. He hugs the crayon box to his chest.

"The Bloody Mary game is easier," Jane says between mouthfuls of chocolate. "We just need a mirror. Don't you have a mirror in here?" Her twin, Jo, says nothing.

Todd stays kneeled over the Ouija board, lined paper with black scratchy markings.

"Is it scary?" says Becky. She clutches her doll as Jane lights a candle.

"It's stupid and not real," says Eddie.

"Is too real," says Todd. "My pop says he saw it done in the war."

"Alright then, genius, so what'll we do?" says Eddie. "Call back General Sherman? Caesar? Jesus?"

"We'll talk to whoever's here," Todd gleams. "We'll talk to whoever wants to talk to us."

Someone is here already? That thought is downright fishy—that the shelter can be infiltrated by the spirit world! But. If it can, then Wilson might as well learn something. *Please be them*, he thinks. Wilson secretly wants Julius and Ethel Rosenberg, because he once overheard Father discuss their trial with Jim Shepherd, and Wilson tucked this particular memory away for later, like a soup can in the shelter, and when the time came, he asked Father who "the Rosenbergs" were, and Father said, "bad people, spies," and that was all. So what Wilson would like to know is: how'd you do it? That, and *why*, though *why* is harder to answer. Because what Wilson knows is this: the Rosenbergs were executed (zapped like lightning in the electric chair!) for giving nuclear weapon designs to the Soviets. They were traitors. They were spies. EXECUTED AT SING SING FOR ATOM SPYING! If this could happen once, it could happen again. Today, tomorrow, next week, next year when he's eleven.

Sometimes Wilson wakes up early and stares out his window. Nothing stirs. Nothing moves. He feels as though he is the last boy alive, which is a very lonely feeling.

"Can we try for someone?" Wilson asks. "Can we try for the Rosenbergs?"

But he's surprised that none of the kids know who they are. (Even Eddie. Watchdog failure.)

Following Todd's lead, they sit in a circle. Using one of Jane's hair ribbons, Todd makes a circle loop, which he moves slowly over the board.

"Is anyone there?" Todd asks. "How many spirits are with us?"

His fingers jolt over the board. The circle loop jumps letter to letter.

"You can answer with Yes or No. You can talk to us!"

Becky pouts. Wilson thinks about Julius and Ethel Rosenberg and wonders if Penny knows who the Rosenbergs are and what happened to them, if she just didn't say anything—if Penny knows about electric chairs and atom spying, if she'd like to join him for some Commie spying later.

He stares still and furtive. Todd hums now and asks the spirit world to please listen to them, they're waiting, doesn't anyone hear him? They try this until Eddie stands up and announces that this is all *chickenshit*.

So they trade more candy. There is a barter system of lollipops and chocolate. Wilson tucks the taffy from the Yuknavitch house behind the water barrel so no one will be poisoned. He chews the Brachs from Eddie's bag and trades his own squares. His left front tooth aches a bit after the fifth caramel, but this is Halloween and he's supposed to eat his weight in candy. Soon, they try Murder in the Dark and make Becky detective so she won't cry through the game and ruin everything. Still, she does. She wraps her arm around Patti Playpal so it looks like the poor doll is being strangled.

Finally, Eddie suggests a new idea: "Let's tell scary stories. I'll go first."

Eddie loves a good ghost story. Most of his stories are a hodgepodge of Savannah lore and comic books (*Atomic Mouse* is a favorite). His stories are roundabout and wild, the settings often the same: the train tracks at night, the bomb plant, the Savannah air force base.

"Oh, don't—" says Penny with a pout. But Eddie smiles, devious, and continues. "It was a dark night. Not unlike tonight. But this was years ago. *Fifty* years ago. The beginning of the Lights of Ravenel."

Wilson cannot help himself. He says, "That one's not scary. You know what's really scary?"

Jane shrugs, and Wilson says, "Bombs."

He lets the word hang in the air like fog before adding, with measured nonchalance, "An atomic bomb dropped on South Carolina three years ago, you know."

"That's not true," says Jane. She opens a lollipop. "How come we didn't see it? That's not true."

"Is, too," says Wilson. He absentmindedly reaches for a tin on the shelf, where he keeps marbles. He spreads them on the floor, rolling them under his palm as he continues. "It just didn't have the warhead attached. Which means we're all lucky ducks. You know what would have happened if it had? We'd be atomic dust."

He saw the pictures—the crater like the pocked face of the moon. The 1958 Mars Bluff B-47 incident. From the sky, there fell 7600 pounds of nuclear casing. A farm was destroyed. Children (his age!) were injured, hospitalized.

"There are planes in the sky with nukes all the time," says Wilson. The other kids shift in their seats, chew softly. "Don't you ever hear the planes? Wake up and hear them flying?"

If the United States government can "accidentally" drop a bomb on their own country, carve a hole in the earth like a clean ice cream scoop, how much worse will it be when the enemy intends to drop one? When the blast is larger than any before, when there is a *hydrogen* bomb?

Father works on hydrogen bombs.

When Wilson asked Father what hydrogen was, exactly, Father called it "an ingredient." Wilson then asked, "Like butter? Or salt?"

Father laughed and said, "Yes, like butter. Remember when you helped your mother make your birthday cake? You leveled off flour and measured the sugar and oil? You add those things together, and they become something new. Salt, for example, is a compound. It's two things added together."

"What two things?"

"Sodium and chloride."

"You blend them?"

"In a way."

"Like chocolate syrup and milk make chocolate milk?"

"I suppose, yes, like that."

"So, what is hydrogen?"

"Hydrogen is a basic element. It's a very simple ingredient, like flour in a cake."

"So, what is a hydrogen bomb?" Now Wilson pictured a cloud of flour, mushrooming, billowing smogs of bleached white flour, making everyone choke on Ground Zero.

"Something very serious for national defense. Do you know what national defense means?"

Wilson nodded.

"Then you know that the nice thing about our country is that little boys don't have to worry about that. Soldiers take care of it. And politicians."

"And scientists," said Wilson.

"Yes, and scientists."

Father then said scientists are like detectives. Some investigate the birth of stars, the cosmic dawn. Others study the invisible particles that make up the world, unique as fingerprints. Father's answers are often like this: vague definitions or metaphors. But Wilson is not stupid. He knows there wouldn't be a perimeter of barbed wire around the Sterling Creek Plant if the scientists were only mixing cake batter. When he's managing a scout post around town, his binoculars sometimes catch the steam rising from the plant, like a chimney or a great atomic baking factory. And he can't help but picture the scientists in lab coats and aprons. Jim Shepherd saying, "We'll need a little bit of hydrogen." Father saying, "And a pinch of uranium."

Wilson looks around the shelter. Above, there are the sounds of the party. Voices rise and fall like a subsonic drum. There is the swell of music. Footfalls, spikes of laughter. The other kids stare at him. Jane sucks her lollipop. Becky says, "Patti Playpal has to pee," and jiggles her leg like a rabbit. Penny hugs her knees to her chest and bites her lip. Todd leans against the shelter wall, smirking.

Wilson says, "Do you know what happens when an atomic bomb drops?" Sure, they've seen the videos in school. But have they—except Eddie, of course—done research? Have they learned what really happens? Do they know how the flash will be so silent? They say that skin will melt from faces, the face will melt off bone. Do they have dreams of the blast, so beautiful until it destroys the world? Wilson has terrible nightmares, and there are always Commie planes. The bombers drop leaflets in the violent Russian script, grim hieroglyphs, warning people to evacuate or surrender.

"You got to watch for the light," Wilson says. He focuses on the marbles, flicks one with his thumb so it collides with another. Thoughts rise through his head like bubbles. They fizz. They pop. They collide—like marbles or atoms! "The light will be brighter than anything you've ever seen. Brighter than a hundred million thousand suns. Then, a cloud. And this will look like a mushroom. Or a tree. Everything will go up in smoke. We will be like skeletons."

This is when Becky starts to scream. Her cry spears the night, echoes around the shelter, startling even Wilson. Becky screams and pees herself, which Wilson notes with dull alarm—pee on the GI blanket on the cot! Perfect. (And what if he needs this cot tonight, *hmmm*? What if the bomb comes tonight of all nights, Halloween, night of evil, night of tricks, and he's left in the shelter with a blanket smelling like Becky Conway's pee?)

Penny tries to shush her. She coos and wraps her arms around Becky, who squeezes poor Patti Playpal even tighter. But Becky just wails. She sits in her pee. Wilson stares, dumbstruck. She must know that this is not a ghost story, but a warning. And what Wilson believes is this: one must have a certain level of fear in order to be brave. He wants them to know the truth!

"Nice going," sighs Todd. He squats in front of Becky and says, "It's all right, he's just scaring you. Don't freak, okay? It's okay."

But still she screams.

Before Wilson can say more, the hatch door swings open. Moonlight pools on the shelter floor. "Wilson?"

Father pounds down the hatch stairs. His hulking shoulders fill the opening. Becky stops her whining.

"What's going on down here?"

Father looks left and right. He takes in the sight of the shelter. Marbles on the floor. Candy in trading piles. The pee-blanket. Wilson in the army cap. (He should have asked permission, darnit!) Wilson wills himself to be invisible. He stays very still. But Father says nothing more, Father breaks the spell, Father has worried-adult eyes. He stoops for Becky and carries her up the stairs first. The other kids follow. Penny gives Wilson a look that seems downright motherly. Eddie is caboose.

"Should have stuck to the grossest joke game," he sighs. He holds the astronaut helmet against his hip and smirks, his freckles making him look extra elfish. "See you tomorrow."

"Bye."

But Wilson doesn't follow. He stays on the floor of the shelter with the marbles.

He knows what remains for this night. Father will come back for him. Father will say: *You disobeyed me, you went out there anyway. You made Becky go home crying. She's only six.* Father will carry him through the party, in the back door, past the kitchen and the living room, down the hall and into the bathroom where he will watch Wilson brush his teeth. There will be the flinging of the bedroom door, the quick prayer, maybe—even—a little spank on his rear, and Wilson will go to bed hot-faced and cursing in his brain. *Chickenshit Commies.* Wilson can't be the boy who did nothing. The buzz in his brain is replaced with a flutter, like a baby robin is trapped in there somehow and can't get out. He sits there and stays very quiet—like when Mama takes her long naps and the sound of a dropped toy will startle her. He stays still. He wiggles his loose tooth with his tongue until it feels like only a tiny string keeps it attached to his mouth. He waits for the sounds, the light, the arms to carry him.

It's not a matter of if, but when.

DEAN

The house is filled with a languishing light. Cups and bottles litter the floor and counter. Chocolate wrappers sparkle in aluminum-silver. Clouds bank in the distance.

Dean closes the door to Wilson's room. Tonight's early bedtime had not come easily. Wilson first clamored that it was *too early for bed*, he *wasn't tired, this wasn't fair*, it was a *holiday*, and he had *things to do*. But Dean didn't care. His thread of patience was already clipped short. There was the steady rhythm and routine of bedtime, before Wilson slid under the covers and asked for a story.

"A war story," Wilson said. "France."

"Not France, not today," said Dean, unease still settled in his stomach. But images rose to his mind like dead fish bobbing on the surface of water. A bloodied arm in the snow, thick ice in the bunkers. Rats. The air veiled with smoke.

Outside, the guests were mingling, waiting. For Nellie or for him.

"You never tell me," Wilson whined.

"You know too much already."

Wilson stared, his eyes searching.

"Isn't that a good thing?" he said, cocking his head. A cowlick of hair slipped from behind his ear.

"Not always," said Dean. He knew that Wilson would understand this one day—hopefully when fallout shelters were no longer needed, when fathers did not have to consider such impossible futures. "War is not for children to think about."

He eyed the room's disarray. It filled him with a kind of sadness, this room: Wilson's toys in heaps. The floor a puzzle of drawings and collected stones for his slingshot. He imagined Wilson rifling through his things with a frightening focus. Paper stars were glued to the ceiling. A rickety model airplane hung in the window, its propellers spinning soundlessly. Dean thought of his own childhood room: coarse wooden walls, a moth-eaten quilt over a thin cotton mattress.

"You disobeyed me, Wilson." He felt more than heard himself say this. The sternness seemed wrong in his voice—like coming from a memory. "I'm disappointed."

Wilson said nothing.

"Do you hear me, boy? You are not to go down there. It is not for playing, for wilding. Do you understand? And you especially are not to take other children down there."

"It's safer," Wilson said simply. And something in his calm made Dean cold.

Now, he steps into the wood-paneled hallway to see April. The dim hall light casts a shadow on her face. She clutches a straw bag with both hands.

"How is he?" she asks, voice low.

"In trouble." Dean cuts his edge with a smile. "But fine. Hopefully he'll fall asleep, but that may be asking for a lot."

"How old is he?"

"Ten this year."

April looks surprised. "He's small for ten. I'd have guessed younger."

Dean just studies April's face. She seems flushed, perhaps from wine. A butterfly barrette is perched in her nearly black hair, as though nesting in silk. She smells of clean laundry, a bright fresh smell. Like a morning after rain.

He steps past her into the living room. April trails him.

"I was hoping to give my thanks to Mrs. Porter. She slipped out before I could catch her."

"Mrs. Porter isn't feeling well," says Dean. *Don't ask me what I want*, she'd said. There was fire in her face, her voice. Nellie was lit with something from within that frightened him. She looked at him with such fury that he wondered, for a moment, if she really hated him. *This whole thing is not what I want.* "I'll pass it along."

"Oh, all right." But April hesitates in the hallway, as if contemplating whether she should still try to find Nellie.

Dean leans against the wall and lights one of his Lucky Strikes. The living room is in chaos, the card table confettied with strips of paper from the women's charades. The ladies have migrated back to the kitchen, where some gather their plates and bowls. Others stack dirty dishes into the sink. There is the clink and rattle of silverware, china on laminate.

"We're glad you could make it," Dean says. He has long sensed the intense fog of loneliness around April, the way she spends her lunch hour alone, writing furiously through sheets of paper, the way she sometimes pauses, dosimeter in hand, and stares blankly out the window and into another world—perhaps the world of her husband, half a globe away on the Okinawa base.

April smiles, then checks her wristwatch, a slender gold band.

"I'd best get home. I'm an old woman trapped in this body," she says. "It's past my bedtime."

"Would you like me to drive you?" Night has already fallen over Oakleigh.

She shakes her head. "Heavens no. I don't want to put you out. I can walk. It's not far. And Bette said she'd give me a ride in the morning."

April filters into the kitchen and says goodbye to the other women before letting herself out the front door.

Dean drags on his cigarette and is suddenly overwhelmed by the desire to retreat to his office and lock the door. Send the few remaining guests home. But Nellie has already vanished. He cannot abandon everyone, too.

Dean slides into his worn leather chair and rubs his temples. Outside, the children shriek, the last to be towed off by their parents.

"Where's the wife?" says Jim, emerging from the kitchen with two Gunther beers. He passes one to Dean.

"Resting. Not feeling well." Dean puts out his cigarette on the nearby ashtray.

"Ah." Jim arches his eyebrows as if to say, *Oh, I see* in manly solidarity.

"Lois walked Penny and Todd back. And listen, don't be upset by the whole thing. I bet you five bucks that Todd put him up to it."

"Doubtful," says Dean. He should never have built that shelter. He knew it then, watching Wilson study the CDA manuals while he sawed plywood and aligned cement blocks. There was a fascination beyond fear, beyond reason. Of course, Dean knew the cinder block floor and paneled trap door would do nothing—knew the CDA knew it, and the president knew it, only his little boy believed the shelter would save him. Was it right to foster that belief? Or was it fostering fear?

Jim stands and peers out the front window. "That's Sander now." He waves. "Looks like the Conways left already. Hal, too. I was hoping to catch him for a few minutes. Did you know he's been asked back to D.C.?"

Dean nods but says nothing. He cannot think of Hal right now.

"You know what Lois wants, apparently?" Jim says. He tips back his beer and circles the living room. He runs a hand along the book bindings on the oak shelf. "A battery-operated pepper mill. Hell, I didn't even know what a pepper mill was! She came and brought the magazine over, and it's this pepper grinder, see? That you plug into the wall near the stove. So you don't have to grind your own pepper. I swear, if any future archaeologists ever dig through America, they'll find automated pepper grinders and they'll realize that this, this is the reason for America's downfall. Plug-in everything. Radios. Televisions. Soon kids will ask how to plug in their toothbrushes."

Jim is the sort of man soothed by the sound of his own voice.

"Don't they already make those?"

"I mean, if they can make spaceships, they can make plug-in toothbrushes. Or baseball bats that swing for them. But what's the point?"

"I guess the point is that your wife wants one."

"Damn right." Jim sips his beer and settles on the couch. He crosses his legs. "It'll be that, then onto the other thing. A bread maker or some gizmo to curl your hair faster. Why does a wife run her hands down her husband's pants? To get to his wallet."

Dean chuckles.

He thinks of Hal at this morning's briefing. *What you see here, what you do here, let it stay here.* In one sense, that is impossible. Work and worry follow him home every night.

He thinks of Hal bent over the lectern, talking slowly as if fatigued. Hal describing the air sampling stations, charcoal cartridges in Nevada, all within the cloud radius.

"No, it's true," Jim continues. "Lois bought a dress for tonight, and she'll want a new one for Thanksgiving and for Christmas and for New Year's. A man needs a private bank account, just to make sure there'll be savings next month." Dean nods, sips his beer. The back door swings shut as more of the women retreat to the lawn. "By the way, did I mention that Lois's sister Ava's in town next weekend? And first of all, I'm just wishing she gave us more of a warning, you know? Second of all, there's the whole mess of Lois wanting to buy a horse. And her sister is all, yes, you should do it, life is short, buy the horse. And I'm saying, but do we have money or space for a horse? We have a postage stamp lot! I have a government salary for Pete's sake! Jesus. Pepper mill and now a horse. Where does it stop? The women get it from each other, you know. It's like kids at Christmas. They like what they have until they see what their friend got."

Dean nods again but hardly listens.

Was it true, the stories about Hal? That he'd been surprised to encounter military plans for the first bomb, even though scientists had long been courting the government with their research and the possibility for a nuclear arsenal?

Sander Preston claims that Hal even wrote to President Truman and begged him not to use the bomb in Japan. Others claimed this was a story spread by Hal himself, to either dispel guilt or appease the wrath of antinuclear protestors, who viewed the ongoing arms race as sinister science. Perhaps he simply wanted to join the ranks of Einstein, voicing dissent too late.

"So, what's with April Gardner?" Jim is watching him carefully, brows raised.

"What do you mean?"

"I mean you invited her tonight, and I'm no fool."

"I was being neighborly."

Jim's silence speaks volumes.

If he's honest, Dean has been wondering this himself. Tonight, April stayed late filing paperwork while he and Jim churned through reports. When they left, she was walking alone to her car. It was the sound of her heels alone on the pavement that got to him. The isolating *click click click* you notice when there's no one walking beside you. And Dean heard himself invite her, last minute. Said, come along with us. She smiled and her nose, splattered with freckles, made a wrinkle. She is twenty-four, a graduate of community college, and her husband, Hugh, is stationed at Kadena Air Base. She rarely speaks of him, though when she does, her face opens like a daylily. At the last Farmer's Ball—Nellie refused to come, claimed to be under the weather—April was alone, sipping a Shirley Temple. Dean sat beside her. They stared at the dance floor. They watched Campbell and his wife teach a white couple to Lindy Hop, and April said, out of nowhere, "I'm afraid we won't know what to talk about." Neither said anything more, but he knew she meant her husband. And he understood the fear all too well. What to talk about when what you share with your spouse is not real life but some other thing? That night, he saw April in a new way. A wife alone in a small two-bedroom house. A wife waiting and worried for her love to come back.

"You're imagining things," says Dean. "We don't all have your charm."

Jim smiles sardonically and sips his beer. "True." He laughs. "Sometimes I miss New York, you know?"

"I don't, actually."

"I'm just saying," Jim's voice dips low again. "If you and April—"

"Don't say it," says Dean, more sternly now. "Don't say anything like that."

He thinks of Nellie in the bedroom; Nellie with her arms crossed, a halo of frizz rising from her curls; Nellie with her hard angles and long legs, her beautiful and wild and blustery presence. He aches for her to come out of that room. He isn't even sure, really, what he did to anger her—at what exact moment things slipped into the irreparable.

Tension pulls between them like a taut thread until Dean changes the subject: "Your boy's getting awfully tall."

"Yeah, Todd's almost twelve now. Says he wants to go out for football, but Lois isn't too keen on that."

Jim keeps talking: the sort of talk that drones into white noise like music played too softly. Dean closes his eyes, leans back into the chair. He has reached an exhaustion that fills his bones. There is too much to think about: the morning's headlines, the day's reports, the data that will be ready on his desk tomorrow. He's almost scared to look. Scared what it will mean. But he knows already, with that same out-of-body assurance that made him know they were having a son before Wilson was born. The plant has buried nuclear waste, destroyed the earth from the inside. He has been complicit. And tomorrow, he must deliver the annual report to the Atomic Energy Commission. He must denounce this behavior or go along quietly.

Rest seems impossible. As soon as he closes his eyes, he is there again: under the economical light, faded and fluorescent. He hears April testing the radiation in the dosimeters, flagging anyone who may have received too high a dosage at the reactors. He sees the soil in test tubes, the cranes lowering boxes into the ground. There is no mental space left to linger on Wilson in the shelter, Nellie in the bedroom, April in this house at all.

Jim drones on, first about a John Cheever story he'd read, then about how ridiculous it was that the Washington Senators had become the Minnesota Twins. And Dean remembers how he met a Minnesotan man—what are the odds, out of only three hundred survivors?—who survived the sinking of the U.S.S. *Indianapolis*. The man visited the plant with the Atomic Energy Commission, toured the facility, and his story was harrowing. He fell into the water, drenched in fuel oil. Treaded for days. Watched sharks glide through the sea. An unthinkable way to die. But this, sometimes, is how Dean feels. He is treading water. Something terrible always seems to swim around him, ready to snatch his life any moment.

"Forty miles," says Jim now, voice lowered. "Forty fucking miles high. Did you read that in the report?"

"Not here, I don't want Wilson—"

"He's asleep. Besides, it was in the paper this morning. Kid'll learn eventually. This here's a fucking nightmare."

"We both know they won't do a bigger test. It's not even usable."

"If that bastard gets on Soviet TV and says, *We will bury you* one more time, then Kennedy better blast them off the goddamn earth."

The patter of small feet. A shadow in the hallway.

"Wilson," Dean shouts, a one-word command. The feet scurry back to the bedroom, and the door creaks to a close.

A darkness wrinkles through him. *Wonderful.* Just what Wilson needed to hear.

"No more of that in the house," says Dean. He flips on the radio, and the voice of the news anchor fills the room, muffling their conversation (he hopes) from the sliver of air under Wilson's door. *News from Washington today show that the deficit is set to increase.*

"You sound like Lois," Jim sighs.

Lois and Jim had always seemed an odd match to Dean. She, an actress trying to make it in New York after a brief London stint—he, a war-haunted POW who threw himself into a physics degree at NYU, desperately trying to forget everything. And by any means necessary. But they both came from old money. Dean himself had never known luxury, could remember days of hunger.

Don't ask me what I want, Nellie had said. As if this is what he wants. What husband wants to be afraid that his wife will buy and hide bottles around the house?

"Khrushchev is a damn coward," Jim says, though Dean missed exactly *what* it was that Jim found cowardly. "Besides, third-degree burns almost a hundred miles away. Think about that. It's like what? From here to Sumter?"

Jim is one of those men who seems to always be thinking of the Pacific. No matter the conversation, there is a connection to be made. Toyota ad? The goddamn war. The local high school puts on a production of *South Pacific*? Jim had a speech to make. He is an athletic type, boisterous, with a frenzied, pent-up energy. Dean never likes to think of

Europe. He wants it locked away like the trunk in his office—though, he thinks now of Wilson ferreting through it, trying on Dean's war clothes like a game of dress-up.

"You know what Todd asked me the other day?" Jim stands and retrieves another beer from the kitchen. "He asked if he should enlist in the army before college. Said he wanted to be like his old man. Only twelve and quite the forward thinker."

"What'd you say?"

"I said it was up to him, of course. But that it would teach him to be a man. He liked that."

Dean says nothing for a minute, then: "I wonder if we'll end up in Vietnam after all."

"I doubt it. The whole thing will fizz over."

Dean isn't so sure. Just days ago, he read in *LIFE* about GIs already training for guerrilla warfare: *The terrain is full of rugged mountains and jungles which provide excellent hiding places. Egged on by Moscow and Red China, who hope by taking South Vietnam to move in on the entire area, the guerrillas infiltrate the long borders, sneak into the towns by night to murder local officials . . . then disappear.* He read about the soldiers in Fort Bragg, only hours away, learning how to knife sentries and suffocate men without making a single sound, how to rig bombs and burn bridges. Was there no end to violence in sight? What was more banal and base—an atomic bomb destroying whole cities or men crawling through the jungle at night, faces painted to look like tropical ferns as they slit enemy throats? Both took lives. Both, to Dean, seem so dark.

He cannot imagine sending Wilson to war. Was this what bothered him about the sight of the army cap on his son's head? His child, so eager to play with violence?

"Korea didn't fizz over, and we thought that then," Dean says.

Jim shrugs, considering this. "It's possible, I guess."

His face darkens, and Dean wonders what he remembers: wonders if Jim is thinking now, this very minute, of life on the choppy water. Life in a five-by-seven cell, standing room only for a waste bucket.

Again, the sound of feet, the creak of a door. Dean turns to see a flash of dark hair as Wilson darts back into his room. Does the boy ever listen?

Dean marches down the hall into the bedroom.

There is the whisper of fabric and a hushed puff of breath. Wilson is a boy-shaped mound under the covers. A tuft of thick hair spills onto the pillow.

"It's *bedtime*," Dean says firmly.

Wilson sits up and throws back the sheets.

"I'm not tired," he wails. Then: "I lost a tooth."

He holds up a baby canine, like a pearl drop.

"You ate too much candy. How many pieces did you have?"

"I don't know. Lost count." He tucks the tooth under his pillow, then flops onto the bed. "Where's Vietnam?"

Damn it, Jim, Dean thinks. Or was he the one who mentioned the possible war?

"Asia," he says. "That's very far away. Very far."

"I want to go there." Wilson says this thoughtfully, earnestly. It's the voice he uses when he asks for a puppy or spare dimes to buy candy. He does not whine like other children his age. He declares.

"No, you most certainly don't." And Dean says a quick prayer to the God he has mostly forgotten, mostly abandoned, mostly doubted all his adult life. God was a bearded presence in childhood, a dark cloud in the war. He prays that his boy, his ten-year-old little boy will never carry a gun into battle, that his ears will never ring with the sound of bombs. Wilson cries now with indignation. Usually tears make Dean angry. He wants his boy to be strong. But tonight he softens, walks to the bed, and runs his hand over his son's face, so pale and clean in the moonlight, bright as Ivory soap. Wilson squirms, murmurs, *Come on*, with exasperation. But Dean prays that Wilson, his boy, named after his father, will never know hunger, never know the weight of another man's dying body on his shoulders, nor how slow the hours can pass in the cold. *Do not want these things*, he thinks. *Never want them.* Terrible days are coming, he knows. More terrible than even he can imagine. This is a world in which men can drop bombs on children, in which children can become soldiers. Would there be child soldiers in Vietnam, sent to

scout the rice paddies or monkey-crawl through camps? Would there
be American boys fighting there, less man than monster, still children
really—not even twenty?

"What's in Vietnam then?" says Wilson.

"There are bad people there doing bad things," Dean says with a
sigh. "Some people think there will be a war."

"Like the war you were in?"

"No. There will never be a war like that again."

Does he believe this?

There is an unwelcome memory: the sky orange, like tonight. Pumpkin and sunflower, winter yet a future worry. Clouds like purple hearts.
And as the sun sank over the hills, the Germans strafed and bombed
them—flames rained from the branches. Dean hunkered in a bur-
row with two men whose names he didn't know. It was dry, but flecks
of ash fell like cotton in the wind. They stayed there all night, awake
and clutching their guns, listening. He tried to remain calm. He laid
back, head against the soil. Still the bombs fell. Smoke floated overhead, blending with the clouds. Bats flew screeching into the night.
Dean buried his face in the ground and coughed. He smelled the soil,
felt the dirt on his face, in his nose, under his nails. He trembled and
thought of the farm back home. His family. Other men toted letters,
pictures of loved ones, lockets with clipped hair, but Dean had only his
father's watch. Father gave it when Dean enlisted, saying, "A day can
feel like a lifetime. But it isn't." And by this he meant: *Come home, son.
You must have a life here.* That day was a lifetime as screams tore the
night. He had not met Nellie then. Did not have the problem other
men had—the anxiety of returning to their girls, the life they'd stitched
in imagination through the long hours of waiting. He only had the
watch. He saw the hours pass. And the clouds moved and the sun rose,
and he was still alive. There was still the hope of something, the hope of
home.

"You're safe here, my son," says Dean. He pulls up the covers to Wilson's chin, as his mother used to do for him.

Then he leaves the room, closes the door firmly behind him.

The house has quieted more. Jim still sits on the couch, his leg bobbing.

He flips through one of the magazines Nellie keeps piled in a wicker basket.

Dean stops in front of his favorite clock, hanging above his chair. This was the first one he salvaged. The scene is of an alpine lumberjack who goes about his task, steadily chipping away at wood that never gets smaller. Zadie Cato, an elderly neighbor from childhood, gave him this clock during her relocation to New Ellenton. The great exodus making way for the bomb plant. The clock was broken then, in need of new weighted chains. He made it run.

"Do you ever think about what you might have done different?" Dean asks, just as the clock strikes ten. The latticed window opens, and the lumberjack's wife appears. She flaps a cloth in the air before disappearing.

Jim flips a page and shrugs. "What do you mean?"

"I mean, without the AEC. If you weren't at the plant."

"After Japan, I knew exactly what I'd do. There was never anything else."

A small scar creases Jim's forehead, the cut from a bayonet. Most days, Dean forgets it's there. But now, in the amber light, as the clocks tick behind him, the scar seems prominent.

"I think I'd be teaching," Dean says. But he knows he could have been just as happy working with his hands. A carpenter. A clockmaker.

He could have taught at Clemson—Tillman Hall on the sloped green hillside, the rusty brick in the autumn, just as the trees changed color. The bell tower that proclaimed the start of the hour. It was Clemson, that little college town, where he'd fallen in love with life again after the war—where he met Nellie and dared to dream. "I'd run a student laboratory. Have an agronomy department. Spend my summer conducting research just for the sake of it."

"Sure, I could be teaching, I s'pose," says Jim, laughing. "Have an office with windows. Have a pretty little TA. Maybe in a few years, you never know how long these jobs'll last."

"Ain't that the truth," says Dean. He knows all too well.

If only there was a way to predict what would happen tomorrow, to plan accordingly.

"Well," says Jim, pressing his hands on his knees and standing with heft, "I'd best be going. Long day."

They wave good night, and Dean finds himself alone now. It is a wretchedly lonely feeling, a quiet but full house.

After turning off the lights, Dean retreats to the bathroom. He washes his face, combs his hair, unbuttons his work shirt. There is no sound from the master bedroom. Nellie has not stirred since their argument—what, two hours ago now? He tries not to be angry by this, but he can't help it. She was the one always wanting to entertain, and yet she abandoned their party guests and left him to fend for their son and the night.

He lathers his face to shave, soothed by the warm foam on his brush. When they were first married, Nellie used to watch him. She stood in her bathrobe with a glass of sherry, watching as he pulled his skin and drew the blade over his cheek bone. She was beautiful—she had symmetry. Heavy-lidded with thick blond hair that grazed her shoulder. Breasts just large enough to fill his palm.

"How do you not cut yourself?" she asked.

"It's a safety razor," he said, laughing as she ran her hand over his face.

"It looks dangerous." This seemed to thrill her.

Had she drawn him to bed in those days? Or did he always ask? He cannot remember anymore. As he drags the blade over his chin, he thinks on that time—not so long ago—when he could coax a sweet sound from her, when she drew her knees by her side, eager with pleasure. He moved faster, almost frantic. Even then, he remembers, she insisted on making love with the lights off, when all he wanted was to see her fully on the bed beside him. See all the folds in her body, every dimple, every inch of skin sheened with sweat.

He believed she'd been happy then. That this was the life she wanted.

A sliver of pain brings him back. Dean stares at himself in the mirror. A thin line of blood runs down his chin.

He cleans his face, but the aftershave stings on open skin.

Dean steps from the bathroom and hesitates outside the bedroom door. Sometimes, after an argument, he cannot sleep. They fight with

turned shoulders and bodies rolled to the far side of the bed. Theirs is a
Cold War marriage—the explosion never happens. Anger hovers in the
silence. The thought of her turned so far away keeps his mind awake.
He can feel the anger radiate off her body like heat from dying coals.

He cannot risk that, not tonight. He needs his sleep for tomorrow.
Everything changes tomorrow.

Dean moves through the house and out the back door into the still
night. Clouds have smeared the sky, but stars still shine through, like
light cutting through tears in cloth. Hardly thinking, Dean descends
the stone steps and marches toward the shelter's trapdoor. In the dark,
it looks like floating jetsam among the grass.

He remembers how Wilson sat on the back steps and watched as
Dean dug the pit large enough to house them for fourteen days underground. Inside, Nellie busied herself with gathering supplies: used
magazines, tools, nonperishable foods. She called it "playing apocalyp-
tic housewife." Dissatisfaction only came when she learned that the
McAlisters, who lived across the street, put linoleum floors in their
shelter. Once Nellie heard this, she begged for nicer floors. After all, if
there was an attack, and if they had to stay down there for God knew
how long, how could they survive with cedar block floors? And how
could they survive in such a dismal space?

"Some people even put running water down there," she said one
night, rubbing cold cream into her skin. "Think of that, Dean. Running water."

"Sounds nice," he said, mildly irritated. Was he undressing then after
a long day? Was he shaving, preparing to shower? Those details escape
him now. But he remembers the words.

"Nancy said that she and Robert plan to install a whole bathroom."

"Well, shelters like that are expensive," he said. "Ours already cost
one hundred dollars. And if there is a war, Nel, and if there is a bomb,
we wouldn't be worried about any bathroom."

"How do you know?"

"I just know, Nel."

As he kneels by the shelter and heaves open the trapdoor, he can still see her face that night, the distance that stretched between them. She said, "You're cheap, you know that? You're a tightwad."

"You don't know what it's like to be poor," he snapped. And when he said this, the words slipped out like river water on stones. "You've never lost anything, not really. You don't know what it's like to be twenty-one and watching your friends die in a foxhole in winter, blown apart. You don't know what it's like to not have food on your plate. I do, Nel. And I'm trying to take care of us, not squander away our money on things that don't matter."

And this is where she chilled.

"You don't know anything about me," she said.

But he did, actually.

He knew about her family, the wealth drained in the wretched divorce. He knew how her mother opened a cotillion school and worked to pay the bills. He knew about the father-shaped hole in Nellie's life. Still. Nellie always had new dresses when she outgrew hers. She never wore shoes with holes. Her mother even employed a cook during the hardest years, draining their savings because it was worse to *look* poor than to *be* poor. Miles away, Dean sweated under the summer sun, picking peaches in June, muscadines in September. As soon as he could read, he had a paper route, and his days were punctuated by the work clock: newspapers thrown at porch steps in the morning, school through the tired hours, then the back-stooping chore of picking sun-warmed fruit.

No, Nellie had never been truly poor. She had always expected red meat at dinner. When Dean told her of whole days where he ate only cornbread and buttermilk, the occasional beans, she laughed, as if the idea was charming—like a folksy picnic from an advertisement.

Dean descends into the shelter. When was the last time he was down here, except to fetch Wilson? Was it after they built it? Was it during a drill? He cannot remember.

The ladder steps are well worn, scuffed by shoe marks. He pulls the cord and a soft light casts the shelter in pale color.

The ground is sprinkled with candy, as if a piñata erupted at a children's birthday. It smells of children—that musty grass-stained smell, mixed with a sweetness like sweat and sun. It is surprisingly warm with the single bare bulb.

On the wooden plank walls, Wilson has pinned drawings. There are hand-sketched maps of town. Dean recognizes their house circled in blue crayon with the words *YOU ARE HERE*. There are CDA bulletins and posters advertising fallout shelters and safety rules. Tear-outs from library books and mail flyers.

ALERT TODAY, ALIVE TOMORROW

BE ALERTE JUSTIN CASE

YOU CAN'T AVERT DISASTER BY IGNORING IT

No wonder little Becky Conway went home crying. He is at once embarrassed and angry—but mostly, just sad.

Toy soldiers stand vigil between soup cans. A broken pair of binoculars—a pair Dean doesn't even recognize—are discarded on the water barrel. Wilson's candy pillowcase lays in a heap beside it. The shelter has become, he sees, a bona fide clubhouse.

Is this how Wilson will remember his childhood? *We hid from bombs underground. We ran drills.*

Dean lies on the cot, avoiding the army blanket that reeks of piss. The cot triggers memories, its coarseness on his skin. But there is a familiarity there, too. After the war, a real bed felt too soft. A pillow sparked guilt. He'd survived to use pillows again, to have unlimited soap, to even dream of *graduate school*, of *life after war*. He knew so many not that lucky.

He falls asleep and dreams of farmland—a thick Carolina clay. He is walking through fields, his father's. The peach trees are so ripe that the branches hang heavy, as if weary. Past the trees and rows of vegetables, Dean runs his hand through the dirt, making finger trenches. But when he pulls his hand away, there is a burning sensation. His skin sheds like a leper in thin strips. Dean writhes in the dream, as though fighting it. He dreams of tiny rivers of radioactivity furrowing through the ground, straight to the red-hot core of earth.

Henry Dean Porter
528 Crimson Crest
Oakleigh, South Carolina 29804

November 1, 1951

My Nellie my own,

I hope this letter finds you well. I apologize for the delay—I've been
working overtime here. They've asked us to stay longer for some meetings,
but there's nothing to worry about. And guess who I ran into on the tour:
old Jim Shepherd. What a small world this is.

You wouldn't believe the number of people here—I hardly do. Right off 278,
I came bumper to bumper with a line of cars as far as I could see. Tourists,
Nel—can you believe that? Tourists come to see the commotion in Ellenton.
They had plates from as far north as Delaware, and I saw men step outside
their cars with cameras around their necks. I laughed hard when I saw
that. Like goddamn disaster tourists, watching as sharecroppers' houses were
transported by train and trailer. But there's also a lot of construction workers.
Yesterday, I met three of the strongest welders, all from California, one as
young as eighteen. They drove here all the way from Loma Linda, can you
believe that?

It really is so strange to be back. I haven't been here since Mother, though
I'm sure you didn't forget. Do you remember that old brick house with the
stables around the back? It was right near that abandoned smokehouse?
Anyway, gone now. The whole town is gone, Nel, you wouldn't believe it.
The depot, the post office, the little white church, the Cotton King. It's like
reading through a book you remember, but there are pages missing. God,
makes me glad in a way that my father never saw this. Can you imagine
him, shotgun and cigar and all, not willing to leave? I don't want to think
about what would have happened, how I would have had to convince him.
Every structure has been destroyed, which I understand. The AEC fears
that any lasting building could become security risks.

Every family I ever knew has left—their farms and cemeteries have
moved, and Nel, I can't help but feel sort of guilty for that, though I know

it's not my choice. They're all relocated to what's being called New Ellenton, a little farm settlement just a few miles outside Oakleigh. Think about it. How would we feel if someone came up to our door and said, 'scuse me ma'am, but we need this land? Last night before supper, I walked through what's left. There was a street already stripped, but the road curb was still there, jutting out of the clay ground. It was oddly beautiful, this curb. Then I saw a little colored girl, who couldn't be much older than five or so, I'd say. She was walking along the road by herself, barefoot in a chicken feed dress. She didn't look at me. She walked sort of zig-zag and every now and then, she'd stop and murmur to herself. When she neared me, she knelt by that curb and I heard her say, "Goodbye curb," before she moved to a little crick and said, "Goodbye pond." Nel, I don't think I've ever been so close to crying in public as I was right then. She disappeared soon after, and I suppose she rejoined her family, wherever they were. But I've seen many like her: old men, some your mother's age, some much older, sit on their front porches, and I feel them mourning for their land.

There's a sign someone put up by the county highway that says, and I wrote this down so I wouldn't forget, "It is hard to understand why our town must be destroyed to make a bomb that will destroy someone else's town that they love as much as we love ours. But we feel that they picked not just the best spot in the U.S., but in the world. We love these dear hearts and gentle people who live in our hometown." Just painted that with shoe polish on gum boards.

I almost wish I didn't read that—or, really that's not true. I'm glad I saw it. But Nel, I have to believe in what we're doing here, as I saw them breaking ground and starting on plans you couldn't imagine. This is not the South Carolina I remember. I remember the tin and timber and unpainted porches. I remember the smell of peanuts and hickory—corn cribs and cotton bolls dotting the ground. I remember the Chickasaw plums in the summer evenings, muscadine wine.

My mind runs away. Forgive me for boring you.

Hope all is well for you and W. Can you believe we've had a month with him already?

Dean

MORNING: COLD AND PEARLY. The grass is wet-tipped, frosted over in the night.

Weak light pours from the kitchen windows. Cars rumble through the neighborhood. Elderly men rake leaves, young boys run lawn mowers. A dark-skinned woman covers perennials with a plastic tarp. The sidewalk is littered with the history of Halloween—candy and bows from costumes and abandoned pillowcase bags.

Wilson has been up for hours. He scouts in the bushes, watches the Royce red and Pontiac blue pass their street. He tramples Nellie's canna lilies, nuclear yellow. He blows on his hands to keep warm. He marvels at the cloud of air, like ghost breath.

The sky still shows the faint shape of the moon in morning. The moon saying goodbye to this, its world.

Then—day splits open. There is the marathon of the morning: ham in the skillet, toast in the oven, water whistling in the kettle. Breakfast, homework tucked in a backpack. The baby tooth wrapped in brown paper, slipped in a pocket. Badge unlooped from the coatrack. A quick kiss, a chill. Dean's car leaves for work. Nellie pours milk down the drain. There is a quick pick-up from last night, all the explosive remains of wrappers and cups and napkins and beer bottles. The wall is scuffed from the card table. Water spots ring the hardwood.

Finally, there is the prodding for Wilson to dress himself. Nellie ventures into his room, as chaotic as if a cyclone wound its way through. Clothes shed like snakeskin on the floor. Toys in pyramids—Colorforms, a pogo stick. And when he slings his bag over his shoulder, he looks—suddenly—adult. A soldier headed for war.

NELLIE

I nside the Sorenson's house, there is a pulsating warmth. There is a bundle of energy. Nellie hugs the front hallway and watches the protest preparation. Everywhere, there are women at work. Some kneel by the parlor coffee table, some write in their laps. Others paint picket signs with jars of black acrylic and bristly brushes. Two women Nellie has never seen before stand smoking by the sliding glass doors that lead to the patio. Somewhere, a child cries. (And really, who brings a child to a protest?) Over it all, there is the voice of Ella Fitzgerald on vinyl.

On the phone this morning, Lois said simply, "Look smart." So Nellie dressed in tweed slacks and sturdy mules with a brass-buttoned overcoat. Dean's two hundred dollars are folded neatly in her pocketbook. When she catches herself in the hall mirror, she thinks she looks severe. And old, like her mother! Gray hair streaks the blond!

There must be fifty women at least—perhaps more? There is Hazel Tuckerman lettering a picket; there is Ida Roskam carrying cigarettes and coffee cups on a tin platter; there are Joan Moran and Barb Braxton, each stamping and sealing envelopes. Nellie has never liked Barb Braxton, what with her horses all named after flowers. Primrose and Dandelion and Queen Anne's Lace. But today, the women look radiant.

The house breathes with light. (If only they could have a house like this.) The living room is open and spacious with an orange couch and gold-tasseled pillows. Silk dupioni curtains bookend the glass doors. Murano vases and Japanese ceramics rest on mounted shelves. On the ground lies an Oriental rug. In place of wood paneling, there is floral wallpaper. In place of ticking clocks, art: Scandinavian paintings, tapestries, framed splatters of mustard and maroon, as though the artist had dribbled paint indiscriminately.

Nellie has been here before, but only once, and she was as struck then. They had just moved to town. Dean was invited to dinner by Hal. If she remembers correctly, there was a fight on the way out the door—something minor, faded with time—but she was sour on the ride over. During a three-course dinner that Myra cooked herself, Nellie sipped her sherry and felt increasingly small as the conversation whorled around foreign policy, the election, Supreme Court decisions that rocked the newspapers, the new school integrations. Even Myra spoke with authority on such subjects.

Now Nellie catches sight of Myra in the dining room. All the chairs have been moved to clear way for pennants. She stands, surprisingly, alone. Myra looks at the full-sized banners and shifts the canvas.

Myra is dressed in all black, as though she's attending a stately funeral. A braided crown adorns her head. Atop it, a simple felt hat. There's a weariness behind her eyes, a slowness to her movements, as though even the slightest nod exhausts her. She is not a beautiful woman—not slender or graceful. But there is power in the methodical way she runs a finger over the lettering. She is the sort of woman whom one stares at, rapt. Crowds part for her.

Myra looks up and smiles as Nellie steps into the dining room.

"Well, look who showed up," says Myra. Her voice is warm as melted sugar, but dark shadows ring her eyes. "I'm glad to see you."

"Last-minute convert," Nellie says and clutches her bag tight.

"The more the better, I say." Myra's attention reverts again to the banners, which she folds gently.

Nellie watches for a moment before venturing, "Is there anything I should do? I mean, do you need help?"

Myra nods to the kitchen and says there are cutouts to finish. Nellie nods and crosses the room, but Myra stops her with a firm hand.

"Listen," she says, and Nellie is startled by the soft tone, like a secret is about to be exchanged. "I just wanted to say that I know we don't know each other well. But it's brave of you to be here. What we're doing— all this—isn't easy. Not everyone will approve."

Nellie nods but also feels like crying or laughing. She has never felt herself to be brave. Other women rushed to volunteer as nurses during the war. Other women lost husbands, brothers, fathers in gruesome ways.

"I know," Nellie says. She wills her voice to be strong, but it comes out like a whisper.

Myra takes her hand off Nellie's shoulder and sighs so deeply that there's a visible weight to her shoulders. Nellie stares at the lines in the woman's face, every wrinkle like a worry thread-thin on her skin. And she surprises herself by asking, "Can you tell me about the bombs? Is it true you saw them at Los Alamos?"

The dark grimace gives Nellie her answer. She chides herself for asking.

"I saw." Myra nods. After a long moment filled with laughter and the voices of women from around the house, she adds, "A lot of us wives knew. We weren't supposed to know, but that's how it was. We watched that first test, Trinity, like a little vigil. You know, later, I felt like Lot's wife. There was destruction around me, and I looked. I looked right at it. I've been a pillar of salt ever since."

This is when Lois enters the dining room.

"You old rascal, you held out on us until the last minute!"

Lois holds a cigarette in one hand, coffee in the other. She also wears all black with a simple cross necklace.

"I'm here now," says Nellie.

She looks back at Myra, who's retreated again to her dignified self, bent over the table.

Nellie follows Lois into the kitchen, where a roar of greeting rises. Around a wide oak table is an assembly line of tasks: piles of paper and scissors, each woman cutting slips into neat stacks. She discards her purse and coat on a sideboard.

She'd imagined—how silly it seems now, how fantastical—an air of illicitness. She'd pictured snake dancing. Housewives gone wild, flowers tucked into hair and shoes discarded at the door. She'd imagined a storm cloud inside the house. The word *protest* implies passion and disorder. But this? There are finger foods on the marble counters:

cucumber sandwiches and watercress salad, punch in a pink bowl. It is a party. Creamy light fills the kitchen, and the women in their brocade dresses and fine wool could just as well be cutting scalloped invitations for a baby shower. Not pamphlets reading ARE OUR CHILDREN SAFE?

Nellie watches the busyness and feels quite small—like that feeling when, on a date with Dean (when was it, '49?) and he tried to explain what an atom even was, this invisible particle of being, and every word he used only reminded her of the chasm between her world and his, so that she left the conversation feeling firmly in the shadow of his knowledge.

"Is Harriet here?" Nellie sits between Lois and the preacher's wife, Clarissa.

"She backed out, sadly. Called this morning and said she'd thought better of it. Which probably means Sander found out, poor thing. You wouldn't know by the looks of him, but that snake's got a bite, if you know what I mean. Cigarette?" Lois pulls a pack from her pocket and offers one to Nellie.

"Thanks."

Lois lights both. She lowers her voice and arcs her eyebrows.

"Listen. I just got off the phone with my pal at the paper, Olive. She said they're sending a photographer to cover this whole thing. Isn't that grand? We could be in the paper."

A scene flashes before Nellie's eyes—her first office, that newspaper in Clemson. The typewriter keys pounding, the musical chime of phones. But most of all, the hive-like energy, the urgent feel of the work. The this-must-get-done-today-ness of it. When she was the sole owner of a set of apartment keys, when she wore new penny loafers and a mauve work skirt and (thrillingly!) had a place to be. She remembers her boss, a stocky and heavy-drinking man, saying, "Better to write the news than be the news."

"I'm not sure I want my picture in the paper," Nellie says.

"Look, I know you're worried, but they won't arrest half the women in town," says Lois. She waves toward the front door as another woman enters. "Besides. Barb's here. Lee was just promoted to police chief, and there's no way he'll arrest his own wife."

Lois laughs, picks up a stack of papers, and passes half to Nellie. "Look, we're making cutouts, see? These are pamphlets to disperse to anyone who wants them. Myra had them printed out all nicely, but we just have to cut them. A few others are writing letters to congressmen."

Nellie cuts a neat line down the first page.

"Does Jim know you're here?" she asks.

Does Dean?

"Well, I told him, but we'll see if he listened. He's not exactly one for long-term attention, unless, that is, he's listening to himself."

Nellie wants to say *I know what you mean!* She considers telling Lois about last night—the teeth, the sense of loss that guttered through her. She longs to put words to that moment when protest became inevitable, when she realized that the man before her was not the man she'd married. Lying had become second nature. Work had become everything. She cannot live this way anymore.

Instead, she says, "That's too bad."

"He can be a little one-track minded," says Lois. In the kitchen, the phone rings. Barb Braxton dashes in from the living room to answer. "Last time we went home to my parents'—my sister just had her fourth, bless her heart—he and my father got into this awful argument. Just terrible. Father works in television, see, and Jim said something like, you know our real danger is the influx of entertainment, maybe even more than the Soviets. Maybe more than bombs altogether. People won't think for themselves anymore, he said! Father just exploded, I tell you. 'Television,' said. 'You're comparing television to the atom bomb?' All through dinner the men argued over whose work was the least terrible. There I was with the children, trying to keep them from hearing, and Penny was just on the verge of tears, I tell you. Sometimes I just want to point to the kids and say, 'They're listening.'"

They fall into the rhythm of cutting. The papers grow into neat stacks, and Nellie finds herself enjoying the cleanness of it, the sheen of the scissors in her hands. As she works, she reads the text.

ARE OUR CHILDREN SAFE?

Did you know that fallout levels hit an all-time high this spring and summer?

Fallout from nuclear testing can contaminate milk and other fresh goods, which significantly increases health risks for your child, including various types of cancers.

But the atmospheric testing of atomic bombs also creates a spirit of fear, which we have seen instilled in our children. So today we march, and we entreat all who identify with our protest to join with your sisters. We believe this is the special responsibility of women—as mothers who bring life into this world—to demand our leaders do better. To demand that humanity deserves more than the risk of sudden and violent annihilation.

Let's make earth a nuclear-free zone.

NELLIE IS AWARE OF her shortcomings as a mother. When Wilson was born—God, she's ashamed to remember!—she kept the windows bolted. Even in summer, when a syrupy heat hung through the house. She feared she would throw her baby out the window in a fit of rage. A tantrum. A soiled diaper. A piercing cry in the night. Even the softness of his sleeping breath could sometimes make her itch with fury. Their home filled with newborn warmth, but she felt cold. She was not there. She was drifting, even then. The parenting books warned of this: that pregnancy could be hard on sensitive, anxious women—well, she was that already. But sometimes, she just needed quiet! A moment to herself! (Dean never understood this: never forgave her for that night when she snapped.) And she remembers how, when Wilson was too young for school but walking and talking already, they played endless rounds of hide-and-seek. She was good at hiding. Once, she lodged herself between the washer and dryer and Wilson, hardly older than three, couldn't find her for so long that he forgot the game. He cried, and still she hid. Even as guilt boiled. One was never supposed to leave a three-year-old to roam the house, never supposed to hide from your child! Wilson eventually forgot the game and his tears and discovered his toy cars, upon which she reemerged and cooed, "Hello, my little baby face, my sweet little baby." She made her great entrance and sparked Wilson's smiles. And maybe, she thinks, as she sips her coffee, that was what she liked most about the game. The emergence. The smile of relief. Like climbing out of a shelter, awaking from a dream.

"TEN MINUTES." MYRA ENTERS the kitchen, trailed by two other women. One carries a cardboard box.

"Ladies, I want you all wearing gloves," Myra says as the conversation stills. Scissors pause mid-cut. "I have extra. Wear whatever you want. I want you wearing gloves not because I give a damn about gloves, but because in the midst of all the red-baiting business, I don't want anyone saying we're not dignified. Right now, nothing is more dignified than what we are doing."

A whoop of approval rises from the living room.

Myra casually adjusts her pearls, sliding the fishhook clasp behind her neck. Nellie imagines that Myra as a mother would never have hidden in the laundry room from her child. She would never have stolen money from her husband.

"Today you are all courageous women," she says. Her gaze moves slowly—too slowly!—about the room, and Nellie reddens under the weight of it. "Sometimes there is no other way than to take to the streets. If we just sit and talk over coffee in our homes, then who will listen? Surely not the people we want to listen to us. If we want to get the president's attention, then we must get the press's attention. And to do that, sisters, we will march."

The telephone rings again, and this time Myra answers. Chatter rises, filling the space in the room. The women pass the box around the table and select a pair of gloves, mostly short and white, some pearl-buttoned, others with mod trim and fringe. Nellie takes a supple leather pair, soft as margarine.

Red-baiting business, Myra had said.

Nellie keeps cutting and tries not to think of this. (Is she foolish for coming? A damn fool?) A vision comes to her, unwillingly—she, standing before the House Un-American Activities Committee. They ask her all those questions: *Have you ever attended a meeting with the League of Women Voters? League of Women Shoppers? Do you believe it is proper to mix white and Negro blood plasma? Are you in sympathy with the working class? Have you ever made statements about the "downtrodden masses" and "underprivileged people"?* All those terrible questions—she was so frightened when they investigated her before. Could she handle it again?

She overhears bits of conversation from around the table. *Said it was a sewing club meeting and he bought it cold turkey.*

The bell rings, and in comes Bev Conway, maneuvering a baby carriage through the door. Bev looks frazzled this morning. Her hair's volume is uneven, and the yellow headband clashes with her turquoise dress. She parks the wicker baby carriage by the kitchen counter as Lois bursts from the table.

"Well, aren't you just the picture of motherhood," says Lois. "I love it. See, I thought about bringing the kids so they could witness this, too, but I didn't want to drag Penny and Todd from school."

Bev smiles at the baby, who sleeps in her cocoon of white blankets.

"I'll tell her about this one day."

Should Nellie have brought Wilson? The moment she thinks this, she smiles, almost laughs. What would Dean say to that? Ha! He'd just about lose his mind—he would deliver one of his lectures in that patronizing scientific voice. *The boy is distressed*, he'd said. As if she didn't know about distress! Yes, the boy was distressed. Well, she was the one doing something about it. She cuts the pamphlets faster and determines to save one for Wilson, for his collections. Yes, she is doing this for Wilson—and for her, of course. (The two hundred dollars still burn a meteor-sized hole in her pocketbook. Will she buy drop-earrings, like twin stars? Will she save it for a day of the blues, when her whole body aches with something shadowy and Prussian?) Tonight, Wilson will recite bomb facts, and she will recite other facts like: "Did you know that fallout can increase health risks? Can lead to various cancers?" She will memorize the pamphlet. Will he appreciate this, her protest? Will he see that their lives are not defined by the bomb plant? Not defined by Dean. Yes, she thinks. This is not just about her husband; this is about her son—she is doing this for Wilson, too. Isn't she?

Bev looks at Nellie with some surprise. "I looked for you to say good-bye last night. Were you feeling ill?"

"Yes. I got one of those damn headaches."

"Methedrine," says Lois. "Try that. Works like a charm. Bill Pace carries it."

"Does he?"

Bev pulls up a chair beside Nellie. "Five minutes, ladies!" Myra shouts. Bev takes a stack of pamphlets and cuts the last few, intense in her focus. Nellie wrinkles her nose. There is the definitive smell of spit-up milk, veiled thinly by baby powder.

Bev leans closer.

"Last night," she says so only Nellie can hear, "Allen heard from one of the other men about the protest. I guess word is getting around. And he asked if I was coming."

"What did you say?"

"I'm a terrible liar, and he'd hate if I lied," says Bev. "I said yes."

"And?"

Nellie is not accustomed to being anyone's confidante, and she feels a flicker of wonder—and almost warmth—at Bev's intimate tone.

"He threw a plate across the room. I still have shards everywhere on the floor."

"What?"

Bev reaches for the wicker carriage and rocks it softly for a moment. Around them, the other women stand, stack the papers, begin to button their coats. Somewhere, someone turns off the record player.

"I told him I wouldn't go," says Bev. "I said, I'll stay home. But this morning, I just had to get out. And I took the baby."

Something dark and unpleasant blooms in Nellie's stomach.

"Well, I'm glad you did," she says.

"Does Dean know?"

Nellie shakes her head. "But he will."

She imagines the bomb plant now—sinister, mythic. Dean and his coworkers drop baby teeth by the thousands into narrow-necked flasks. She imagines Dean taking Wilson's teeth from under his pillow, and the thought fills her with an inking anger. She can hear the voice of her mother: *It's undignified, unladylike—women marching in the street like that. It's unnatural.* But here she is, a bomb plant wife like Myra, ready to join the protest. She will get her husband's attention; she will protest this, their life, his work, their marriage. The way the Sterling Creek Plant has polluted every part of their world.

Oh yes. Dean will most certainly know.

February 2, 1950. Panic was in the air. The war was over, but not over. The president had announced plans to increase the nuclear arsenal: TRUMAN ORDERS HELLBOMB MADE. And Nellie had started her first post-college job as a newspaper secretary in Clemson, in a small bureau office near the university. She wanted to learn about Linotype—longed to watch the cylinder of the printing press as it turned copy into typeface. Instead, she was fetching nylons from Lewis Drug for her boss's wife. She was picking up doughnuts for the staff break. This morning: cold and dove gray. Her breath, a cloud. In her arms: two brown paper bags, one with a carton of milk and the other with still-warm muffins from the bakery, often populated by students. She walked through the quad, back to the office—this is when she saw him. He wore dark tweed. He was tall, angular, and swayed as he walked. Suddenly, he knelt to the ground, rubbed the dirt between his fingers and smelled it. How odd, she thought! So odd that she stopped watching her path, tripped on a misaligned brick, and the carton of milk slipped through the bottom of the bag. He was upon her in seconds saying, "Are you all right? Is anything hurt?" Dean insists she said, "Only my dignity," though Nellie has no memory of this. She has never been one for quick wit.

He was an agronomist working at the university's research facility. She found him brilliant in those early years. Oh, how his thoughts were so orderly! He saw the patterns in the world, layers in the sand. He told her about the composition of soil, how groundwater moves like an estuary. He spoke of Oppenheimer and Fermi, names she barely recognized. This was during the "courting months." He was courting her. The plant was courting him. How she loved him then, or wanted to. She was like a pioneer's wife, facing uncharted territory.

DEAN

Wilson was one month old when Dean was sent by the AEC to complete the environmental baseline in the Oakleigh area. This was November 1951. A part of him hated leaving, though he was never much good with babies. He can remember standing over the lace-trimmed bassinet. Nellie was mixing formula in the next room. She was in a stage of wearing too much makeup, trying to hide the tired from her eyes. Wilson looked so small and red-wrinkled among the blankets. His skin was paper thin and petal soft. What Dean loved most were the baby toes, like little pebbles.

"Tell him I'll miss him," Dean said as he carried his leather suitcase to the door.

Nellie looked up from the stove, her face misted with steam.

"He's one month old. He doesn't know anything."

"But tell him anyway. When he wakes up every morning this week, tell him Father misses him. I want him to know. I want him to know subconsciously."

She rolled her eyes, but playfully. "Tell you what. Why don't you call when you can, and I'll put the receiver to his little baby ear. Got it?"

He would call. He was gone only two weeks, but it felt so long then, a little deployment. He called from the post office, too eager to wait. His team was all staying at a boarding house in Augusta, and his carpool waited outside, the blue car parked next to a fire hydrant.

After several rings, Nellie answered, breathless, expectant.

"Hello. It's been raining," she said.

He remembers this distinctly, that tinge of complaint, her first few words, as though he controlled the sky.

"How's Wilson?" he asked. He wanted nothing more than to press his lips to those baby toes.

"He keeps crying. I can't tell what cry it is. I read in this book that babies make different sounds. Only, I can't tell the difference. It just sounds like crying to me."

"Put him on. I want to talk to him."

"For God's sake, Dean, talk to me, *please*. I've only had an infant for company for a week now. Please just talk to me."

He thought that she might cry, and if she cried on the phone, he didn't know what he would do. His hands were still soil stained. His boots smelled like swamp.

"Okay, Nel, okay," he said.

There was silence for a moment. The post office was busy at this hour. A gray-haired woman in a gardenia print dress waited for the phone. In the absence of Nellie's voice, Dean heard no Wilson.

"I don't hear him crying now," he ventured. "Is he sleeping?"

"He's fine."

"Okay—" Something in her voice, her dismissive tone, made him uneasy.

"I swear I'd give anything for a sunny day right now. A walk in the park. Anything."

"Nel, where's Wilson?" A cicada roved up the post office wall. It caught his eye—funny how he remembers this. The most obscene details.

"He's fine," she said again. But her words ran together, melting like butter on a skillet. The softest of slurs.

"But where is he?"

This was the first time he felt fatherly panic.

"I don't think I'm so good at this mother thing," Nellie said at last. He heard then what he would hear many times later: a definitive thickness, a liquor voice. "I think other women know what to do. They don't feel like I feel. But I love my baby."

"It's hard on anyone," he said carefully. A beam of afternoon sunlight cut through the west window, filling the post office with buttermilk light. The cicada was still making his journey toward the ceiling. When it entered the light, its wings turned rainbow for a moment, briefly iridescent. "Your body just made life. It's hard on any woman."

"Something terrible happened to me today, and I'm too tired to talk about it, but I wrote you a letter. Call when you get it?"

That kernel of dread—he would always remember the way it rubbed his throat raw.

"Nel, where's Wilson?" he asked again.

"I put him outside."

They lived in a three-story walk-up. There was no outside—only a musty old hallway that led to neighboring apartments.

"Outside as in—outside our front door?"

"No one will take him," Nellie said, as though she were telling him the clouds would pass.

"I didn't think someone would take him! I think his mother should bring him back inside. He's one month old, Nel."

"If you knew what kind of day I've had." There was a razor edge to her voice that actually frightened him. He glanced around the post office, watching a few patrons go through the line with their packages wrapped in brown paper.

"So help me God, Nellie, you take care of our baby. Or I will drive home right now and get my boy."

This was the first time Dean thought about a Wilson-shaped hole in his life. The many possibilities for accidents and infant fatalities, the way a baby can slip through fingers and become a memory. He'd only known his son a month, but already that hole was impossibly large— the thought of losing what makes life beautiful.

WILSON

He sits by the window in Room 3. The window chair is prime real estate, offering a clear view of town. Outside, the sky is stormy silver. Clouds hang low. This means a plane could easily hide, so Wilson glances out the window every five minutes to be safe. Penny Shepherd sits ahead of him, Eddie to the right. In his rucksack is the necessary Watchdog gear: a key ring, a chocolate bar, a roll of coins, his radio, his flashlight, a map of South Carolina, a map of Oakleigh, an Altoids tin with bandages and licorice, a comic book. As usual, he wears light-colored, loose-fitting clothing. He never has the sleeves rolled up. Better to prevent flash burns. And usually, there are the aviator goggles, but he's learned not to wear the goggles during class. The other kids stare at him. They call him Odd Ball or Weasel. Operatives shouldn't be stared at or called names.

"All right, class," says Mrs. Jenkins. She wears a dull purple sweater, and her chalk makes a scratchy sound on the board. "Who can tell me how many senators there are in Congress?"

Penny raises her hand. God bless Penny.

"One hundred," she says.

Wilson threads his tongue between the gap in his teeth, and remembers how three years ago, there were forty-eight states, not fifty. It's important, he thinks, stealing a glance out the window, that they have Alaska now. It's a strategic location for the U.S. border, a place to scout for planes.

"Very good," says Mrs. Jenkins. She pushes her glasses up the bridge of her nose. "Remember the differences we talked about between the House and the Senate?"

She rattles on. She is not a nice teacher. Once, on Communism

Training Day, she made them play a game Wilson hated. She asked them to take their lunches and place the food on their desks. His: a sandwich and wrinkled apple, a Twinkie for dessert. Then she walked between the aisles and collected everything, passing them out again as she went. Wilson ended up with Donny Lisle's potato salad. "This is Communism," said Mrs. Jenkins as they wailed over the new food. "They take what you have and give you something else instead. This is called redistribution of wealth." Wilson hated that.

While Mrs. Jenkins describes the makeup of Congress, Wilson oscillates between staring at the sky and Penny's braids and that Soviet spy Annie Yuknavitch, who sits in the front row by the door. Her dress is plaid with an embroidered cat. Red ribbons are tied around her blondish curls. Those red ribbons taunt him. Annie catches his eye, sensing the stare, and he returns his gaze to the sky.

Though Wilson likes sitting by the window, it also makes him panicky. Here, in the far back corner of the room, he is the farthest from the door. Which means that in the event of attack, he'd be toast. He'd be glass-splintered. While that Soviet spy Annie Yuknavitch could escape down the hall, evade the bomb and capture.

Mrs. Jenkins talks on. His head pounds, his eyes burn.

Wilson opens his notebook and begins the day's field log. The only thing he has to report is Annie Yuknavitch's red ribbons, which he writes by sounding out "ribunz" because, though he's a good Watchdog, he's not good at spelling. A cluster of birds flock past the window. He watches them, imagines a plane hiding in their V formation.

Though windows are necessary for scouting, they also give him the heebie-jeebies.

Once, a Commie snuck in through his bedroom window. This was late, the sky still black. Wilson woke up, blinked, and there he was. Dressed in a suit with a felt hat and red tie. (Typical Commie attire.) He stood by the window, near the curtains. He was slender, swarthy-faced like a pharaoh. Wilson freaked. He leapt from bed, flipped on the light. But the Commie was quick and escaped out the window before Wilson turned around. Wilson prowled through the room for a good hour. He hunted under the bed. He threw open the closet doors and ruffled behind the clothes. He kicked over toy baskets, stepped on army men and building blocks, crinkled comic pages. But alas, the Commie had escaped, which was a bummer.

Another time—this was March, during a late cold spell—Wilson felt bugs in his hair while he slept. The shiver on his scalp like a creepy-crawly nested there. He woke up and smashed his fist into the pillow. *Smack, smack, smack!* He saw no bugs, only his crumpled sheets. He wriggled and writhed and shook his head about, but nothing fell! He flew to the bathroom, took Mama's soap and scrubbed at his scalp. Still, he felt them. And there's a legitimate concern of biological warfare, yes sir. Operation Big Itch—he's heard rumors of the government testing fleas and mosquitoes. (Think: infected mosquitoes dropped in $E14$ bombs, descending on cities like a plague!) Maybe that Commie had snuck back in, planted the bugs. Maybe they knew he was onto them. (Mr. Yuknavitch the spy?) Maybe they wanted to squash out the Watchdogs like beetles, so they were increasing their scare tactics.

Wilson doesn't sleep well anymore.

His mind is always spinning. Spinning like the world—though the world never comes off its axis and the brain never falls out. And he can travel at the speed of light in brain time—to the USSR to the bomb plant to the bathroom sink with soap and bugs to the pharmacy to the Mars Bluff crater to dinosaur days to the shelter to the moon and back—and still be in the window seat in Room 3 listening to Mrs. Jenkins lecture on the three branches of government, though he isn't really listening because the sky is like ash and the planes are gunmetal gray and no one else from Room 3 is looking out the window except him and sometimes Eddie, but Eddie is more interested in folding paper and coloring dioramas. So Wilson must watch. He must!

When Mrs. Jenkins isn't looking, Wilson writes a quick note and slips it to Eddie.

retfa evif rewot eht yb teem, or *meet by the tower five after*

Five after recess, is what he means, and the water tower that looms over the playground. But Eddie will know that. Eddie giggles, casts him shifty glances that are downright conspicuous. Wilson has a feeling that if Commies were present—if that creeper had appeared in Eddie's room—that Eddie'd be caught red-handed. He'd spill the beans.

Sometimes, Wilson thinks he'd be better off as a Watchdog-singular. Or maybe, by teaming up with Penny instead. Penny can take things seriously, and she is good at math. To Eddie, everything is a joke or a game. Eddie is a *my way or the highway* type. But then again, he is a good sleuther. He swipes medical supplies and candy from the pharmacy when Mr. Pace isn't looking, which is often. Eddie's three shining moments in life have been: throwing rocks at a moving train, falling out of a sapling, and eating three worms. (This was on a dare, and Eddie's one weakness, besides ice cream sandwiches, is a good dare. Wilson once dared him to touch a flame for ten seconds, and Eddie tried but failed.) He once even stole the costumes for the school's Christmas pageant, left them a cardboard rocket ship in the school gymnasium instead. Wilson is a more restrained animal. Eddie is untamed. His mother died when he was born, so it's always been him and Mr. Pace, a watery man who walks slowly and talks slower. But he pays well. This is the other benefit of teaming up with Eddie: their pharmacy job.

Mr. Pace's dollar a week goes a long way. While Mr. Pace manages the clinic—carbuncles and bee stings and hives—Eddie and Wilson run deliveries, hopping on their bicycles with brown bags of antibiotics and sleeping pills and insulin. They bike down Main Street, past Kendrick's Shoes and the flower shop, past Olly's newspaper stand where they buy comics on the return route. This is a good way to learn town secrets. They learned that Pastor Jones of First Baptist has diabetes, that Mrs. Bird has nail fungus, that the old woman on Hickory has a set of false teeth, that Mrs. Beverly Conway buys a lot of sleeping pills. (Wilson has his eye out for a Yuknavitch delivery. That could be evidence.)

When they proved they wouldn't swap delivery bags as pranks—an everyday temptation, still—Mr. Pace let them package the drugs themselves. He has a simple system. There are Wets (cough syrup, aloes, iodine) and Drys (Beecham's powder, Epsom salts, pills). These are delivered in large vats from a supplier, dropped off biweekly and taken to the storage room where Eddie and Wilson stand at a fold-up table spooning salts into plastic bags, measuring the Wets in small brown bottles. Wilson loves this part. He imagines he is Father in a white lab coat, standing over a vat of hydrogen. "A pinch more uranium, Jim!" Other times, Wilson pretends he is a CIA operative. The fine white Epsom salts? Poison, really. From the KGB. The storage room is an interrogation chamber. He pulls the single bulb chain, shines his flashlight on Eddie, and tells him all the things the Reds would do if he doesn't *talk*. Eddie hates this. He'd rather sneak candy from the counter when Mr. Pace pops his first beer. He'd rather they sample ice cream with their fingers and try the gumdrops and lemon sours. He'd rather lick the pills and joke that people will swallow his spit.

All in all, partnership with Eddie has its perks. And Eddie does have good ideas. It was Eddie's idea to try one of Mama's cigarettes in the shelter, stashed behind the cans of tuna. It was Eddie's idea to stake out one night—Wilson left via the window—and watch Todd Shepherd meet with Irving, the seventh grader, behind the skating rink. Hidden by the bushes, they watched the kissing, the hand going up the shirt. And while Eddie giggled all the way home, Wilson thought how he wouldn't live long enough to do that. He wouldn't live long enough to ask Penny Shepherd to marry him. He was thinking how they've started saying, *What do you want to be IF you grow up.* And the thing is, Wilson wants nothing more than "just to grow up, please." He wants the bombs to hold off long enough.

Eddie is still giggling about the "five after" note. Wilson makes a slashing sign with his finger across his neck. Eddie doesn't notice. He's busy scrawling a note, which he passes back: *K.O.*

They also need a better code language.

Mrs. Jenkins has barely added the word *Legislative* on the board when—bright and bold!—the drill bell rings. Wilson snaps to attention. He drops from his chair and crawls under the desk. *1.5 seconds, .5 seconds faster than Eddie.*

There is the scuffing of shoes and chairs as the other students hide beneath their desks. Mrs. Jenkins says, "Good, good," as if they're puppies. (Wilson also hates that. She is all around a terrible teacher. It's quite probable that he's more the expert on nuclear bombs anyway.)

Now she tells them to stand, that they're going to practice filing into the gymnasium all quiet-like with their hands around their heads. They crawl from under the desks. Wilson counts—how long until the bomb if this was real and not a drill?—and they file down the hall, past the second grade drawings of three-legged horses and comic characters. Still he counts. He sees that Soviet spy Annie Yuknavitch at the front, watches Penny shuffle ahead of him, and thinks that the bomb would go off *now*. But as they walk down the hall with their hands around their necks, he is calm. He is watchful. He is sly. This is a drill, not a real alert. They walk in single file through the school, Eddie behind him, Eddie breathing heavily and whispering, "At least we got out of class, Geez Louise."

They enter the gymnasium. Other classes stream from the east hallway—Ms. Orion's third grade class, Mrs. Harrison's fifth grade, then Mrs. Delaney's first and second graders. Wilson sits between Eddie and Penny. The gymnasium echoes with the sound of shuffling shoes and hushed voices. In the chaos, Wilson leans to Eddie and whispers, "Did you get any more cards?"

Eddie ferrets through his jacket pocket. One of Eddie's few irreplaceable Watchdog contributions is in the form of swiped-things-from-the-pharmacy, including the Bowman Gum's "Red Menace" trading set. These cards are good research.

The new card he produces from his inner pocket is *Ghost City*. Wilson stares, riveted. The image is a destroyed New York with the Grim Reaper watching from the clouds. *This picture is an artist's idea of what an atom bomb could do to a great American city. The Reds like us to think of this. They think it will make us afraid. But actually, we are growing stronger by realizing that this could happen to us. We are working to make America stronger day by day, week by week. We must continue to work for peace through the United Nations and in every possible way. But an America fully prepared to defend itself is not likely to be attacked. The Reds understand this language. FIGHT THE RED MENACE*

"Interesting," says Wilson. He nods solemnly.

So far, they have collected:

Red Rule in Manchuria

Visit by Red Police

Slave Labor

Landing at Inchon

Berlin Kidnapping

Concentration Camp

Ambush in Indo-China

Red Guerrillas in Greece

War Maker

There are still thirty-one more to go for the Watchdog records.

"What's that?" Penny's voice like a breath of air. She leans to see the card.

"Nothing," hisses Eddie. He tucks the card back in his grubby pocket.

A hush falls over the gymnasium like a blanket. Wilson stays very still. As soon as everyone has settled, the all clear resounds through the school. Mrs. Jenkins marches to the front carrying a cardboard box.

"You have all done a stellar job," she says. "On behalf of Principal Hayes, I want to commend you all for your diligence as we've operated safety regulations at Oakleigh Elementary. Today we have something very special for you." She opens the box and lifts out a chain necklace. "These are for you to wear at all times. Say a big thank you to Principal Hayes when you next see him. He took a tip from Uncle Sam and made sure each and every one of you has this personalized identification tag for free. Many kids your age in New York City and other places have had these for a while, but we now have funding approved. And I'll wear one, too, you see? For safe keeping." She lifts up her own chain, twirls it between her fingers, then tucks it in the fold of her angora sweater.

Wilson blinks. His heart stops. Starts again. He reminds himself to breathe. He has trained himself to be calm in tricky situations, and this is a tricky situation. He watches the teachers stroll through the bleachers, dropping the dog tags in open palms.

This is bad. Because here's the truth: if the adults are increasing their protections, that means they know something. That means danger is imminent. (Is a plane on its way already? Has Mr. President launched a full-fledged attack?) Wilson knows what these dog tags are for. *Death.* They are to identify bodies in the event of nuclear attack. First responders will wade through the rubble and cinders and flesh and identify his body. Or what's left. Maybe they'll find only an arm here, an ear there. Maybe they'll find a skeleton. Maybe nothing. They'll look at the tag in the shuddering cinders and say, "Oh, what a shame. Mr. Wilson Adley Porter. Only ten! Well, at least we'll get the tombstone right."

Mrs. Jenkins stops in front of him. The dog tag falls into his hand with an unceremonious *plop!*

He stares at the etched words:

PORTER, WILSON ADLEY
405 BRUNNELL STREET
OAKLEIGH, SC 10-7-51

The floor seems to tilt beneath his feet. He wants to run from the gymnasium. He wants to scream and hide and vomit. There's a rustle in his hair—those darn bugs!—and he scratches violently.

When Mrs. Jenkins is out of earshot, Wilson whispers to Eddie, "I say we have Code Orange." His voice rattles.

The Watchdog Code system is how they identify possible threats. Red is imminent danger (an air raid signal); Orange is an insinuated threat (increase in drill procedures, check-ups from the CDA, teachers panic); Yellow is a suspected threat (Annie Yuknavitch); Blue is the all clear.

"Okay," says Eddie. "Why?"

"Dog tags."

"Again. Why?"

"Don't you know what they're for?"

Eddie shakes his head.

"Graves," Wilson says. "They'll be able to ID your body. I heard that on the radio."

"Gross," says Eddie. He shivers a little.

Wilson puts the dog tag around his neck. It lays against his skin like a talisman. Then Penny slides next to him on the bleacher. The hairs on his arm tingle with excitement as she cups her hand to her mouth and whispers, "Are you scared?"

She leans back, wide-eyed and expectant like a deer. He licks his lips. He wants to wrap his arm around her like he's seen in the movies, but the other kids are watching, and they already call him Oddball. He'd be teased relentlessly for this. But here is Penny, scared, and oh God, he thinks he loves this girl. He wants to ask her if she'll agree to marry him in ten years if they don't find someone else, ask if she'll be his temporary fiancée. You know, for practice? Or for just in case?

"No," he whispers back.

But he is, he is! This fuzzes up everything. Recently, it seems, things have gotten incredibly *worse*. His life has become a matter of waiting to see if tomorrow will come.

Mrs. Jenkins returns to the front of the gymnasium and says, "It's the Communist incentive to derail our Civil Defense whenever they can. To question and challenge and ridicule these safety efforts. Children, these are difficult times. But we want you to be warned, not frightened. Remember that if you sense someone harbors Communist sympathies, you can always come speak to me or one of the other teachers."

She keeps talking, but Wilson feels like he's listening to her from underground. Her words are blurred by layers of grass and dirt, by cement walls. He can only think of the dog tag. The air raid signal. Signs of warning.

The recess bell rings, and Wilson flinches, heart racing. The other kids move in a sweaty horde, but Wilson cannot budge. His head spins. Eddie stands and says, "Come on, geez Louise," but the dog tag weighs him down. The heart of a Watchdog is not always brave.

Wilson stands and follows Eddie and Penny out the side door, toward the playground.

"Meet in five," hisses Eddie, darting toward the water tower, that white monolith at the end of the school yard. Yes, they're supposed to meet, organize their missions and scouting zones for recess.

Wilson blinks. The playground blurs—is it melting into metal soup? He sees—no, please no!—a flare of sun, like a spotlight. He hears movement, a whisper. That darn Commie with the red tie, is he back? Wilson clutches his rucksack for dear life. It has all his survival needs, of utmost importance right now, and right now is confusing. Right now is quite possibly the end of the world, and does only he know it? Penny looks at him in an odd way, lip trembling. She clutches at her dog tag—SHEPHERD, PENNY ELAINE—and oh God, oh God does she know, too? Wilson can see it all. He knows how it would go down. There would be the ring of the air raid signal, the blip of warning, not enough time to make everyone evacuate, only enough for the people with fallout shelters. And then, what about the people who don't have shelters? What will they do? Father says the plant has secret bunkers underground. But enough for everyone? That's what Wilson wants to know. This whole shelter thing is fishy, like not having enough lifeboats aboard the Titanic. And that went over real well. Would people let other people into their shelters? If they did, would there be enough oxygen and food to go around? It'd be like a big game of sardines— desperate families pounding, begging *Let us in!* Oh, the questions! The details! The impossible logic of death!

Penny Shepherd's family doesn't have a shelter, but right now, with the way Penny is looking at him, Wilson knows he'd open the hatch for her. He'd say: *Join me, there's room for one more. I'll keep you safe.*

"What if a bomb comes?" says Penny. She draws a circle in the dirt with her toe.

"It'll be okay," says Wilson. "I know what to do." He is shaking, but he tries to calm himself. He can't let Penny see.

"What if it falls on the school? Or on my house or your house?" Penny bites her lip.

"It won't."

"But what if it does?"

"It won't."

"But *how* do you know?"

"I just know."

She looks at him for a long minute. Then—she darts forward. He smells her breath, her shampoo. It is at once brightly floral and citrus. She leans in and kisses his cheek.

Wilson jumps.

Had Penny Shepherd—lovely Penny with the dungarees and the bare feet and the braids that sway like jump ropes—had this Penny just kissed him? Here on his right cheek? He didn't even ask her to. She simply did. This is wonderful, since she is the only girl who doesn't call him Oddball or Weasel. She calls him Wilson and maybe, if the world doesn't end, he will tell her about the Watchdogs. She is his Irving, only better since he didn't have to pay her fifty cents.

He stands dazed. He watches Penny run across the playground. She passes the tire swing and turns back with a *Well, are you coming or what?* look that makes her seem decidedly older, like in the movies. He wants to cry, he wants to scream, he wants to whoop for joy. But maybe whooping is premature. How is he to know? How does one prepare for love and death at the same time? Destruction approaches, and only he knows.

"Geez Louise, you just stood there. You just stood there and said nothing!" shrieks Eddie, running from the opposite end of the playground. Giving up his scout location, darnit! "What's wrong with you?"

Wilson stays silent. Penny's kiss still warms his cheek, and he wishes he could have locked that moment into his brain like a freeze-frame. He could have smiled, shown off his tooth crater. He could have *done something*. But no matter. Penny Shepherd likes him, and he likes her, too, and right now that's all the strength he needs to finish his work. To complete his mission.

It's good to show your emotions, says Mama. *It reminds you that you're real.*

But then. A flash of crimson like a cardinal. He is on Red Alert. (And why do they call it Red Alert in the first place? That's what he would like to know. Red is Russia. Red is also the highest color of the rainbow. Red is first, Red is strong. Red is the universal color of STOP.) There she goes, that Soviet spy Annie Yuknavitch with her red ribbons, and he is reminded. *They're coming. This is it. The dog tag is our warning.* He has that scalp itch sensation like bugs are crawling through his hair. Like—like he's waking up in his room and he knows someone is there. The bugs creep along his scalp. They scratch at the skin, digging to enter his brain. The sky slips lower, as though the person holding up the clouds has slouched. Wilson drops his rucksack, bends, and scratches wildly at his head. Eddie's voice comes from somewhere distant—"What are you doing? You look crazy!"

"Bugs!" Wilson cries.

"There's nothing," says Eddie, irritation tinging his voice.

But Wilson feels them. Their insect legs, so delicate like spider webs! Their wings, like paper!

"Geez Louise, come on," Eddie says, breathing heavily. He is not, for all their bike riding, what anyone would call "fit."

Today is Wednesday. An ordinary day. But the destroyer of worlds can come on even ordinary days. On mornings that are gray like silver dollars and dust and doves.

It would be better, he decides, slinging his rucksack to his shoulder again—it would be better to die. For there to be no "last" and no shelter. To accept the end, right? To accept the end without ever knowing it's coming.

Unless. Unless there is a chance to stop it.

Father said that's why there was war: death was coming like an oil spill polluting everything, but they could stop it. They could march to battle and contain it. (Like a jar over a spider!)

Wilson takes inventory of the playground.

On the jungle-gym, Penny carries herself across the monkey bars. A few older kids climb over the fence and dart across the street to the pharmacy, likely for candy cigarettes. Annie Yuknavitch and a group of girls sit on the grass playing string games—Bridge and Cat's Cradle—making suspicious shapes with their fingers. Others skip rope, play jacks, hopscotch, marbles. So many precious lives!

His radio fizzes. It sounds angry and urgent. He brings the speaker to his ear. There's the wooly sound of static. And then, and then, does he hear something? Is there a warning? He pushes the radio closer, closes his eyes. Somewhere, within his brain, swims a voice.

Your attention please, Agent Wilson. This is Dick Chapman, one of your official civil defense broadcasters with a special message. Military authorities have advised us that an enemy attack by air is imminent. Repeat, imminent. This is a red alert. Keep your radio tuned to this place on the dial.

He's heard this voice before, but never so clear. At times, he's felt it like a sixth sense. He knows when to check his radio. The hairs on his neck tingle when there's danger.

Tucking the radio in his backpack again, he cups his hand to his eyes. He glares at the sky. He must ascertain this danger, scan the landscape for threats so he can warn and protect everyone in Room 3.

He knows what he must do. He marches toward the water tower.

DEAN

The river valley is filled with the mechanical purr of the plant: the drone of conveyer trains, the motor-hum of military trucks, the burn of incinerating organic solvents.

Past the security checkpoint, flag whipping in the wind, Dean approaches the laboratory. It is gray and oblong, rectangular and obtuse. Electrical conduits are enclosed in cement pillars, the windows mounted in transite. A narrow, high-rise fence encircles the property and operations trailers. Tight coils of barbed wire catch the pale gray light.

Dean parks his Chevrolet in the private lot, then strides into the building with a mechanical air about him. His eye catches the warning welcome, black letters on nuclear yellow.

KEEP IT INSIDE THE FENCE — THE BIGGEST GAP IN SECURITY IS AN OPEN MOUTH

"Morning, Dean," says Susan, the front desk receptionist. She shines a gap-toothed smile.

"Morning," Dean nods back.

His feet know the way. As he walks, his briefcase bumps against his leg.

The laboratory is all white walls and dark laminate. He passes the shoulder-high partitions dividing test rooms from personnel offices. There's the familiar whir of machines and phone calls. The corridor walls are patchworked with newspaper clips and Security Team cutouts—ACCIDENTS DON'T JUST HAPPEN, THEY'RE CAUSED, or DON'T SUPPLY THE AMMUNITION (LOOSE TALK!) OR WE MAY BE THE NEXT TARGET. Usually, he finds these signs almost endearing. Like political sketches in the newspaper: nuggets of truth hidden in cartoons. Today they seem ominous, like the sight of black clouds.

The winding staircase to the basement glassblowing workshop is on his right. Carlton is the chief glassblower, a former self-employed artist from Asheville who now blows custom flasks and tubing. The conference room on his left has a security meeting underway for new lab technicians straight out of undergraduate chemistry courses. Dean glances through the door panel and smiles at the sea of white shirts and khaki slacks, crew cuts and clipboards. He sat in many such meetings during his early days here.

Voices of the women clerks rise from the technical library. The door is open when Dean passes, and he sees the attendants shuffling reports into the storage vaults—some research is from here, some shipped by the Department of Energy for cross-reference. Ahead, a narrow hallway leads to the administrative offices, where Hal and the other managers, Lisle Gringott and Pete Murphy, spend their days in meetings. The locker rooms and Geiger stations are a door down—then the "Fab Lab" where Jim and his team of metallurgists study the fabrication of fuel elements. Word was, they were onto a new bonding process for uranium slugs, the enriched turrets inserted into nuclear reactors. There had long been hiccups in the process. The cellular structure would swell and crack. Jim was finding a way to bond the uranium with aluminum.

Dean passes the "caves" where radiochemists stand lined behind shielded windows. Dressed in white lab coats, they steer cables attached to robotic pincers inside the cells. The technicians mark notes on the solvent reactions behind the protective cave wall. Dean is grateful not to work in that lab in such close proximity to hot fuels.

The Health Physics lab is the last room in the building. Dean pushes through the double doors. Inside, the walls are lined with CDA posters.

A HAND COUNT IN TIME SAVES NINE:
HEALTH PHYSICS FOR YOUR PROTECTION

RADIATION NEED NOT BE FEARED: BUT IT
MUST COMMAND YOUR RESPECT

HEALTH PHYSICS SURVEYORS ARE
TRAINED AND EQUIPPED TO HELP YOU
AVOID RADIATION EXPOSURE

Dean is pleased to see his techs already hard at work. They stand in rows at the workstations, clad in lab coats and gloves. His lab is state of the art, all the best equipment.

There's the survey meter, which measures the average ionization. Stan Turrek is stooped over the device, his eye to the telescoped lens. Input from the machine feeds into the electrometer—a black box small as a radio—and the ticker measures the amount of ionization. There's the boron counter and scintillation monitor, which track the atoms when a particle passes through the material. Dean has always found their corner of the laboratory rather beautiful: here, they do not hide behind thick metal "caves," here they work with glass, the shapes so intricate, like instruments. He has always loved that word, *instrument*. An apparatus for measurement, a stringed and stemmed mandolin, both mechanical and musical. Books from the plant library are stacked high on the far table, where two techs exchange notes as they type a report.

"Morning, Mr. Porter." Lloyd Thatcher approaches, clipboard under his arm.

"Thatcher." Dean nods.

Lloyd is young and ruddy, eager to please. He was a former All-American baseball player before a shoulder injury put a stop to his athletic career.

"We have the new stream samplers just in this morning," says Lloyd, nodding to a steel-lined crate in the far corner. "Also, Henry was wondering if you signed off on the numbers for the air monitoring stations? We have them in from Macon and Greenville."

"Not yet, but I'll get to it. Did you run those final samples from Area Twelve? The ones I noted last night?"

"Yes," says Lloyd. "Everything is on your desk, sir."

"And was it?"

"Yes, sir. And we estimate a 99 percent accuracy rate."

The air seems to thin. Dean blinks, swallows hard. "Yes, thank you, Lloyd."

Lloyd raises his clipboard, lifts the front page. Dean keeps walking, but his legs are lead. He hears the thud of his own heels on the floor. There—his office on the right. 731A—the metallic nameplate reading H. D. PORTER. The results will be on his desk.

"Sir?" Lloyd has followed him.

Dean turns.

"Sir, we still have thirty-two remaining from Lanigan Rill and sixteen samples from Sterling Creek. Do you want those run today?"

"No, that's fine. We have enough." And then, when Lloyd seems expectant, Dean adds: "Let's turn to the groundwater monitoring report, they want that up to management by the end of next week. Tell Bette and April to pull everything we have on the bedrock sampling." Dean checks his watch. "I want those geological reports on my desk by eleven, got it?"

"Yes, sir."

Dean lets himself in and closes the door. Here are the industrial walls, here is the bleached, runny light. Here is the picture of Nellie and Wilson, Christmas 1959, she in one of her golden spells. Here is the one dust-rimmed silk plant on the windowsill, a pitiful fake fern. Along the back wall, rows of papers and pamphlets, a copy of his doctoral thesis, leading manuscripts from the Atomic Energy Commission. Dean sets down his briefcase on the desk. A few pencil shavings and paper cups of coffee are scattered on the tabletop, along with his Olympia typewriter. The data from Lloyd sits in a crisp manila folder.

Dean stares at the folder but doesn't open it. He reads a brief note from Bette about his phone messages from the morning: one requesting him to guest lecture on agro-climatology at Clemson, another asking for a peer review. He lights a cigarette, focuses on the smoke, wishes it were a pipe or cigar. He watches the gray fade into nothing and feels a distinct envy. The small, paneled window shows the tips of trees in the distance, forked and feathered things, cypress and pine that bleed into the sky. Dean stares outside and remembers, fleetingly, what it was like to run through these woods as a boy. He can almost feel the pine needles on the soles of his feet. Feel the hot summer sun, his hands still stained with news-fresh ink. All those summers, he'd longed to leave the fields. He watched his mother peel potatoes, make soup from beans and broth, watched his father cart fruit into town and sell what he could. Promised himself: I will never let my boy go to bed hungry. Dean taps his cigarette over the ashtray, watches the light shift as a cloud covers the sun.

He can never escape the soil.

What he wouldn't give to be in those fields now! To feel the skin of fruit in his palm, sun-warmed and sweet, ripe to bursting. How he would love to carry that bucket of peaches through the tree line and see his house—all wooden slats, really *shack* more than anything else—waiting to welcome him home. The world was more wonderful than he knew then. Innocence is lost on young people.

The cigarette burns to a smoldering nub. He puts it out, lights another. There is the rise and fall of voices, the heel-click of steps. Dean pushes away from the desk and throws his cigarette pack across the floor. The office is too small to pace, but he does—six steps to the bookshelf, his thesis smiling at him, white letters on leather. Six steps back.

One of the techs laughs. Then there is the ice-clear sound of glass breaking. The lab goes silent, followed by four letter words.

Dean bounds to the door and throws it open. One of the younger techs, a man named Ricky Ivy, hardly twenty-one, kneels beside a broken sample slide. A small circle of sludge is smeared on the ground.

"This here's a lab, not a school gym," Dean snaps.

He isn't one for shouting. Was that his voice, that edge? The men stare back at him. Ricky hurriedly brushes the broken glass into a dustpan.

Dean's office door closes with a clatter.

Another cigarette. (His third?) Six steps there, six steps back. The light bulb blinks, almost dead. Nellie smiles from the photograph. Her eyes follow him. She is beautiful in gray scale. There is that knowing cocked smile, a playful mystery in those lips. *Nellie, don't despise me.* Even if he loses his job, he will be unable to tell her why. He will be unable to explain this shadow that has followed him for years now, since those early sampling days. *Nellie, I'm trying.* That was the Christmas they visited Carol in her old white house. In the picture, Wilson, so scrawny next to his mother, holds a pair of binoculars—a gift from his grandmother for bird-watching. He would use them for anything but birds. Dean remembers thinking, *Do you know your grandson at all?* Then again. Does he know his son at all?

Smoke and watery clouds in the window. The desk, chipped and worn from his chair scraping it every day. *Nellie, I wish I could tell you everything.*

He sits. He opens the folder in one swift movement. He reads slowly. *A statistically significant increase,* Lloyd had typed.

There is stillness, like a breath. A resigned acceptance settles on Dean's shoulders. He's feared this day for so long that it feels, now, inevitable. The pinprick of doubt has been needling at the fabric of his conscience.

And today is the annual meeting with the Department of Energy and Atomic Energy Commission.

With the data on his desk, he pulls the typewriter forward. Usually, he would give his handwritten notes to April or call her in to dictate—not today. Today, this information is too important. He starts to type, slowly so as not to miss a key.

From: H.D. Porter
To: H.A. Sorenson
Copy To: S.K. Seymour, P.R. Moore, D.E. Walters, J.H. Horton,
P.B. Marten, W.J. Endorf, A.A. Thompson
Date: November 1, 1961
Re: The Imminent Danger of Faulty Waste Management

Could it really be ten years ago that he stood in waders, knee-deep in the creek? That he was filling vials with sediment? A water moccasin jerked by him, awakened by the disruption. Around him, the construction crew cleared the swampland. They drained the muck in the river basin. They whacked down trees. He and his team had little to go on, just a few charts and flypaper to catch airborne radiation. Particles clung to the flypaper which, when in contact with x-ray film, showed the amount of radioactivity. It was so primitive, Dean remembered thinking. *We're making bombs, and yet we have this primitive science.* Fly-paper in the woods. Men in waders with glass tubes, measuring poison in water and air. "We must have a baseline," Hal said then. "We need to know how much is already here, so we know how to measure our foot-print." There was the time crunch, as the Nevada testing increased out west. Dean was eager to be home. Wilson had just been born.

This document contains information relating to the activities of the United States Atomic Energy Commission. Not to be reproduced or released without prior approval. Health Physics Department for Works Technical, AEC.

SUMMARY
Total management and containment of radioactive waste—liquid and solid—is what guides all Health Physics laboratory operations at the Sterling Creek Plant. The goal is to decontaminate the waste when possible, store the waste when necessary, and complete sustained environmental monitoring.

He shakes as he pounds the keys. He has always been a "do what you're told" man. He has followed orders. He has approved reports that made him doubt. He sees himself at a security hearing: all shouts and disseminated papers, the board demanding "absolute loyalty," the board saying that even doubt was unpatriotic, un-American. To doubt, to dissent, was to be disloyal.

Oppenheimer's hearing proved that a scientist had no right to protest. The scientist's job was to study, to document, to be silent.

However, the Health Physics department has found gross incompetence on the part of the waste management disposal methods that are currently underway. Without steps to ensure a long-term solution, the immediate environmental consequences of nuclear fallout and unmanaged waste may prove to be catastrophic.

DISCUSSION
In the surrounding 40 miles of the plant's outer perimeter (OP) there is a population of roughly 500,000 civilians. The largest

surrounding populations are in Oakleigh, Augusta, Aiken, and
Savannah. In this region, the soil is nonuniform: there is sandy
soil and clay soil. The basin receives an average of 45-50
inches of rain. There is a significant source of groundwater in
the basin, from perched water tables and artesian aquifers.
Though we can estimate the direction of this groundwater,
it's near impossible to accurately predict the trajectory due to
environmental variables. Regardless, the groundwater does not
have to travel far before reaching one of the five tributaries of
the Savannah River.

He keeps writing. He writes with a fury that astounds him and remembers his first day in this office, after construction was complete,
when Hal gave the grand tour. Dean jokingly called the lab "homely."
Hal shrugged and said, "But it's sturdy. The windows would blow up,
but the life source of the building would last. And it's easy to rebuild."
That day, Dean just stared out his window. He watched the trees.

Someone raps on the door just as he finishes the first few pages, placing them neatly on his desk. April lets herself in.

"I have the geological reports from the University of Florida," she
says, thumbing through a series of folders. "There's also a few from
UGA. And Bette is pulling the cross reports from Tennessee. Were
there any others you needed?"

"No, that's perfect." He nods, and she discards the stack on the desk.

He musters a smile at April. She wears a cream-colored sweater and
embroidered outer vest. Her skirt is short, just past her knee. A single
pearl rests on the nape of her neck, threaded by a delicate gold chain.

"I had a nice time last night," she says. "Thank you for inviting me."

"Course," he says. "Glad you could make it."

"And how is Mrs. Porter doing this morning?"

He starts. Why does it bother him when April mentions Nellie?

"Fine, she's fine," he says. But he sees Nellie's face last night, her fury.

It seems that at every turn, she is hot fire mad about something, no
matter what he does or says. The latest tooth is wrapped in brown paper, in his slacks pocket. If only Nellie knew—if only she knew what

the real risk was! If only he could tell her. "She can be easily overwhelmed sometimes."

"Understandable." And then: "It's not easy being married to important men."

She says this with meaning, and he wonders when April last saw her husband, when his next furlough would be. April sits alone every lunch hour, writing pages and pages—and for what?

"Do you write to him, at lunch every day? Your husband?" He surprises himself by asking this.

"Oh. Yes." She glances at her white shoes. "I feel like I'm talking to him then. It's like a one-way telephone call."

She speaks with tenderness. Dean longs to say, *Sit down, just stay and work here for a while.* April moves a hand to her right ear and massages the soft lobe—a nervous tick he's noticed. Suddenly, he's aware of himself.

"I'm sorry, I didn't mean to intrude. My head is all fogged up. Bad morning."

"Oh no, it's fine," she says too quickly.

Dean stands and maneuvers the tooth from his pocket. "Listen," he says. "Can you add this to the sampling stock? Date, yesterday. Sam is running point on that."

"Of course." She takes the package, but her eyes study him. "Dean, is something wrong?"

She used his first name.

"No, I'm fine," he says. "You get on now. Long day ahead."

"All right," she says and turns to go. "Don't forget. Delivery was moved to ten."

She slips from the office, leaving the smell of lavender and clean clothes.

When she leaves, he returns to his desk. He rereads the report. There is time, still, to do nothing. He has not done anything irreversible. He could always destroy this report, ignore the data. He would not sign a false statement, but perhaps he could downplay the consequences. Say everything is fine.

Even as Dean thinks this, he knows he cannot do it. He must speak to Hal.

SEVERAL WEEKS AGO, THERE was a terrible moment. It was a Saturday, windy and autumn-colored. He'd been called into work. Wilson was spending the day and night at Eddie Pace's. Dean came home love-hungry after ten hours in the lab. His feet ached from standing. His temples throbbed from reading small numbers under fluorescent lights. He showered, ate reheated food in front of the television while Nellie flipped through a magazine. Then he moved beside her and placed a hand on her knee. "Come on, Nel, it's been weeks," he said. "Wilson's out—just you and me. Let's go to bed early." But she stiffened visibly at his touch. He longed to carry her to bed, slide into her in one grace-ful move, but not if she would recoil like that. Not if she would roll her eyes to the ceiling as though waiting for him to be done. *What do you want from me?* he wanted to shout at her, but he knew that would only make things worse. Why can't they ever have it out, loud and heated? Say what they need to say?

Dean bursts out of his office again, ignoring the stares of his techs. Through the lab, down the hall, into the corridors. Conversations rise in clouds from behind closed doors. It amazes him how everyone else seems to be going about their day as normal. To them, it is simply an-other Wednesday at the office. Men make plans to meet for drinks at Bar Ursula. The women exchange hopes for the holidays while they file paperwork, measure the film badges, read the plant newspaper. Dean walks with his head down, eyes on his shoes. He almost runs into Carl-ton, who enters the hallway with two flasks, both narrow on one end, bulbous on the other. "Careful," Carlton shouts, "you'll make me drop these. Took ten hours to get right." Dean murmurs an apology, then slips down the admin hall.

Irene, Hal's secretary, sits typing outside his office.

"Is he in?" Dean asks.

"He's got a meeting," she says around her cigarette without looking up.

"I need to speak with him."

"Day's booked, sonny." Irene glances up and studies him for a moment. "Christ, what happened to you?"

"Who's in there now?"

"A rep from the DOE," she says. Dean feels the panic ripple through him.

"I'll just be a minute," he says, then knocks quickly before entering.

Irene trails him into the office, exclaiming, "I told him you were busy, sir!" She casts Dean a look when Hal waves him in.

Hal's office is not much larger than his own. The walls are decorated with diplomas, a few newspaper clippings, a photograph with Einstein. A pale blue globe stands in the corner beside a portrait of Myra in a checkered suit. Hal sits in a worn leather chair, his face lined with Churchill-like gravity. Across from him is a man in a pinstriped suit.

"Porter," says Hal. His voice is slow and languid, like he's just woken from a long sleep. "Meet Martin French, with the Department of Energy. He'll be here through tomorrow for the week's briefings. Martin, this here's Dean Porter, our leading agronomist. You two share an alma mater, I believe."

Martin is a lean man, his hand delicate when Dean shakes it. He wears gold-rimmed glasses, and his hair is parted in thick, oiled gel.

"Nice to meet you," says Martin. "I've read many of your reports. Good to put a face to a name."

"Oh, thank you." Dean looks fleetingly at Hal, hoping to catch his eye, exchange a private glance. "Sir—I was wondering if I could have a minute of your time."

Hal studies a stack of papers on his desk and seems lost in them. Hal is often like this, giving the impression of half listening, of not really being fully *here*. But he is a brilliant man. He was one of the participants when Enrico Fermi and Chicago Pile-1 created the first nuclear chain reaction. One of the minds behind Los Alamos—he was there with Robert Oppenheimer. He witnessed Trinity, he knew Louis Slotin. He'd lost friends to the cause of the bomb. Had he testified for or against Oppenheimer, Dean often wondered. Did Hal believe the allegations?

Hal clicks his pen on, then off, then on. "We have a security meeting in five, I'm afraid. Some new engineers coming in this morning. One's from Boeing, has real promise."

"That's wonderful, sir." Dean checks his watch. The shipment will be at the burial ground in less than fifteen minutes.

"You all set for today's briefing? One o'clock, am I right?"

"Well, sir—"

Hal stands and arranges the papers in his black briefcase.

"We'll also have Ross K'Burg, George Henderson, and something Butler. I forget his first name. AEC is eager for an update on our progress." Hal looks up. "Who's presenting with you?"

"Just me today."

Can Hal hear his heart pounding in his chest? Sweat beads on his skin. *Oh God, oh God,* he thinks. He is not sure if he believes there is a God at all, but how he wishes he had faith now. How he wishes he believed in prayer. Though he doubts prayer could save his job. He doubts prayer could keep invisible particles of tritium from flowing slowly through the earth, like radioactive rills. He checks his watch again, hardly thinking. It's almost ten. It's almost ten, and he has only three hours before he must deliver this report. Martin French is watching him, Hal is latching his briefcase, and Dean is suddenly aware of his intrusion.

"I'm looking forward to your report," says Martin.

Dean nods and manages a "Thank you" before slipping out the door.

Irene says nothing, but he can feel her gaze follow him down the hall. He must hurry now to meet Campbell at the waste deposit.

First stop: the lockers. Dean strips from his jacket and pulls on a white laboratory coat and dosimeter badge that are hanging from a copper hook. He then takes the hand-and-foot counter, mounted against the wall, and runs the receiver over the sole of his shoe. He's clean.

The burial ground is across the plant, roughly three miles away. He moves almost thoughtlessly—out the locker room door, through the parking lot, into the plant truck. The paved road runs parallel to the train tracks, so he follows the railway line north and catches up with the cooling rod train on his left. Every half mile or so, the trees clear away to reveal another unit of the plant. Reactors shaped like hourglasses. Heavy water tanks and canyon frames at the separations facility.

The wasteland is ahead. Out front, there is a sign:

SAFETY FIRST AND LAST ALWAYS!
DAYS SINCE LAST ACCIDENT: 578

Dean parks at least fifty feet from the trenches, then walks the rest of the way.

Beneath his boots, twenty feet deep in the Carolina clay, lie years-worth of radioactive waste. The land here is a silty brown. The trees are razed like a field tilled for planting. He stares out at the open earthen trench, ready for the latest shipment of hazardous materials, anything exposed to plutonium, tritium, cobalt, strontium. The forklift and crane are parked at the edge of the trench, for lifting the heavier materials.

A truck pulling a high-level trailer barrels through the waste management gate. Campbell waves out the window. He's a jovial man, the son of a former sharecropper, now a driver in the Traffic and Transportation department. Dean has always been fond of Campbell. He attends every Farmer's Ball, him and his wife Marjorie. He boxes sometimes for sport and once brought Dean a whole bushel of tomatoes, fresh from his garden. "Best you'll find north of Atlanta," he proclaimed. "You can slice 'em, dice 'em, or bite right in like an apple."

Dean waves as the truck approaches.

"Sorry for the holdup," says Campbell after parking at the trench rim. Two Black men descend from the truck with him. All three are dressed in denim-blue coveralls. "There was a slight paperwork mix-up at the P Reactor. Shift problem, most likely. Old Owen's home sick today. All cleared now."

Campbell hands Dean a complete inventory.

"We got quite a lot today." Campbell laughs. Dean does not laugh back.

Dean fills in the plot points while the men lower the trailer bed and haul crates of waste.

He scans the list. Most of today's run is personnel-related items. Everything from cardboard boxes, electrical cords, overalls, and shoe covers to steel pipes, tarpaulins, Mylex suits, polyethylene bags. The men handle the loads with thick surgeon's gloves. Pile after pile is thrown directly into the concave pit. Dean feels sick to his stomach as he watches.

"Land, that's all that matters, boy." The voice of his father, pressing dirt into his child hands. He must have been around Wilson's age. Spending hours picking fruit, planting vegetables, worried about rain levels and bug infestations, about whether the land would grow enough food to feed him.

The refuse items are packed in paper or plastic, tucked in boxes, barrels, bundled in cloth. They are crisp white, black lined, nuclear yellow. They fall into the earth with a cascade of color.

"We're Carolinians. You know what that means, boy? It means we protect this here, our land. It means we know its ways, its seasons. We know its sights and smells, we can listen to the land, hear when it thirsts, when it's fertile. It means we got dirt under our nails and in our veins."

It's been so long since this was Ellenton. What was here, then, when he was a boy? Are they standing where the post office used to be? Or the depot, where old women sat stringing beans on hot evenings, shaded by the portico? What crop grew here, before tritium, plutonium? Who was buried in this ground, before this waste? The worst part about the town's move was the transportation of graveyards. He could not bring himself to watch as the crew moved his own family, carted their decomposed bodies to a new lot miles away from their land.

"How old's your boy now, Mr. Porter?" says Campbell, as they work.

"Ten, last month."

April had said he seemed younger than this. She was right, really. Wilson was small for his age, almost delicate—and yet so adult. Ten going on fifty.

"My boy's almost sixteen. Name's Marcel. He was just a little thing when I started here."

"You were a custodian first, weren't you?" Dean asks.

Campbell laughs and nods. "They had all the physicists in the world. What'd they need? Someone to clean the damn floors. Now I'm still cleaning up, just different."

"You're good at your job."

Campbell wipes at his brow with his shirt sleeve. The younger men move more quickly around him: papers slip from the cardboard boxes. Boots and gloves and gas masks slide into the burial ground, raising a soft cloud of dirt.

"I don't know what I'm doing half the goddamn day," says Campbell, leaning against the trailer. "They tell me go here, and I go here. They tell me go there, and I go there."

"You and me both," says Dean.

As the men work, Campbell launches into a story. He talks about his son, Marcel, and how he's been busy shooting rabbits, considering it's prime rabbit hunting season, and how, when Marcel was first learning to shoot, he was too damn scared of the shotgun and lost his balance at the first sign of a cottontail. The kickback struck his eye socket—but he could see fine now.

"Does your boy hunt rabbits?" Campbell asks as a box of scrap paper falls into the pit. A few pages catch the air, fall gracefully.

"No," says Dean. "He's been asking to try my rifle, but he's a little young, I think."

"Ten's not too young," says Campbell. "Long as he isn't gun-shy. Take him out sometime, you'll see."

A gun is the last thing Wilson needs, but Dean doesn't say this. He just smiles and nods.

Soon the boxes are done. What's left: the heavier steel-lined barrels, all marked with the yellow triangle for radioactive waste.

Campbell steps into the crane platform. The machine roars to life, and Campbell maneuvers the sheave to hook the steel-lined barrels and lift them into the air.

Is there any solution that will last? For high-level liquid waste around the plant, they use underground tanks, buried on pads of steel, encased in concrete. Inside the tanks are cooling coils, for fear that fires could erupt in the ground during waste decay. And yet, even concrete can crack, even tanks can leak, contaminate groundwater, sand, clay. Besides— the radioactive half-lives mean the waste will last thousands of years longer than the tanks that hold it.

One year ago, alarms sounded through the laboratory. A Type-II tank had leaked. Radioactive uranium seeped from the steel-lined vault into the outer cavity. Hundreds of gallons leached into the soil beneath the tank. Yet how many times had Hal—and the other managers— claimed the tanks were invincible? Said they could withstand seismic forces, from strafing bombs to an earthquake rippling through outer crust? Instead, there were hairline chemical cracks. Alkaline nitrates in the waste reacted with the steel walls. Stress points at the welds gave way. Waste met the ground.

"Beautiful day," Campbell shouts from the crane's deck. "But I smell rain. Glad this here's an early shipment."

What would Wilson think of all this? A radioactive landfill, the sort that unwitting artists write into their comic books, warning children that exposure to nuclear waste would imbue their bodies with powers, make them mutants. He's seen the comic books Wilson lugs home and leaves strewn about the living room, left in piles on the GI cot in the bomb shelter.

Toro—Genetic Mutant. Parents exposed during laboratory work.

Captain Atom—The Galactic Scourge. Atomized when a rocket exploded, leaving him irradiated with nuclear power.

The Atom—The World's Smallest Super Hero.

Atomic Knights—World Out of Time!

Atomic Mouse.

Atomic Bunny.

Atomic Anything.

Once, one of his techs—Dean forgets who now—said jokingly, "The wife doesn't want our girl to know about the *Titanic*. Says it'll scare her to know boats can sink!" His girl was twelve. Dean remembered thinking, *What twelve-year-old child is scared of the Titanic in a world where atomic bombs exist?*

Campbell clambers down, and the men strip their gloves and

coveralls, throw them into the trench, too. There is the stupefied whir of the train, carrying crates of enriched uranium to the separations facility. More trucks roll to the waste management operations. Engineers carry toolboxes. Surveillance crews circumnavigate the trenches.

"You're doing good work, men," Dean says. Though he feels a certain heavy sadness in saying this.

Campbell nods and climbs into the driver's seat of the trailer. He waves as they rumble back to the depot.

FBI, Atomic Energy Commission, Transcript Part One
Interview Case File #41940
November 1, 1951

Buford O'Connor: Please state your name for the record.
Nellie Porter: Cornelia Elisabeth Porter. But I go by Nellie. Does that matter?
O'Connor: That's fine. Mrs. Porter, we're going to ask you a series of questions that pertain to your husband's security clearance. Please don't be alarmed. This is standard procedure.
Porter: All right. I wasn't alarmed, but now I am.
O'Connor: Is it true that you attended school at Clemson?
Porter: That's right. Class of '47. I was a humanities major. I liked poetry.
O'Connor: And before that, Ashley Hall Private School for Girls?
Porter: Seems like if you know the answers already, there's no need in me telling you.
O'Connor: This'll go a lot faster if you just answer the question, ma'am.
Porter: Yes, I went there. It was a beautiful school, a boarding school. I had a roommate named Marina, I remember her. But that was only for about two years. During the hard times —
you know how it was, I'm sure. My father's work and all. It was public school after that.
O'Connor: Your father. Tell me about him.
Porter: How long do you have?
O'Connor: Long enough.
Porter: He was an account manager at a law firm in Charleston. They handled train companies, I think. He did well, but my mother was the one with old money. We had a beautiful home, white with a wraparound porch. Gardenias in spring.
O'Connor: And he lost his job, when?
Porter: When everyone did. I don't know, '31, '32?
O'Connor: Is he still alive?
Porter: I don't know. You probably know as well as I, if not better.

O'Connor: When did you last see him?

Porter: I really don't understand how this pertains to my husband's security clearance. Who did you say you were with?

O'Connor: It pertains because we say it pertains. When did you last see him?

Porter: Oh God. It must have been . . . the summer of 1947, the year I graduated. I saw him in Columbia with his new wife. They had a little girl. The wife couldn't have been much older than me, can you believe that? I don't think he saw me, though. And that was years ago now. But look, I'm not so sure I want this in any report. I have no contact with my father. Whatever he's up to, I know nothing about it. He left me and mother when I was ten years old, just left us. Do you know what it was like to be a divorced woman in South Carolina back then?

O'Connor: Mrs. Porter, do you know where you were on the night of September 8, 1934?

Porter: I was eight years old.

O'Connor: So that's a no?

Porter: That's a no.

O'Connor: On September 8, 1934, one Oscar Lee Carraway held a meeting in the basement of the Free Masons building on 5th and Cherry in downtown Lamming. Your father attended this meeting. Do you recognize the name Oscar Lee Carraway?

Porter: No.

O'Connor: He, along with James P. Cannon, are self-identifying Trotskyists and founding members of the International Labor Defense, which, as you may know, Mrs. Porter, is a Communist-front organization.

Porter: I don't know. I've never heard of them before. But look, my father — I wouldn't be surprised if that's true. He took it personally, the job loss and everything. I wouldn't be surprised if he were registered in any labor defense groups.

O'Connor: So, for the record, you were not aware of your father's socialist interests?

Porter: No. Look, ask my mother if you want. She still lives

in that old house, refuses to give it up after all this time. Me?
The place depresses me now. But look, she'd know more than
me. Name is Carol Garrett Smith. She remarried when I was
in school. She'd tell you everything you'd need to know. Like I
said, I was eight years old at the time.

O'Connor: Did your father ever read you Communist writings,
or take you to any subversive meetings?

Porter: Oh, Lord no. When he was at the house, he really never left his chair in the parlor. He read the paper or listened
to opera on the radio, not much else really. I haven't spoken to
my father since I was ten, like I said, so I can't be much help to
you. And if you'll excuse me, my baby is going to wake up any
minute. He isn't sleeping well. Is there anything —

O'Connor: Just a few more questions, ma'am. Is it true that,
while at university, in the fall of 1946, you attended a lecture
entitled "The Freedom of the Chinese People?"

Porter: I have no memory of that.

O'Connor: And did you or did you not enroll in a course, while
an undergraduate, entitled "Russian Literature and Language:
An Investigation."

Porter: That I did do. It was with Dr. Rudford, I think, in the
Classics department. I remember that he studied at Brown, and
he had a nasal voice, very slow. But I don't remember his first
name.

O'Connor: Mrs. Porter. Are you familiar with the House Un-
American Activities Committee?

Porter: Of course. I'm not a total ignorant.

O'Connor: Right. Well, did you or did you not —

Porter: Excuse me — forgive my interruption. But you don't
mean to imply that I have Soviet sympathies, do you? Because I
read a few novels in school? *Anna Karenina* or *War and Peace*?

O'Connor: I'm implying nothing of the sort. But Mrs. Porter. The
work your husband is undertaking is highly sensitive, of the
most delicate nature.

Porter: I'm aware.

O'Connor: And your husband. How did you meet?

Porter: Here in Clemson. I worked at the newspaper before Wilson was born. Dean was working at the laboratory already, though I don't know what he did. It was the agronomy department, soil research of some kind.

O'Connor: Does your husband ever speak with you about his work?

Porter: Only in vague hypotheticals. But no, nothing more than that.

O'Connor: And has your husband ever professed any Communist sympathies?

Porter: Dean is as red, white, and blue as they come. If you cut him open, he'd bleed stars and stripes straight from his veins.

NELLIE

The clocks are what get to her—

Nellie will be sitting on the sofa alone. It will be half past ten. The house will have been family-free for three hours. She will be on her second cup of coffee and wish it were stronger. The radio will be on—it is always on—and suddenly, a blistering itch will come over her. She will feel it in her toes, up her bones. The offbeat ticking around the house, so maddening! She will fantasize about throwing each cuckoo in the trash, crushing the fine wood paneling with the heel of her shoe.

And yet the silence is worse. Sometimes she retreats to the bedroom just to escape the clocks, the endless sound of time passing. She lies on the bed in her dress and shoes. She places her palm on her forehead. It is only morning. But then the silence is what's unbearable, as though the house has been gutted, is waiting for life to resume. But this is what she can't understand, what she can't put her finger on. What does she want exactly? Sometimes, she doesn't know, but she looks around at this, her house, her life, and feels only an immeasurable sadness.

And here is the terrible part. She is lucky. She knows this, of course. Already her luck has surpassed her mother's: she has a husband who stayed, a house that is paid for. She has a healthy boy. But she wants more. She wants different. It was the teeth—yes, that terrible thing! The teeth and the party and the bomb and that secretary woman and his tone, his, *Just keep doing what you're doing.* That is exactly what she cannot do. How had it taken her so long to realize that he lives in a world she cannot share? His is the outside world, beyond the town, hidden behind the plant perimeter. Her world is nine hundred square feet deep, with the sounds and chimes of Dean. Everything is Dean. (If she floated away, would he notice? Would he miss her? Would his love ripen in absence?) She is lonely. So desperately, desperately lonely, and should a woman in love feel loneliness like this? Should she hide away in her bedroom, shrouded from the sounds, from the hammering inside her head? Should she march in the street, put her husband's work at risk?

DEAN

It was Hal who first planted the seeds of doubt.

They sat outside the laboratory on a warm metal bench. This was 1954, a humid and heavy Saturday. It was exactly two weeks before the Oppenheimer security hearings were set to take place—Dean would make this connection later. On this Saturday afternoon, Dean watched the cars through the geometric shape of the fence, slivers of color. Hal was peeling a peach in one long coil with a pocketknife, his hands wet from the meaty orange core. Both men had folded their coats beside them on the bench, their sleeves rolled to the elbow, shirts licked with sweat.

"It was so goddamn hot there," said Hal. A piece of peach skin fell to the ground. "But a dry heat. Desert winds in summer, dry cold in winter. It was my first time out west. You ever been out west, Porter?"

"No, sir."

"Myra hated it. Said she could never get the dust out of the house. She taught at the school but never fully settled there."

"I can't imagine," said Dean. He was staring at the ground where a trail of tiny ants had discovered the warm peel.

"You know I still have a hard time talking about it." He was slicing the peach now in perfect slivers, dropping them on his tongue like candy. "I can't quite separate myself from thinking of it as Project Y, as P.O. Box 1663. You spend so many years in such a hurry. We were always rushing—always. I slept in the lab more than my bed. Poor Myra would be worried sick when I came home exhausted, smelling god-awful. Like Tiger Balm, she used to say. I still feel strange talking about it, as if my phones are tapped, as if they're listening. There was always someone listening. But then again, you know how it was, the urgency. There was a rush then. There was no hurry up and wait, there was only *go go go*. Sometimes a man can miss that, if you believe it. Even that."

Dean wondered why Hal was telling him this. They were friendly, sure. They shared the regular smoke break, but Dean wouldn't necessarily consider Hal a friend. This was Hal Sorenson, laboratory manager. He'd appeared in *TIME* magazine alongside Dr. Robert Oppenheimer himself, before the allegations churned up like brine. Dean was a humble soil scientist. He'd been fighting in Europe while Hal helped develop the greatest weapon known to man. But when Hal Sorenson asked to join you on the bench outside the lab, you said yes. You made room.

The full scope of the Sterling Creek Plant was finally up and running, so perhaps, Dean thought, Hal was feeling the stress of it all. The reactors had gone critical at the start of the year. The AEC was breathing down their throats. "I never fought in the war," Hal said. His knife struck the pit. "I was too old, of course. Already at U of Chicago when they tapped me. You ever been to Chicago, Porter?"

"No, I'm not much of a city man."

Hal smiled and shrugged.

"Big and cold, but a rush. The opposite of Alamos."

Dean was just about to excuse himself, self-conscious about the length of his break. But then Hal's voice changed, the register deepened.

"You were in the war, right, Porter? Army?"

"Oh—yes, sir."

"Did you kill anyone?"

That purple sky. The foxholes, scouting points. His head against the soil, bombs flaring in the sky like fireworks, like constellations, like nothing but bombs. Yes, he'd killed. The German relieving himself behind a tree, hit in the back. The sentry hiding in the patisserie, abandoned.

"Yes," Dean said slowly. "I don't know anyone who didn't, except maybe our medic, our chaplain."

"I did, too, Porter. I killed a hell of a lot more than you." Silence for a moment. Hal paused, the pocketknife midslice. Peach juice dripped from his hand. And then: "Did I ever tell you that I was one of the ones they sent?"

"Who sent? Where?"

"Japan." Hal started slicing again, gentle, methodical. He waved as a Works Technical van rumbled through the lot, and Campbell whistled back. "September. They sent me, Morrison, a few other radiation experts. I was with Colonel Warren in Nagasaki. I had a little Geiger counter with me and a camera. That's all. They gave us one week."

Dean could only imagine walking through the rubble of a broken city. Hospitals filled with children, limbs gone, parents incinerated. Babies crying for dead mothers. Clothing tattooed to their skin.

Dean said nothing, only lit a cigarette.

"It's different," Hal continued, "when you see them, the children whose parents you've killed."

"But you didn't—" Dean started.

"You know, my father was a lawyer, and he got a lot of people off scot-free for terrible things. One man, arson. And he walked away clean. Had murdered his wife and kids in their own home. Just awful. But there was a loophole somewhere in the investigation, some mistrial thing, and my father found it. I remember him weeping about it, my father. The only time I saw him cry. He was in his office, hunkered over. I was young, maybe eight or nine. And I remember him telling me later—this was before he died, liver failure—to do something I could live with. And you know what I decided?" He'd forgotten all about the peach, maybe even about Dean. He stared at the parking lot, the chain-link fence that surrounded the lab. A bead of sweat bubbled on his nose. "I decided, I won't go into law. It's not for me. I'll do something to help people. I'll go into science. Isn't that goddamn funny, Porter? The world has twisted me." He sighed, then looked at an astonished Dean for a moment. "I don't know why I'm telling you this. Except for, you're a good man—and I have not always been good. I have done things I cannot live with."

Just then, the laboratory doors opened, and out came other members of the Health Physics department. Sleeves all rolled in summer heat, two smoking, one singing a baseball chant while someone else scoffed.

Hal stood, smiled, retrieved his coat. He greeted the others warmly. But this, this is what Dean would remember most: the rest of the peach Hal left on the ground for the ants, which clustered around this sweet and golden gift.

NELLIE

Myra leads the demonstration. With two other women, she carries a wide banner that reads, WOMEN STRIKE FOR PEACE.

It's a delightful shock to see the street filled with women. Much more than fifty, Nellie now notices. And others seem to join as they walk, melt on in. The crowd expands like dough on the rise. It's as though all the houses burst at the seams and the women came spilling out. They are here demanding peace in this town with the cinema red-lettering WEST SIDE STORY and the piano hall with the Irish pianist who only knows Scott Joplin—this town with the secret underbelly of nuclear life.

They pass Pennelton's, advertising alligator shoes on sale; pass the grocery, where women emerge holding brown paper bags. They stop and stare. Nellie approaches some of the passersby and hands out pamphlets.

A stream of cars has piled behind them. Some are impatient, others interested. Sidewalk conversations drop to a whisper as the onlookers watch the protest and read the placards. Some murmur to their friends behind gloved hands. Others ignore them, march into the butcher, the pharmacy, the post office. Still others wave at their friends in modest support. Nellie sees one woman in a maroon coat and hat who shields her child's eyes and hurries along the sidewalk.

Where is the warmth from yesterday, the pulpy sun? It's cold. Every breath a cloud.

Ahead, Bev Conway pushes her baby carriage. Beside her is Sarah Hatfield. Sarah runs the "Ask Abby" column in the town's newspaper. It's supposed to be anonymous, but Sarah cannot keep a secret to save her life, and word spreads like a wine stain. There is Irma Ryland, and doesn't she work at the bomb plant herself? A technician or assistant of some sort. On the street corner, under the striped awning, is Bill Pace. He rubs his glasses and watches ruefully as the women pass his pharmacy.

They turn onto Main Street. Police line the road now, pressed against the glass storefronts. One has his hand on his holster. Another holds a nightstick.

The dark feeling in Nellie's stomach takes a turn. She remembers—suddenly—that day in 1954 when she first saw Dean sob. Wilson was small then, asleep. Robert Oppenheimer had just been revoked security clearance by the AEC. The papers lost their minds. OUTCAST OPPENHEIMER! OPPOSITION TO THE H-BOMB PROOF OF GUILT? MCCARTHY CLAIMS PROOF O WAS RED! And though Nellie had not followed the hearings closely—had picked up tidbits from the radio and friends—she was secretly frightened by the idea of a Red nuclear scientist. Not just any scientist, either. The father of the atomic bomb! One of the most powerful minds on the planet, he was a man who'd seen the elegance in atoms and also their potential. What did that mean for the future of the country if Soviet spies could infiltrate the likes of Los Alamos? And the likes of Sterling Creek, for that matter!

But Dean seemed to take the scandal personally. After putting Wilson to sleep that night, Nellie found Dean bent over his knees on the couch. She stepped slowly. She sat beside him and watched as fat tears rolled down his cheeks, and something about this terrified her. Seeing him broken that way. He did not even cry at his parents' funerals, only stood solemn and stoic as marble. She sat in silence until he said, his voice barely a whisper, "My God, they've exiled him." He sat and cried, and when he'd finished crying, he stood and stared out the window, and then something seemed to tear through him. He circled the living room, talking more to himself than to her: "They've been after Oppie for years, Nel. Years! And, of course, they couldn't catch him on real *evidence*, they catch him on moral objection. So a man can't object now? Is that it? He's supposed to follow blindly? God, Nel, what is this world coming to?"

After a few minutes, he caught himself and blinked at her for a moment, as if realizing who he was speaking to. Was he about to confide in her, she'd always wondered, about to say more than he should? "Tell me," Nellie said, with all urgency and yearning. She watched him close again. He rubbed his face with those strong hands (it was perhaps his hands that she loved most of all, thick and calloused and rippled with veins) before retreating to his study.

Only last night, she herself voiced a warning to Lois: *Aren't they calling people in for less all the time?* And here they are marching, demonstrating.

Worry needles at her. Will Dean's job really be in jeopardy with her demonstrating? She thinks this, even as she despises the bomb plant. Then again, Lois is here and Myra, other plant wives. Surely the plant managers wouldn't fire staff based on their wives.

Ahead, Myra does not flinch at the sight of the officers. She walks boldly. She rolls her shoulders like a panther. Her coat is midnight black. She is thick-boned, tight-lipped, cat-eyed, severe.

They pass the Ramsey Hotel on the left with its stately white columns. Guests crowd the portico, holding beaded glasses of iced tea. Cynthia Barnes sits on a rocking chair. The Barnes family owns the Barnes and Bros. stables on Wesley Avenue, and last spring, their horse Iris placed third in the Oakleigh derby.

Nellie squints and looks forward, focuses on her steps.

Shouts echo down the street. Someone has entered the protest. There is a woman's cry. Nellie recognizes the voice. Allen Conway has marched into the crowd of women. He calls for Bev. Nellie can barely make out the words. "Beverly . . . my God . . . what in Christ's name?"

Nellie freezes, stricken. Through the gaps in women's shoulders, she sees Allen take Bev by the arm. Bev shrieks, but softly, a gasping chirp. She drops the sign she'd been holding with one hand. WAR KILLS. PEACE SAVES. The baby howls. Other women part for Allen. Only Lois cries and runs forward, shouts back at him, her voice muffled and indistinguishable. Nellie stands still. Her feet are weighted suddenly, like she's been nailed down. There is no movement left in her, no breath. Bev shrinks at Allen's grip, a small flinch that speaks volumes.

"Beverly, let's go home, Bev—come on now, Bev, let's go home and talk about this, Beverly." He says her name over and over, as if that eases things.

The police stand idle by the storefronts.

Bev wilts visibly. Lois still shouts until Allen turns and shouts back at her, "You better be thankful I don't tell *your* husband you're here."

There is the awkward procession of leaving. Allen hoists the wicker carriage onto the sidewalk and pushes the baby firmly up Main Street, toward his pale green car. Bev trails him. Nellie tries to catch her eye but doesn't.

The women briefly hesitate. (Should they continue? Part and leave?) But Myra strides ahead, unfazed by the altercation. Her gaze is on the courthouse, still two blocks away.

"Unbelievable," murmurs Lois, returning to walk beside Nellie. "Unbelievable pig, that's what he is. A real *pig*."

The thought occurs to Nellie that Dean might be here, that he might be waiting on the sidewalk, like Allen, to watch her walk by. That he might take notice. The thought of this both terrifies and exhilarates her. (What would she say? What would he do?) Dean is not one to make a scene. He has never raised his hand to her, though she's heard stories from less fortunate wives. She scans the sidewalk for him, but there is no sign of his tall frame.

A crowd of onlookers has gathered now. There are shouts from the sidewalk, husky voices: "Why don't you go home and wash some dishes?" "Go feed your children!" "Get back to the USSR, you Commies!"

Well, who's to say what's right? She doesn't know what's right! Her husband has lied to her—that's not right! She has stolen from him, but he has lied to her for years. He has taken Wilson's teeth. He has run tests on their son! He has kept secrets. He has contributed to this mess, this war, this nuclear arms race.

And what was it her mother had said, years ago? The day before her mother's second wedding—a simple, modest affair—when Nellie whispered, "Do you love him?" And her mother grunted back, "Can I love what I distrust?" It was no surprise her mother was singed with fear of the world, of men who would fail her. Nellie was, too. Nellie was afraid of everything under the sun. Afraid of loneliness, afraid of marriage, afraid of divorce, afraid of having children, afraid of what she was capable of. But in that moment, she thought, *I'll do better than this, Mother, I'll show you.* And all this time, since the divorce, her mother's remarriage, she had been hoping to prove her mother wrong.

They approach the courthouse. The American flag whips in the wind. Thunder rolls in the distance, and clouds darken the horizon. Lois waves to her friend Olive, who stands beside two photographers. Flash bulbs emit blaring light, freezing them all in frame.

This is when Nellie sees her, the young girl with cinnamon freckles. She stands beside her mother, a lean woman Nellie recognizes vaguely from some church luncheon or company affair from long ago. But it's the girl who catches her eye. The Holly Golightly child from last night. She carries a sign that reads, LET US BE THE NEXT GENERATION. (How had Nellie not seen her yet?) There is something terribly sad in this sight: a girl who is not yet a woman, not yet a mother, drawn into the adult worries.

Nellie is glad that Wilson is not here to see this, that he is safely tucked away at school.

The girl is dressed almost dollishly, with lace-hemmed fabric. Seeing this dress, Nellie is reminded of a day in that first dreadful year after her father left. She, not yet eleven. The cotillion, newly opened from their home. Mother was leading a group demonstration of the waltz step. Little Nellie sat in a white dress with scalloped edges—new, a rarity. Little Nellie needed to pee. But Mother said no, no, she had to stay seated through the lesson, hands folded like a lady, legs tucked under her skirt. She tried to stand and leave, slip away unseen, but Mother glared at her, speaking wordlessly: *Don't you dare!* What embarrassment flooded her face when, in front of all the girls, a warm, wet stream of yellow trickled to the floor. The girls snickered. Her mother ignored it. She did not dismiss Nellie to change but made her dance in front of the others to teach her a lesson.

Nellie has not thought of this memory in years. She has tried to store it far away, in the same place she's locked up the smell of fresh silver polish, the sight of her mother's heels, or the weight of rules at dinner.

The Holly Golightly girl breaks her gaze.

Nellie blinks as Myra climbs the white courthouse steps. When Myra turns to face them, she seems downright presidential. The silence is heavy and expectant before she speaks.

"We women hail from different backgrounds." Her voice is slow and granular. "We leave our homes, we stand here together as sisters, bonded by something greater. We are not merely housewives. We are also teachers, writers, social workers, artists, secretaries, saleswomen. We have different beliefs, different dreams, different backgrounds. But we are all human beings." There is an energy through the crowd now. Do the other women feel this? Something in Nellie burns. Where there was a distaste in her stomach earlier, there is now a ripening. "If I'm honest, I myself am surprised by the boldness of this great declaration. We are ordinary women. We are not politicians or experts. We are humans who want humans to flourish. Many of us are mothers, though I myself am not. Just yesterday, we passed out candy to children who knocked on our doors. They said 'trick or treat,' and to them, the world was nothing more than a great and beautiful game. We know better. We know how they will lose this awe of the world.

"This morning, someone called me one of the originals, and I laughed because it made me feel old. But I was there, in Los Alamos, during Trinity. My husband, as many of you know, worked on Manhattan before being transferred here after the war. The wives did what wives did. Some ran seamstress shops from their homes. Others baked and kept busy. I recorded what I saw. I taught in the schoolhouse and kept extensive journals. In the days leading up to the Trinity tests, there was a premonition around the town. The men slept in the labs, came home smelling of camphor and sweat and that thick clay. The wives weren't supposed to know what was happening, but some of us did. Kitty Oppenheimer knew. Jane Wilson. I knew. The night before the test, we met together. We stayed on a place called Sawyer's Hill, right near on old ski run, giving us a view of the valley. We prayed. We waited. We wished our husbands would be alive in the morning. I remember being up all night, candles and lanterns lit, shutters closed, some music. That was how we saw it—like light swallowing the world. The sun was about to rise, and there on the horizon was the flash. I remember how I closed my eyes, but I could still see the light burning behind my lids."

Nellie tries to imagine the sight. Yellow light blooms, surrounded by the Sandia. The ground, rust-red, with desert dunes in the distance. Trinity: a fitting name for God-players.

Myra continues: "Our husbands were only six miles from the test site. Perhaps that was the moment, seeing such destruction, like a doomsday image, like the fist of God in Revelation. Perhaps that was when my beliefs on the danger of nuclear war crystallized. I saw that bright light in the sky, a light that no one but God should be able to make. I saw how it burned in my husband. Something seared in his soul that has never gone away. But I am not here to debate the ethics of employing the bombs, nor even man's right to hold such knowledge. That tree of knowledge has always tempted humanity, and I fear it always will.

"So back to last night. I sat in my rocking chair and listened to June Christy as children knocked on my door. I dropped candy in their baskets. And I confess, ladies, that I resented this. I thought, here are children who believe, without doubting, that the world will still exist tomorrow. That the air they breathe, without even thinking it, will not poison them. And I thought—will they even live to reach adulthood? Will they even live to have children and learn to fear in a whole new way? There comes a moment when one's fear is not for oneself so much as for the ones you love: your friends, your spouse, your children. There's no knowing what will happen, ever. That is the great curse of life. But I have lived these past sixty years, often disbelieving my own power to press for change. Yet I've become convinced of one thing. This is not a men's issue. Not a men's war. This is no longer something that can be left to a government of power-hungry men. They talk in headlines. They talk in measurements and give us dimensions of the bomb, as if this were a war game, not a toxic threat of annihilation. They tell us, 'better dead than red.' I for one refuse to accept such an ultimatum. The suffragettes reminded us of the power for good, the potential for power, in each person. And today, in the largest gathering of its kind since our mothers and grandmothers, since I myself was there to claim the right to vote forty years ago, we proclaim the need for peace. Today, you join women around the country, I daresay around the world, who are interceding with government officials and school boards and local mayors. There are marches in Washington, Los Angeles, Philadelphia, St. Louis, Baltimore, Denver, Cleveland, Cincinnati."

Oakleigh seems different now, as though light has slipped through the clouds, illuminated the entire town in a shroud of color, when before there was only gray. There: the Oakleigh playhouse with its stark white building now seems to glint pearl. And the maple trees and the crape myrtle, bare after the frost, seem like canvases ready to hold hues again.

"For many of us, this is our first time protesting. Our first time on a picket line. We spend the years of our lives bringing up children to be healthy individuals and good citizens. Others of you have spent your years perhaps in poverty, serving someone else's child." There is a murmur through the crowd at this. A shuffle. There's a shout from one of the men on the outskirts, but Myra keeps going, unmoored. Her voice rises, her vibrato strengthens. "War and peace are the great equalizers. We are all affected equally by fallout. And we all want better for our world. Now, in the atomic age, all women, not only mothers, have an urgent duty to work for peace in order that the children of the world may have a future."

Above, a rumble interrupts them. Heads crane to the hazy sky. A plane tears past and then vanishes. A flock of birds take to the sky, startled by the sound. Nellie looks up, too, and wonders what it must be like to look down on the world from a cockpit, to see this protest in miniature, to see the squares of light that make up homes and the homes that make up towns. They must not seem like people from way up there. It must be possible to hold out one's thumb to the fiberglass and imagine that those are not real homes down there, only models. Perhaps that is how a human can drop a bomb on another human—by ignoring their humanity.

Myra continues, the sound of the plane silenced.

"I want to read you something from last year's *Newsweek*, an article called 'Young Wives with Brains: Babies, Yes, but What Else?' Listen: 'The educated American woman has her brains, her good looks, her car, her freedom . . . freedom to choose a dress straight from Paris (original or copy) or to attend a class in ceramics or calculus; freedom to determine the timing of her next baby or who shall be the next president of the U.S.' But ladies, I say to you today that we have much more than this. Our freedoms are not limited to buying a dress from Paris, nor even the vote. We have the right to speak out, to demand change. And look around you! You're part of history today. This is a new revolution. We may be challenged. We may be questioned. But today, we march, and we ask the powerful women, Mrs. Jacqueline Kennedy and Mrs. Nina Khrushchev, to please help us in pushing for a test ban treaty. Help us keep the world free of fallout. But more importantly, free of fear. How can we raise children under the threat of nuclear proliferation?"

Yes, yes! Nellie feels a surge of pride. Applause swells through the crowds, not just the protestors who raise a racket, waving their banners, but the onlookers. Nellie feels herself holler from some deep and secret place within her. It feels like a scream more than a shout of agreement, but she keeps hollering. Myra turns to the photographers now and stands serene and unsmiling as flashes of light capture her on the stone steps. Still, Nellie whoops with a great unladylike cry. Finally (after everything!) she is a woman striking for peace. Nellie is a woman brave. Because this is what she knows: wars can exist in the great wide world and in the small crevices, too. In the house's dust-filled nooks. In the space between the wedding band and the finger. Yes, explosions happen daily, but sometimes you swallow them. Sometimes, you explode on the inside and the shrapnel stays there forever. The fallout builds like a tumor.

She has the disorienting sense of waking up. As though she's been living a dream. As though she's been submerged in an underground shelter lined with clothes and drapes from Sears all for her. She wakes up and remembers with searing clarity all the things she had once dreamed of, before the house on Brunnell Street, before she fell in love with a man who bent his head to study the earth.

Today she stands with the women. Today she has two hundred dollars in her pocket, and her protest has just begun.

DEAN

His office is a mess of manila folders and stacked memos. A steaming cup of coffee sits beside the typewriter, likely left by April. There are also the remaining geological reports, cross-referenced from Oak Ridge.

He has barely sat down to review the material when there's a knock on the door. Dean jumps, then shouts, "Come in."

Jim Shepherd sticks his head inside.

"You on break yet?"

"Too busy for a break," says Dean. "And it's early. I feel like I just started."

Jim strolls into the office, hands in his pockets. "Wahl's got his arm up my ass pushing for this report for Works Technical by end of day. No one ever mentioned how many write-ups there'd be, am I right?"

When Dean says nothing, Jim frowns.

"What, what'd I say?"

"Nothing, I'm just tired is all. Things at home."

His mind spins. There are so many aspects to consider. Will he lose his job? If so, will they have to leave Oakleigh, uproot Wilson from his school and life here? He'd surely be stripped of his security clearance. There could be investigations within the AEC, the FBI.

Jim nods. "Come on out, you old man. Smoke break at least. You can bum a cigarette off me. How's that?" When Dean says nothing, Jim narrows his eyes. "What? What is it? Something's been off with you for days."

"Nothing." But Dean's eyes flicker to the report neatly clipped on his desk.

Jim picks it up.

"Imminent danger?" Jim says, scanning the page. "Dean, what is this?"

"Nothing." Dean folds his hands and leans forward against the desk. Jim's brow furrows in concentration. "It's not your department. You shouldn't read it."

"We have the same clearance code." His face darkens as he reads. Dean says nothing, and the seconds slide by. "You going to Hal with this?"

Dean nods. "At one."

"Are you pulling my chain right now?" Jim laughs hesitantly, then stiffens when Dean doesn't laugh back. "You can't be serious."

"More than I've ever been."

"So, you're what now? A conscientious objector?"

"God, no—Jim, I'm just concerned."

"Fuck that." The report drops to the desk.

"It's not what you think," Dean says.

Jim takes a cigarette pack from his pocket. He lights one languidly and eyes the feather of smoke.

"Do you know what's happening in town today?" He taps ash over the papers and sits in the faded plaid chair across from Dean. "I heard from Allen, who's losing his mind about it. God, you shoulda heard him on the phone. There's an antinuclear march, and you know who's running it? Our wives. Because they're hearing from people like you in the press who're saying—how did you put it?" He picks up the front page and reads, "The immediate environmental consequences of unmanaged nuclear waste may prove to be catastrophic."

"Well, it may. It will."

Dean remembers the crane lowering the waste into the unlined trench. Recalls watching the polyethylene and Mylex suits fall to meet the earth.

"And what do you think we're doing here but trying to avoid just that?"

"We're making things worse, Jim. I know that. You know that. Half our lab knows that."

"You sound just like Simon." Simon was an Atoms for Peace delegate before leaving the plant to work as a university lecturer. He was a Zionist Jew whose wife had escaped from Poland during the war years. He

himself was from Brooklyn and had worked at Hanford before coming
to Sterling Creek. "For God's sake, Dean, you and I've been through a
lot together. And you didn't even tell me about this. I would have told
you from square one to drop this."

"I wouldn't have done it, Jim."

"That's the thing about you, you know. You're so principled. You
make a man feel like he's in goddamn church all the time."

Outside, clouds have eclipsed the sun. A low rumble reaches
them—the train loaded with cooling rods, headed to the Area 700
reactor.

"Did you know he demonstrated outside the White House once before joining the president for dinner?" says Jim.

"Who?"

"Simon."

"I didn't, no."

Jim stares at the desk for a moment.

"Don't do this." His voice is low and serious. It's lost all sharp-
ness. "Don't go all Quaker. Please. The AEC, they're up to their eye-
balls in crap-shoot accusations every day, don't go feeding them more
nonsense."

"What kind of a man would I be if I didn't say anything?" Dean stands
now. "What kind of father to my son?" He runs his hands through his
hair and turns to face the bookshelves. Wilson's school photo from '57
stares back at him: all freckles and baby teeth, hair buzzed close to
the scalp. He thinks of Wilson last night, camped in the shelter. Wilson begging for a war story. Wilson tramping through the bushes this
morning, binoculars around his neck—and looking for what, exactly?
"You know my boy believes, really believes, that a bomb will come.
When I was his age, I knew nothing about war, not really. Just what I
read in books. But I've heard him pray, Dear God, please protect me
when the bomb comes." Dean turns back to Jim, blinking furiously. "He
doesn't say *if*, Jim. There is no *if* for Wilson's world. Do you understand
that? And I can't help feeling like a hypocrite. The *me* here and the *me*
there. I know what the real danger is, Jim. And it's not in the sky, not
when we have ballistic missiles ready to take anything down. And hell,

it's not in the goddamn teeth. It's in the ground. It's in the water we drink. But of course, I can't tell them that. I can't tell anyone. I don't want this kind of life for my son or for myself."

He thinks, as he often does, of an article printed in *LIFE*, written by a fourteen-year-old boy. "The hydrogen bomb reeks with death. Death, death to thousands. A burning, searing death, a death that is horrible, lasting death. The most horrible death man has invented, the destroying, annihilating death of atomic energy. The poisoning, killing, destroying death. Death of the ages, of man. The lasting death." Eleven times out of forty-nine words.

Jim looks aghast, almost offended.

"You think I want this for my children? At least I'm not lying to myself. I know what would happen if we stop—"

"I'm not saying we should stop production, I would never—"

"Then what? What's your grand plan?"

Dean hesitates because he doesn't know. Because he fears there is no answer, not really—not for the disposal of dangerous elements that will outlive them, perhaps outlive this country.

"I don't know yet," says Dean. "I don't know, I just—we can't keep doing what we're doing. It isn't safe. It isn't right."

"This? This wouldn't fix your boy's fears," Jim smacks the front page. "They'd still have drills in school. The Soviets would still have the H-bomb. The only thing it'll do is drag your name through the mud and your family with you. You won't accomplish anything."

"I refuse to believe that."

"Hell of a patriot you are," Jim says quietly.

"Now that's enough." Dean hears more than feels himself strike the desk. Jim sits back, surprised. "I fought in the war. I love this country. I don't want to see us destroy it from the ground up. I want there to be a country for my grandchildren to live in. I want there to be a blue sky and grass, a land worth protecting. Instead, we've welcomed the world into the atomic age, and now we live to see the consequences."

Jim steeples his fingers.

There is laughter in the corridor as several clerks walk by Dean's window. Bette pushes a cart of dosimeters for registration and Marge

O'Connell carries a stack of paperwork. Through the half-lowered blinds, Dean sees April glance his way. She raises her eyebrows, as if to ask, "Everything all right?" He breaks her gaze. Stares at the mounted map across the wall. A map of Ellenton from before the plant broke ground.

"Forgive me," Dean says after a moment. "You didn't deserve that."

Jim rubs the scar on his temple.

"You know what appalls me?" he says. "Honestly appalls me? I don't understand how the Los Alamos folks can act like they're immune to any responsibility. That really pisses me off. They build the bomb, they discover fission, they lose men trying. And then, at the last minute, after *they themselves* entreated the War Department to look at their new weaponry, they send around petitions. They warn Truman not to use it. Act like they're not responsible. Pontius Pilate washing his hands."

"I'm sure they felt guilt." Dean sinks into his chair again. "When you're afraid, when you're in war, you do things you don't want to do."

Lord knows he did.

"So you think we shouldn't have used it?"

The atomic bomb, he means. The question of all questions.

"I can't answer that," says Dean. Had they not dropped the bomb, the invasion of Japan would have been exactly sixteen years ago, to the day. November 1, 1945. It's true that they put an end to the war. They stopped countless more deaths. Had the war continued, how many more would have been lost? The quartermaster general had ordered 370,000 Purple Hearts in advance.

"Thank God I didn't have to decide."

Jim leans forward. There is a grimness on his face that Dean has never seen before.

"Do you know what they did to me over there? What they did to everyone?"

"I was in the war, too."

"Not in the goddamn Pacific. You didn't see what I saw."

"I saw enough. War is war."

"Not like the Japs do it. They lined us up in rice paddies, turned out our pockets, and if we had any yen, they shot us. Thought we stole it from soldiers or civilians."

"You're not understanding—"

"Made us strip naked in the sun." Jim speaks faster now. "No water. No food. Hundreds in these goddamn train cars. And then Tokyo."

"You don't have to talk about it. I know I can't talk about it."

Dean remembers. The sky was sea-gray, the snow higher than his knees. Dean hunkered in a foxhole with Ernie and Sergeant Burrows. It was colder than cold, colder than death. Shots fired, and Dean could not tell if the white flakes in the sky were ash or snow.

"Clearly I do because you've lost your mind, and you're talking like a goddamn Commie, and you're sure as hell going to lose your job."

"But we bombed civilians, Jim. Women, children, grandparents. We targeted hospitals! Isn't that different to you? We were soldiers. We knew what we were getting into."

A sound like a train through the air and a blast so loud that he heard nothing for hours after. His ears rang. His mouth burned. The man next to him, Ernie from Iowa, was clipped in the neck when he stood too high—and Dean buried himself against the frozen soil.

"Those Japs aren't like normal people." Jim pushes away from the desk and paces the small office. "They're hardly even people at all. They put their own women and children in those factories on *purpose*. They were just asking for it. And it was a *war*. Bombing comes with the territory. Slaughtering and castrating your POWs does not. A couple years ago, Lois said she wanted some Japanese car, and I said, to hell with that. Not buying from those animals. To hell with all that."

"War makes animals of anyone."

Dean remembers: late one night, the war newly over, roused from his barracks by the sound of a woman's muffled cries in the camp. The soldiers had become wild. They had lost any filter of behavior, even the good ones. They raped French women, then offered food as if in penance. They liberated towns. They brought English and Old Glory and rotting rations and the reek of bad breath and women-hungry men. The war was no longer ally and enemy, the war was no longer black and white, moral and amoral. Could war even be moral? Love had no place in war. War takes a moral compass and cuts out the north. He couldn't question, he couldn't think beyond tying his laces in the morning, beyond the snow-laden trek through France and western Germany. When they reached the camps, there was no north—only a tar-like anger, heavy and settling in the gut. When they watched blade-thin bodies spoon food into their mouths, there was no north. There was only, *End the war. Leave the war.* There was only, *Do what it takes. Survive.* Any reflective American knew that most Germans felt the same. He was only a soldier. He had orders to follow. When the commanding officer said shoot, he shot. When the officer said march, he marched. Only later would he hear about Dresden and the Biscari. About Hiroshima.

North comes later.

Moral direction takes distance and reflection. Dean knows this. How could he possibly know what he would do as Truman, as Fermi, as Oppenheimer, as General Marshall? He only knows what he knows. He's only done what he's done. And what he knows is that now—sixteen years after hearing the woman outside his tent—he can do something.

"I had a buddy named Coop who sent his fiancée back in Arkansas a Jap's skull," says Jim. "The whole gang signed it."

"If the war had been different," Dean says slowly. "If the Japanese had surrendered first and we were left fighting the Germans. If the last stronghold was not Tokyo, but Berlin, do you think we would have dropped the bomb on the Germans?"

A crack of thunder resounds outside the window. There is the early patter of rain on the roof.

"Jim."

"The original goal for the bomb was to beat the Reich." Jim is lighting another cigarette, the other one burned to a red nub.

"For Pete's sake, answer me. At the end of the day, would we have dropped it?"

"I don't know."

Dean can't help seeing the faces. Imagining what he'd feel if that was his son, his wife. If the keloid scars were raised on their bodies. He knows what the blast does to a person, of course. He knows about the 3-D sunburns inside the body; knows what happens to flesh in ten thousand degrees Fahrenheit. Organs melt, eyes boil. And after the blast, the lingering cloud, the problem of waste and radiation. (Like

Louis Slotin—who died in Los Alamos when the demon core went critical.) Tens of thousands died immediately, burnt alive. Thousands more would succumb slowly, gruesomely. They would bleed internally, excrete mucus and stool. The radiation would cut through their flesh, divide their cells, cause the body to cease being a body.

And now, they are not just poisoning people. They are poisoning the earth. He has stood by and watched as cranes lowered atomic waste into the dirt. As they covered it with soil. As they walked away from the trenches, colloquially called "graveyards"—the problem temporarily buried and forgotten.

"I'm not addressing my concerns over what happened years ago," he says. "I'm concerned about what's happening now. Not just to our own country and to our own children, but to every country. I'm concerned about the things we don't know about yet."

"Listen, I know you, Dean." Jim drops his voice, glances fleetingly to the closed door. "I've worked with you for a long time, and I know you're no sympathizer. They? Out there—they won't know that."

Dean studies Jim's face for a moment and weighs the risk of telling him too much.

"Jim," he says, pocketing his hands, "tritium is leaching into the groundwater. And it's reached the river."

Jim considers this with a calculating expression. "How much?"

"Enough," says Dean. "That same water irrigates the forest that surrounds the riverbanks. Then there are the worms that come in contact with radioactive materials. The birds that eat the worms. The boys that shoot down the birds and collect their feathers. The diatoms that are absorbing uranium in record numbers. The fish in the contaminated water and the alligators that eat the fish. And this? This is only from what management deems low-risk waste. What we bury in cardboard in unlined trenches, straight into the dirt."

"We're doing a hell of a lot better than Hanford."

"Not by much. Their tunnels are weak, but we have the chance to prevent this. Prevent the contamination of public drinking water. Prevent more animals from becoming irradiated. Prevent cancers, Jim."

"You yourself signed off on the storage procedures years ago."

Of course he knows this.

"We didn't know enough then," he says simply. "We know now. My techs have analyzed 958 stream samples for uranium and plutonium, 1000 for nonvolatile beta, and another 800 for tritium. I know what I'm talking about."

Dean pulls out a map of the plant. Jim rolls his eyes, says, "I know where we are."

"Just look," says Dean. He points to Sterling Creek. "The creek is here, right? In the 12 Area effluent."

"Right," says Jim.

"The C Reactor storage basin is here. Now the creek runs south-west and hits the Savannah River at this marsh tributary. The river then runs south, where it meets Coal Run, Lower Stream, and Rabbit Branch. That means any irradiated content in Sterling Creek can con-taminate—and disrupt our data—at the other tributaries. I could lose my job for even telling you this."

"You'll lose it anyway if you keep this up."

"All these solutions, they said would be short term, so I signed off. I signed off thinking we'd fix it, thinking it would be fixable, but it's been ten years. We have all this waste that will last thousands of years. Thou-sands, Jim! And it *will* continue to leak, and it *will* only get worse. Until our groundwater is fully contaminated, until the river where our own boys play, where they catch fish on the weekends, will be dangerously radioactive. Do you understand me?"

"I can't have any part in this," says Jim. "Please don't ever say I knew anything about it."

Jim stands and leaves without another word.

NELLIE

For the past six months, Nellie has had a recurring dream.

What she sees: a papery light. In neat, economical lines, there are rows of shoes. Wallets, purses, fragrances. Dresses of every color. Peacock blue and bruised purple, like knees after prayer. Elegantly, Nellie runs her fingers along the leather, the chevron sweaters, the alligator shoes. The single lightbulb (with a pull cord, how odd!) is small and filmy and yellow and flickering. Overhead, dreamily, the air raid signal warbles. The sound shakes the floor. Still she walks. Dust falls from the rafters, but still Nellie shops. There she is in Women's Wear! There she is in Home Decor! Her arms are full of fabric when she stops short and sees it—in the corner, is that the rick-rackety ladder, the ramshackle hatch? And there, across from cosmetics—are those her soup cans and batteries? Is that Dean's Geiger counter! Yes, yes! She is inside the shelter, a subterranean Sears. Meanwhile, in the world above, Oakleigh is being bombed. Oakleigh: small derby town, town of hats and camellia shows and Little League and Halloween parties and the bomb plant. Is the plant being destroyed, obliterated with a fifty megaton blast? The bombs sound like thunder or hail. Around her, the store clerks are unfazed. They slip mohair shawls off the hangers. They spritz Chanel No. 5. The air raid signal wails and wails, competes with the store's harpist. She shops. She cradles beautiful things in her arms. From her purse, she retrieves the money. She is wild, she is daring. She is Nellie gone rogue. She is a woman in love with her life, shopping underground.

In the morning, she awakes and curls herself in the sheets, but she cannot hide from the sound of the bombs. She smells the plaster dust, feels the silk dresses. Then, voices. Vapid, muted. As though she is underground—shopping, living!—and the sound wafts from the world above.

WILSON

Hand over hand on the ladder rungs. He is thirty feet off the ground—now forty—now fifty. He towers above the pines. Sweat beads on his face (his rucksack is heavy with supplies), and the dog tag weighs around his neck. Still he climbs. It's important to reach the top of the tower in time. He must scout. A Watchdog needs a watchtower.

Eddie wails on the ground because Eddie is chickenshit and chickened out. But this was no surprise, Eddie being more of a wimpy Watchdog anyways—and this whole day only proves Wilson's theory that Watchdog-singular or Watchdog-with-Penny may be a better plan of action.

He'll determine that later. If there is a later. If—and this is a big *if* given the situation, given the level of threat (RED!)—he succeeds in thwarting danger.

Onward he climbs. He doesn't look down. Past the network of steel pipes and tangled wires. Up the ladder, toward the top, he goes to his own observation deck. His senses tingle. His ears are pricked. Eyes, alert. He's breaking pretty much every school rule. *No hopping the perimeter fence; no getting too near the tower, government property; no trespassing.* Federal offense maybe? Not important now. His scalp itches, but he can't stop midclimb. Can't stop! He is a Watchdog, and this is his first real mission. This is much more important than trick-or-treating, than hunting Commies in the neighborhood. (Unless his suspicions prove correct. Unless Mr. Yuknavitch even now taps Morse code in his basement, betraying lab secrets!)

Wilson's radio buzzes its CONELRAD warning, so he climbs onward, up and up. He has been training for this. He is ready. He has all the necessary skills. He knows how to mimic the sound of the siren, how to leap over Sterling Creek without getting wet. He knows how to stare into the pharmacist's lamp—he can withstand great brightness. These eyes are trained eyes.

At the top of the ladder, Wilson hoists himself to the deck. The white bulb of the water tower is squat like a turnip and casts a shadow over him. This must be where the older kids stand, drop their pants, and piss. Or exchange girlie magazines and beer stolen from their fathers. Scratch their names with a nickel on the white paint.

Below him is the playground, so tiny! The other kids from Room 3 dot the grass. Mrs. Jenkins points at him. He can tell because of her ugly purple sweater. Other teachers stream from the school. There is Annie Yuknavitch, Becky with Patti Playpal, Todd Shepherd and Irving. And there, camouflaged by kids, is the Commie with the red tie. The Commie watches him.

But Wilson will be sneakier. He's made it this far.

The clouds look wispy like the strands of gray in Mama's hair. Birds fly in triangular patterns. And he's higher than the birds! Has he ever been this high? Doubtful. The wind whistles past, and he wishes he had his bomber jacket. Then he rifles through his rucksack for the aviator goggles and straps them around his head. The yellowed plastic dulls the sun's light. All around, Oakleigh is spread like a blanket. The treetops are like broccoli heads, people small as apple seeds. Water cuts downstream in the river. Cars honk. Crowds of people in town walk and wave banners like a July 4th parade. He can see his house from here, the soft slanted roof. How toyish the world seems, how delicate. Walls can tumble like Lincoln Logs. Roads look drawn like zigzagged chalk. He holds out his thumb, imagines squashing town hall like putty.

Then he leans against the railing and steadies his gaze on the horizon.

Father said an atomic bomb will always come from the air. And Wilson asked why, why couldn't it come from the sea? Why not from a submarine? And Father said, unlikely, but possible. And Wilson asked why, and Father said planes are faster, easier with their aerial vantage point. The downside to this is that planes are fast, which means there's less time to evacuate whole cities, descend to the shelters. The upside? Wilson is trained in planes.

This is because years ago, he was a secret member of the Ground Observer Corps—not officially, which was a bummer, because Father wouldn't sign the paperwork. Father said, "What business does a seven-year-old have doing such things?" What Father didn't understand was that Wilson was a savvy seven-year-old. And other kids were doing it, kids from the elementary school and teenagers and even their mothers! What made this so unfair was that Wilson was actually skilled. Wilson actually knew things. He would have been a great scout. He longed to speak into the radio receiver and say things like, "Come in Air Defense, this is Wilson Porter reporting." It even rhymed! "We have an air flash, sergeant! One—multi-jet—very high! Urgent, repeat, urgent. Fox-Hole-Papa-Zero-Two-Two-Black." He'd say that last part to identify location because apparently Fox-Hole-Papa-Zero-Two-Two-Black was the code name for the local Observer Corps' location: a pen of plywood near the American Legion building, with stairs leading to an observation deck.

At the time, his not being allowed to join officially was a particularly sore subject. Wilson pouted about it the way his friends pouted for a puppy or the way Mama sulked for a bigger house. He dropped hints at the dinner table like, "I'd be the youngest, you know." But Father insisted: civilian war efforts were not for children.

Wilson did it anyway.

Todd Shepherd was an official member for a while, which meant he was Wilson's inside man. In exchange for smuggled gumdrops and cigarettes from the pharmacy, he told Wilson about the logbooks, the maps, the charts of wingspan and altitude. Todd even passed along his manual for research, which Wilson never gave back. (It's still in the shelter, hidden behind cans of green beans.)

The requirements for joining the corps were simple and Wilson met all of them, which is partially why he should count as an honorary member:

1. Normal hearing
2. Normal eyesight
3. Ability to speak clearly and distinctly so that the Aircraft Flash message can be accurately received at the Filter Center
4. Ability to exercise good judgment and make proper decisions
5. Definite loyalty to the United States, which can be checked by a personal clearance. (And Wilson was definitely loyal. He'd signed the school loyalty oath and everything.)

Wilson learned fast. He studied the shape of the planes, the color, the sound. He learned to differentiate between single motor, bimotor, and multimotor. Between jets and normal aircraft. He didn't need a wings badge to be an observer. He had new binoculars. ("For bird-watching" Grandma Carol had written on the Christmas card. Ha!) The radios shouted, "It may not be a very cheerful thought, but the Reds right now have about a thousand bombers quite capable of destroying eighty-nine cities in one raid. Won't you help protect your country, your town, your children?" Yes! Wilson's heart raged. Yes, he would. He would help protect his town, his family. This, he could do.

Now, perched on the water tower, he scans the sky, observes the world in miniature. He feels that he is finally a Ground Observer. He is earning his wings.

With one hand on the banister for balance, he inches along the ramp and looks south. Surrounded by cushions of green, steam snakes from the bomb plant.

His heart beats wildly. What a day! What a week! Everything hurts. He has that wishy-washy feeling in his stomach from eating too much candy, from thinking about the dog tag, from looking at the hundred-foot drop. What would happen if he fell? Would he crack into a million pieces like glass? His cheek burns from where Penny Shepherd kissed him. He has so much to report in his log later. But first: Must scout the sky. Must watch for planes. Must, must!

The radio drools sound. He'd forgotten it, stupid! Wilson kneels to the deck, shuffles through the rucksack again, presses the transistor radio to his ear.

We have your coordinates, Agent. Be on the lookout. You are at Ground Zero. Repeat: you are at Ground Zero.

Roger that.

We're counting on you, Agent.

Roger.

Will there be a pilot in the plane? Will it be a plane at all, or one of those missiles? And maybe, he thinks, the Reds have moved past all that. Perhaps, there's a dog in the cockpit, like Sputnik. Poor dead dog in space. Now that's a horrible way to die, overheating in space and alone. He heard a rumor about "lost cosmonauts" from Todd Shepherd, that the Soviets lost men in space, they went up and never came back down, all before Gagarin. And though he knows he shouldn't feel sympathy for Commies (they aren't even human, according to Donny Lisle; they're more like robots) he knows that's a bad way to go. Did they burn immediately, or did they float away into the galaxies, watch the world fade little by little, until it was no bigger than a marble?

Once, during a Watchdog training session, after he and Eddie timed races around the playground, Wilson asked, "What do you think's the worst way to die?" and Eddie said, "War, obviously. Bang, bang, bang!" Here, he pretended to shoot an artillery rifle, like films of U.S. soldiers barreling down the Germans. This was during Eddie's obsession with the Marine Corps.

But Wilson wasn't so sure. "What about freezing? Or drowning? Would you prefer drowning?"

"We don't get a choice, dumbbutt," said Eddie. He pretended to shoot Wilson with his invisible gun. "Got you. You're dead." He kept shooting until Wilson fell on his knees and convulsed as though he'd been shot.

The worst would be atomization.

Years ago, Wilson sat on the living room floor while Mama watched the *Ed Sullivan Show*. She fell asleep halfway through. Father was working late. A cartoon came on the screen called *A Short Vision*. Wilson couldn't tear his eyes away. What he saw: people asleep in their beds and animals perched in their trees and a beautiful starry sky. An amorphous shape appeared in the distance like a gray disk. He was small then, but he knew. *Because it was so far away, it seemed very small at first. And because it was so big, it seemed to move slowly.* It was not an alien ship, not a blimp, not a weather balloon, not a superhero, not a rocket ship, but a silent, stealthy invader. Wilson watched as the bomb fell from the plane's tail—as the animated city on screen erupted in a helix of light. The worst part? The drawings of faces. Eyes melting in their sockets, dripping red down the skin as flesh evaporated. God, god! The nightmares that ensued for weeks after this! The tinny music that echoed in his brain!

The Commie appeared in his bedroom soon after. Commies can smell fear.

Now Wilson stares at the sky. He holds his thumb to the horizon. A plane is coming, said the radio. A plane is coming, and he must wait for it. Must note the dimensions, the size, the altitude, the type. He must do this for his parents, for the bomb plant, for Penny—lovely Penny who loves him. He will call into Air Defense, report any findings. He will warn them in time to take shelter!

Wilson looks down. Behind the fogged and filmy layer of the goggles, everyone seems shrouded in moon dust. That pharaoh-faced Commie is still there. Wilson sees the red of his tie beside the red of Annie's ribbons. (Signs, symbols, clues!)

If he succeeds in his reportage, then what? He knows there are jets always poised at the bomb plant, ready to intercept an enemy plane. Would there be a jet war above town? Would the American pilots shoot into the sky, thwart the Commie plan and plane? This is where things get fishy. Because if the U.S. fighter jets shoot down the plane, then wouldn't the bomb still explode? Wouldn't the nuclear warhead still rain down on the town? Wouldn't there still be a fireball?—four miles wide. Lots of fire, enough to cover buildings, cars, and people? (No ordinary fire.) And wouldn't there still be radiation? Gamma rays so strong they penetrate the body and kill within hours? And there would be the air blast, another five miles—wind that ruptures ear drums, collapses buildings, carries away cows and dogs and babies. (No ordinary wind.)

It would be like Hiroshima, only worse. He's played Atom Bomber, and nine times out of ten, he succeeds in bombing the city. He's become skilled at timing the automatic bomb release, dropping it over the board.

Apparently, Father has seen actual pictures. Wilson overheard this once, a late night conversation. Father saying to Mr. Shepherd, "Wish I never saw." Hiroshima happened before he was born, when he was still a little bean in Mama's belly—or maybe before even then, when he was, as Father says, just a "thought." Wilson likes to think of himself this way. "A thought." A "thought cloud Wilson" floating above the world like a comic book bubble or a secret satellite, invisibly watching, waiting to be born. Perhaps when he was still a "thought cloud Wilson" he was this high then.

What would happen is mass panic. A run on the bomb plant? Would there be mass evacuations? That sounds tricky to Wilson with everyone lined up in their cars like sitting ducks on the highway. No, no! He'd bike straight home, yessir. No good being up here when the bomb hits. He'd fly off his bike, fling himself inside the shelter, pull the hatch closed. He'd whoop and holler because *he made it in time.* He would check his supply kits, crank in fresh air, then he'd sit and wait and watch and wait and listen. There'd be a rap on his shelter door—Penny Shepherd out there in her bare feet and dungarees. She'd be screaming, "Oh, Wilson, you saved me!" And he'd say, "Get in here, darnnit!" He'd open the door for her. He'd risk exposure, radiation. He'd pull her down the ladder steps and then, they'd be like fiancés in a way, but not really. They'd sit crisscross and play Parcheesi and Monopoly. They would not play Uranium Rush or Atom Bomber because those would be depressing at this point. Wilson would show her how to tune into CONELRAD 640 AM, how to open cans with a pocketknife. He'd light candles, she'd tell stories. She'd make shadow shapes with her hands. He'd show her how to filter water using clay, a can, and a terry cloth. He'd share all his research with her, and if that's not love, he doesn't know what is. He'd explain how fallout is propelled into the atmosphere, like debris from a volcano. He'd say that they're safe so long as they're not in the *high impact danger zone,* which will probably be a city like New York or

Washington or San Diego. Unless the bomb plant is the target, then it's just bad luck! If other kids come by and knock and wail, Wilson likes to think he'd open the hatch for them, too. (Except not Becky Conway, given the pee-blanket situation. And not Annie Yuknavitch, she being a spy and all.) But he and Penny, they'd survive together. That's important, because surviving alone is not a much better alternative to dying, that's what Wilson thinks. Would he like to emerge from the shelter and be the last boy alive in Oakleigh? He thinks not. It would be apocalypse. The country would be invaded on every coastline by pharaoh-faced Commies ready to burn churches and flags and dress him (sole survivor!) in red-Commie gear. No, no, he can't let it happen.

He breathes slowly. He stares at the sky. He is waiting for the GAR-GANTUAN NUCLEAR BLAST. *The Doomsday Clock is ticking.* There is a purr, softer than the hum of cicadas. Wilson shields the sun with one hand.

A small black dot approaches. Slender, a streaking star. Sunlight gleams, bright as a meteor. It moves slow.

The radio bleats.

Central control, come in, central control.

This is Air Defense, central control, go ahead.

We have an aircraft flash. Elliot 84106.

The blip approaches with its oblique metal wingspan. Wilson brings the binoculars to his goggles. The sun glints off the plane's underside, so he can't detect the make or model, or if it's even American.

And the kids are still down there, still exposed. God! Where is the CDA? Why isn't the plane being intercepted? Won't anyone do anything? There is an unidentified plane in the sky.

Sirens scream through the air. Below, two fire trucks have arrived by the school yard. They must have seen the plane, too! But why isn't the air raid signal going off?

His stomach churns. He pukes a little, then swallows it. He can't give up now, not now—he remembers the Observer Corps template. He holds up his hand and sees that two of the planes could fit in his thumb, which means it's about five miles away. There's time still!

He fumbles with his radio.

One multibomber, probably. Flying low. Bravo Hotel, 35 west. Flying south, over.

What sky—what light—his thumb can block the sun! It's approaching, the little silver demon. He shifts his goggles, steadies his feet. Presses the radio to his ear: RED ALERT, RED ALERT, RED ALERT, THIS IS NOT A DRILL. It's inching closer—oh, it's closer!—and there is the belly, pewter gray like a fish. And the red crest of the Soviets. His stomach twists. It makes a double knot.

He inches toward the ladder's edge. He begins his descent. He has alerted Central Control and completed the mission. Back to Room 3. Back to recess, then social studies at two o'clock. He will tell Annie Yuknavitch that he thwarted her subterfuge. He will tell Eddie Pace that he's *chickenshit.* He will thank Todd Shepherd for his top-notch training. He will inform Mrs. Jenkins that he wants his ID tag stamped with additional info, please, to be extra sure he's identified properly.

A bird flies by. He pauses, watches. Time slows. The world swims. A firefighter has jumped the fence and begun to climb the lattice of ladder rungs.

He thinks: he does not want to be gunned down or frozen or burned or atomized. There is so much left to live for.

Then he is airborne. He is windswept. He is falling like a bomb from the belly of a plane.

DEAN

It was his father who used to say, "Time is what you pay the earth for the gift of living. It's like money you never get back. That's why we say *spend time*."

He said this during winter, as he waited for the earth to heal from the cold. He said this when he was dying, when his heart gave out like a broken-down engine. Dean's parents died within a month of each other, his mother succumbing to loneliness, he assumed, more than physical failure. He buried them both himself. He shoveled the dirt until he stood in six-foot-deep trenches, until red soil streaked his pants and lodged under his nails. When the plant construction was underway—reactors traveling on barges up the river, men with machetes cutting down vines and cypress knees—Dean had half a mind to hide his parents' gravestones. *Samuel Wilson and Gloria Jean Porter, d. March 1951.* He yearned for them to rest in peace on their land. But the thought of their bodies disrupted by a bulldozer was even worse. He let them go.

Every time Dean checks his watch today, he thinks of his father. Samuel Porter, his face jagged with wrinkles, his hair prematurely gray, pressed this watch into his hands when Dean said goodbye in '42. He never said Dean didn't have to go. Never said, *come back and farm with us.* Dean knew he never would, but he could not tell his father yet that the army would pay for college. That he'd been accepted already.

Now, he checks the watch with obsessive repetition, counting down. He checks the watch—the band worn soft like butter, his father's one possession of value—and thinks, this day does not seem like a gift.

Instead, the morning moves with painful speed, like fishing line slipping through his hands. Impossible to reel back. Everywhere he turns, someone needs something from him. *Sign here, Mr. Porter. Approve these numbers.* He confirms the techs' math on the Curta calculator. He signs for the new aqueous samples from Sterling Creek. He helps Lloyd recalibrate the colimetry machine. He takes a phone call from an editor about notes for a peer-reviewed journal. Over it all, the meeting. Hal. The calm collectedness of Martin French. The report on his desk.

By noon, there is a lull. The lab hushes, creating a cavity of sound as the techs take a break.

One hour.

The thought of food makes Dean nauseous. The thought of staying alone in the lab is worse. The commissary is in the administration building adjacent to the Sterling Creek Laboratory. Dean storms through the lab's winding corridors. Some employees smoke in the halls, others sip bottled sodas in the small break room off the lockers. Dean stares at his shoes when he passes Jim's metallurgy lab.

In less than an hour, he will stand in a small conference room. Coffee will wait, untouched, on a rolling cart. A scribe will sit with her glossy typewriter. The security posters will catch the shaft of window light. SILENCE MEANS SECURITY. DON'T LET THE AMERICAN DREAM BECOME THE SOVIET NIGHTMARE. He will see these for a moment as Wilson sees them—not as warnings but as truths about the world. He will be surprised as he sometimes is by the folly of it all: making decisions of consequence in a small twelve-by-twelve office room with prefab walls and faded green carpet. Hal will enter with his briefcase; he will murmur under his breath in that faraway voice. Martin French will trail him, followed by the other committee members. Dean has delivered innumerable reports before. He has stood under the warm, bald lights. He has reported that *they're well under the federal minimums, they are causing no lasting harm.* He has reported on the viability of drilling into bedrock, using steel-lined trenches for everything. What makes today different?

Dean walks and feels like a ghost of himself. Someone calls to him, and he manages a "hello" back, without registering who it is.

He moves down the labyrinth of hallways and into the covered corridor that connects the two buildings. Three women he doesn't recognize—all blond—swing through the doors, almost clipping him in the shoulder.

What's different today is that he no longer believes the things he's said before.

The doors open directly into the commissary. Jim is returning his tray on the conveyor belt just as Dean arrives. He catches Dean's eye briefly before skirting past, headed back to his lab.

The cafeteria smells of over-burnt grease and canned vegetables, a rancid sweetness. The menu today is meatloaf, sliced ham, and whipped garlic potatoes. A few open tables are strewn with abandoned newspapers. *HURRICANE WRECKS HONDURAS. PLEA FOR TEST HALT NIXED BY THE U.S.* Carlton and Sander have a card game going between them. A fit of laughter rises from their corner of the hall. Ricky Ivy stands against the west wall, talking on the mounted phone. In the far corner, Hal pours coffee into a paper cup. Martin French stands beside him with a paper tucked under his arm.

"Porter!" Sander waves him over. "You look like hell, old sport," he slaps an open chair for Dean, but Dean stays standing.

"What's the game today?"

"Rummy and nothing else," says Carlton. He smells of wax and heat from the glassblowing workshop.

Sander leans across the table, grinning wildly. He always looks like this, impish with a secret. He is a man who likes to tell stories and jokes, who fidgets when bored. He likes opera. He paints birds with watercolor. Sander is an organic chemist from Boston, an Irish Catholic.

He lowers his voice.

"You heard about Allen?"

"No, what?"

"Filed in sick around ten."

"Not sick," Carlton chuckles and collects the queen of spades from the open deck. "Lest you call being lovesick *sick.*"

"More like love angry. Hey, I mean I heard this morning, too, from Harriet, and we put an end to that. But around ten, Allen got a call from, who was it, Eugene?"

"Eugene," Carlton nods.

"Got a call from Eugene that Bev was planning to march with some of those antinukes in town today. He must've seen her leave the house or something. Anyway, ole Allen gets all hot and bothered about it, walks straight out of a meeting with Works Technical. Jim was pretty pissed about it, too. You know he was actually quiet all through lunch? Jesus, it's a miracle." Sander studies his cards for a moment, then discards a two of hearts. "You gonna sit or what? Like I said, you look like hell. Get some coffee in you, Porter."

"I need a Coke," says Dean.

The men return to their game. Dean goes to the vending machine by the tray rack. He reaches into his pocket for change and pulls out two dimes and two nickels. He was no older than Wilson when he ran to the local bank, saw the line of men in overalls and torn flannel, straw hats on their heads, all pounding the door, demanding their money, until they peeled away and walked in slow, lazy circles around town, their faces flecked with dirt, freckled with sun. GREATEST CRASH—*Deluge of panic selling overwhelms market*—*Prices tumble like an avalanche.* He had $3.85 in the bank when the market crashed. He would get thirty cents back.

Dean drops a nickel in the machine and selects a Coke. He fists the cold bottle and downs it in a few long sips.

Don't hate me, Nellie, he thinks. *You'd understand if you knew.*

April sits alone at a round table. She is encircled by a spray of yellow paper, and she writes furiously. A half-eaten bowl of potatoes and a cup of tea occupy the open scraps of space. Smudges of ink decorate her middle finger.

"This seat free?" he asks, settling down before she can answer.

She looks up, surprised, and collects the papers in a neat stack.

"What happened to you?" she says.

"Nothing." He checks his watch: *45 minutes*. "What are you writing today?"

She picks up the first page, her lips turning up in a half smile. "I'm writing about this party I went to for Halloween, and I'm trying to remember some of the costumes the children wore. Hugh likes the details like that." She bats the pen against her palm. "And then I'm telling him about some plans with Bette for the weekend. She wants to take me to the Barnes and Brothers stables. I've never ridden a horse before, and she just can't believe that."

Dean nods. Hal and Martin have moved from the coffee counter now. They carry trays of food to a table near Dean and April.

"Do you smoke?" he says to April.

"Sometimes."

"Walk with me."

He means this as a request, but it sounds like a command. His voice has entered a deep register that sounds foreign.

"I only have a few minutes," she says. "My break is almost over."

But she tucks the papers in her purse, brings her steaming cup of tea, and follows him out into the covered corridor.

The buildings seem spartan in the gray light, all beige concrete, uniform and warlike. Though the roof extends between the buildings, April steps out from under the colonnade. She tilts her head toward the sky and leans against the outer wall. Dean joins her. The air is crisp and water-heavy. The clouds are thick and dark and raggedy.

"My sister called me this morning and asked if the clouds she was seeing were from the test bomb," April says, holding her tea with both hands. "Can you believe that? She said she read it somewhere. She asked if I could confirm it."

"What'd you tell her?"

"I said I do paperwork. And that my security clearance is nil. But I also told her not to believe everything she reads."

A bird trills above them, then lands on the fencing between the lab and the road.

"Do you remember the Farmer's Ball?" Dean finds himself asking. "When you sat in the back with your Shirley Temple?"

"I'm surprised you remember," April laughs. "I think I wore my mother's old pageant dress. It was horribly out of style with those white ruffles."

"You said you were afraid you wouldn't know what to talk about. You and Hugh. I think about that a lot."

She reddens. "I shouldn't have said that. Hugh wouldn't like for me to have said that."

"No, it's all right. I understood. I understand."

She runs her finger around the rim of the cup. "Hugh is sensitive. He doesn't like me talking about him or about us, what with him not being here. I get it. He's proud and stubborn, but I love him."

Nellie is proud and stubborn.

"My mother told me once never to tell her anything bad about my marriage." In saying this, he has a sharp ache for his mother. She was a time-wearied, sun-dark woman who could weather anything, she said, with prayer and a good slice of bread. "She said she'd always side with me. That I should never let her think anything poor of Nellie."

"And did you take that advice?" April asks. She reaches her hand palm-out to the sky. "I think it's going to rain."

"I tried to."

He knows why his mother said this. She worried when they married.

He first took Nellie to his family farm when they were already engaged. It couldn't have been long before the wedding, one month or two. She stepped from his car, and her kitten heels sunk into the loamy ground. She kept her gloved hands at her waistline, as though afraid to touch anything inside the farmhouse, which was much cleaner than when Dean lived there. His mother tried to play hostess. She showed Nellie how to pour boiling water over garden-fresh tomatoes so the skins slid right off; she showed her how to cut off a rhubarb's crown and stew the pink stems for sponge cake. His mother knew how to make food from anything. Dean was proud of this. She knew what to do with milkweed and dandelion, how to grate them over corned beef like sprinkled lettuce. She knew how to save every last part of a chicken for broth, how to conserve watermelon rinds for pickling. Growing up, their cellar was stocked with stewed tomatoes, canned peaches, pickled dill, black currant jam. She was a small woman and Baptist to the bone. During the hard years, she made money where she could, stitching quilts, turning chicken feed sacks into towels or aprons, selling advertisement space on their barn. For as long as Dean could remember, there was a rusting metal billboard on the wall that faced the road: TRIPOLI QUININE, ONLY THE BEST. But in her lavender day suit, Nellie seemed awkward in the setting, a bulb planted in wrong soil. And Dean watched as his mother moved with a new frenzy through the small kitchen, explaining everything, sliding the salt pork into the cast iron as though justifying herself. "We do it like this," she kept saying. *We.* Though it was warm, Dean lit a fire. He stoked the flames and waited for the drop biscuits to bake, for the sorghum molasses to congeal on the stove, and for the black-eyed peas to boil. When at last they sat at the table, lined with the freshly bleached lace and the best family china, he saw how tired his mother seemed. And how old. She would die eight months later. Dean gulped down the buttermilk. Nellie picked at her beans. She nibbled like a rabbit in lavender. After supper, his father played dulcimer and his mother brought out her quilting, a beautiful Solstice Star, and Nellie sat awkwardly by the fire, picking at a loose thread in her skirt. When his mother tried to give Nellie a gift—a homemade beeswax candle, rose-hued in a glass jar—Dean saw the hesitation and thought she was about to refuse. Instead, she held the jar gingerly, smelled the wax, and gave a soft, "Thank you, Mama." It was the *Mama* that betrayed her insincerity, and he saw his mother recognize this in the proud tightening of her lips.

Was it his fault, how far they'd fallen? Had he refused to see?

"How did you two meet?" Dean asks, remembering himself.

"High school," says April. "I was a majorette at Oakleigh High, if you can believe it." He could believe it. April in those white boots, April in that brass-tasseled skirt. "Hughie played baseball. Funny how I thought we were so grown up then. A lot happens in a life after high school."

"Why didn't you go with him?"

To Okinawa, he means, and she knows. She says nothing for a minute and sips her tea. And then: "My mother isn't well. I couldn't leave her. I don't know if Hugh completely accepted that, but it's what I had to do. He wanted me to come."

"I would give anything for more time with my parents," says Dean. "There are days when I wish I never left them."

"It's breast cancer," says April. "She's hanging in there like a champ. But Hugh and I've been apart for ten months now. So I write him letters."

What she doesn't say: *I write letters because I'm afraid my husband will forget me. Because there are other women there, while I'm eight thousand miles away.* But Dean sees this in her eyes and the smile that tries to cover the tremble.

April drains her tea, then sets the paper cup on the ledge behind them. Her hand moves to her ear, massages in a steady rhythm. Her nails are white crescents.

A thought wafts through his mind, cloud-slow. He could take April's hand and lead her through the lab into his office. Close the blinds and lock the door. He could erase the light, unbutton her pearl by pearl. He could awake every muscle in her body with his hands, his mouth. He could see the soft whiteness of her like dough or snowfall.

He blinks. This is not why he asked her out here. (Is it?) Why then does he feel himself hardening? Why is there a distinct pang in him now like a lightning bolt of hunger?

"What about Mrs. Porter, what is she like?" April lights a cigarette. When she brings it to her lips, it seems almost delicate like a kiss. "I never see her at any of the women's socials."

Nellie. She is the lush voice of night. She is often drunk. She is always unhappy. How to describe his wife—all the beauty and all the thunder that she evokes? She is a body rolled to the far corner of their bed, silent and perfumed in anger.

"She's bored right now," he says.

"I don't think I would like being home all day, all that quiet to myself."

There, on the green carpet of his office, her legs could tuck beneath his desk. Her back could arch under his. Would he draw sound from her, like beckoning music from an instrument? Would she tell him where to touch her, what she likes? Would she whisper his name so only he could hear?

When he's thinking of April, he realizes, all thought of his meeting with Hal—the report on his desk—evaporates like water on leaves.

April checks her watch, then taps out her cigarette against the wall. "My break is almost over," she says. "I'm supposed to meet Bette in records. Are you sure you're all right?"

The first whisper of rain hits the ground. The drops fall, delicate as petals thrown at a wedding. Dean doesn't move, but April flicks her head to the sky. A drop strikes her nose and rolls down the button onto her upper lip. This is when he kisses her. It is not as he expected. It is not with passion but with sadness. He kisses her slowly, deliberately. She tastes of smoke and salt and something herbal. He kisses her, his mouth searching, his mind suddenly relieved of anything else: the shelter at night, Nellie in the morning, the meeting so soon—just minutes away. April's hand reaches to the small of his back, and he kisses her more deeply then. He reaches up her spine until he meets her hair, thick as wool and soft as silk.

"April," he says her name gently, pulling away. "April, April."

Like April showers, like *April is the cruelest month*, like his birth month, when the peaches are still green and firm, not yet ripe. The rain wets his face, thins between them. He can feel the drops speckling his shirt, running along the gel of his hair.

She whispers his name back to him. His senses return, and he's aware that they're standing in front of someone's office window, the blinds at half tilt. He pushes her lightly, until they are tucked beneath the roof awning, just behind the gutter, near the service door. A shadow covers them. The rain falls more steadily now in a thin river from the roof. Lights wink from the highway as workers drive across the plant for lunch. Would she use her mouth, her hands? He doesn't care—he just knows that he needs this, needs to feel alive, needs his body loved this way.

With one hand, he cups her breast outside the sweater. He can feel the boned bra and the whirlpool lace through cashmere. *My office*, he thinks. *My car.* They could slip away for an hour—no one would miss them. *A storage closet. The locker room.* He would be fast, so fast! It's been so long! *A sampling trailer. The stairwell.* He will be so gentle when he enters her. Against the wall, on the floor? Anywhere. He wants to make her gasp, but he will be so gentle. April leans against the cinder block, and he moves his mouth to her neck, to her earlobe, where he bites her softly. She will be so smooth, he thinks. And she will not roll her eyes in boredom, she will not be stiff as a board. Her nails run down his back, and he kisses her harder, pushes against her until her mouth forms a soft O.

The service door swings open behind them.

April leaps from Dean, quick as a wild rabbit. It's only now that he sees her bewilderment and her tears. Two buttons on her sweater are unhooked. (Had he done that?) He stares at the pearl around her neck, watches it rise and fall with heaving breath. Suddenly, she seems so small. Her black hair has slipped from the barrettes, and a rain-streaked curl sticks to her forehead.

"Hey."

Dean knows that voice. He turns around, trembling, to see Jim in the open doorway. Jim's expression is unreadable, a rarity. His jaw is hard and heavy as he raises his eyebrows at Dean.

The rain falls more steadily now. The sky has darkened to indigo, surprising for the early hour. April glances between the two men as if unsure what to say.

Jim speaks first.

"We've been looking for you everywhere." His eyes bore into Dean. "There's a call for you. It's urgent."

Nellie Porter
7716 Upper Ridge Lane #145
Clemson, SC

November 1, 1951

Dear Dean,

You won't believe what happened to me today. Goodness—I've had such a fright that I can hardly write straight! Mother would be horrified by my letters, so excuse that. But a man came by here and asked me all sorts of questions about you and my father, questions about Communist ties, and Lord, it was awful. He was terribly rude and asked so many things about my father that I almost felt a dizzy spell coming on. W started crying eventually, which put an end to that mess, thank God.

I hope it's nice there. We've had rain only, which has been dreadful, if I'm being honest. Hopefully the flowers in the planter will grow, and that'd be nice, but I've been stuck inside with W all day, all week, and I'd give anything for a walk outside. I've been entertaining myself by watching the birds at our window. One cardinal keeps pecking on the glass, as if wanting to come inside. I have half a mind to let him.

I've been thinking a lot about what you said before you left. I don't know if you remember or not, but I do. I think about things a lot. Sometimes I feel like I just need days to untangle a single, simple thing. Do you ever feel like your brain is all knotted? It's hard to follow one thread of thought that way, it's one mess of yarn up there. I hate being angry over a letter, so please don't be frustrated with me, but I just have to write it out. And I want to say what I mean, so I think this is better than waiting until you get back and I've been here thinking about it, getting hot like a kettle on the stove too long.

Do you remember the clipping I showed you? They were for curtains, a fabric with birds. I had cut out the picture to show you while W napped, *and I waited all day for you to come back. I feel silly writing this now, but it's true. I waited all day. While you have your work, I have this now. I have clippings and a baby. And that's fine, Dean, because I'm happy. When W coos at me, I'm just full to bursting. But what you said when I showed you the fabric and how I'd measured the windows in the kitchen and calculated the cost—you said, "It's just curtains."*

Now that may not sound like much, Dean. And I'm sure to you, it sounds like nothing. Not even an argument. You've probably forgotten all about this. But I have thought about the word "just" ever since, and I thought about it through that horrid interview, and I thought about it as I waved you off down the street with W on my hip. I have thought about it when nursing in the middle of the night while you've been gone. (Do you have any idea how lonely it is to wake in the middle of the night, alone in an apartment, to nurse a hungry baby?) To you they were just curtains. Just part of the house—but to me, they were a project. Work, something to create and do. Something to do with my hands, Dean. I'm afraid I'm not explaining myself clearly enough, and I don't want you to be angry. It's just that I want to know that what I'm doing means something to you. Because darling, I am so terribly proud of what you do. So terribly proud that I wish I could be there with you, watching as they build this important place.

I had a letter yesterday from Mother and I wrote her a postcard back telling her you'd been scouted for government work. I'm tickled to see what she will say.

W sends his love in the form of messy diapers and baby cries. Ha ha! That baby keeps howling. Is there anything we can do to fix that? Any medication? I can't get a moment's quiet in edgewise. Maybe I'll ask my doctor about it.

Come home soon.

Yours always,

Nellie

PART II

We have had the bomb on our minds since 1945. . . . How can we suppose that something so monstrously powerful would not, after forty years, compose our identity? The great golem we have made against our enemies is our culture, our bomb culture—its logic, its faith, its vision. —E. L. Doctorow

The stars are not wanted now: put out every one,
Pack up the moon and dismantle the sun,
Pour away the ocean and sweep up the wood;
For nothing now can ever come to any good.
—W. H. Auden, "Funeral Blues"

NELLIE

The bus doors creak open. "Columbia town center," announces the driver, a squat man with an unfortunate purple birthmark across his cheek.

Nellie stares, hesitant. She grips her handbag and hears, from across the street, the sirens of emergency. Behind her, the protest has fizzled, but women still claim the streets. She has slipped away unnoticed, leaving the leftover pamphlets on the courthouse steps.

She climbs into the bus and siphons herself toward the back, the last row before the COLORED PASSENGERS sign. Through the window, the stout nose of an ambulance rolls to someone's rescue, bright triangles of sunlight reflecting off the hood.

A gray chill seeps through the glass. Ahead, a young mother bounces her toddler son on her lap. The woman has a picket sign tucked beneath her seat. Another protestor. The boy intently folds a paper airplane, or perhaps a boat. As the bus lurches forward, the howl of the sirens fading, Nellie watches this child, this mother. Sees the woman brush the boy's hair from his eyes, examine the paper boat, listen to the child's description of why it will float. The mother leans to kiss her son's ear.

Nellie looks away. She leans her head against the glass and watches the town wash by, parabolas of shape and color and impossible light.

HERE IS WHAT HAPPENS at the plant's burial ground:

The boxes and bags and irradiated coveralls meet the earth, the soft wet dirt. There is rain like today, the cold fall drizzle of Carolina. The rain when it meets the isotopes: the first drops create a small chain reaction, invisible but precise. Surface water becomes puddles, then becomes streams that dip into the nuclear cemetery. The movement depends on the type of ground—clay, silt, sand. In clay, the isotopes move the fastest, slipping and sliding through the earth. Tiny veins move around pebbles, like a river splicing a boulder. This is how tritium reaches the groundwater, the aquifers.

This is how it reaches the river.

This river is flat and alluvial. Near the Sterling Creek Plant, the area is swampy like the mouth of a bayou. It is populated by alligators, cat-fish, and diamondback terrapins.

The animals will become irradiated. The water, the fish. Plant staff will joke and say there are "tritigators" on-site.

But to the scientists, this will not be funny. It will be terrifying, this rain. The way the earth is trying, so desperately, to cleanse itself.

DEAN

A certain paralysis of horror came with war. For Dean, this was not the same as battle shock. He was prepared in those moments. His muscles tensed. It came in the quiet stretch when war life seemed bewitchingly ordinary. When he and three comrades went into the woods to relieve themselves and came across a mass grave with bodies piled in a ravine. He saw a girl's body, her dress ripped from shoulder to knee. They were not yet decayed, but wild dogs had found them. It came on the hot morning, the trees yellowing, when a soldier went to the water pump, only to flip a trip-wire bomb left by the Germans. The tolling in Dean's ear lasted for hours. He could do nothing but watch as the body that was no longer a person collapsed into the dust.

It came when a woman's screams tugged him from dreaming. He could not swim back to sleep. Grogged and drunk with exhaustion, he stumbled from his bunk and followed the cries, chased by thin laughter.

He found them. Three men, whose faces Dean can no longer remember, and her. This was August, maybe. A French woman. He'd seen her in town. Her face was thin and her cheeks sunken. Her head was shaved, a shearing done publicly because she was accused of fraternizing with the Germans. "No, no, she's a maid," an older woman had said to Dean in the street, in troubled English. "A maid, a maid, la femme de ménage!"

In the night, on the ground, this woman locked eyes with Dean. There was animal desperation in her. Though it was pure dark, he could see her so clearly, the way her face pressed into the dirt, the way her nails clawed helplessly in the air as though reaching for him. *Oh my God, oh my God, oh my God*, Dean thought. He stood, stunned. It seemed like minutes that he watched, stricken and horrified. He had never been with a woman. But he knew it was not supposed to be like this monstrosity he'd come across.

He was barely twenty-four. April's age now.

The soldiers saw him and shouted profanities. One pushed Dean back, demanded, "What you lookin' at, farm boy? Get outta here 'fore we do worse to you."

They would beat him to a pulp, he knew. They were body-hungry, they were wild, likely drunk. They would break him in all the ways he learned were possible since joining the war. He was afraid. North came later.

How long would he blame himself for doing nothing? For stepping back, palms up, and saying, "Sorry, sorry," as though he were the one in the wrong. The woman gave one last desperate kick as he turned to leave. As Dean walked, he hoped that (maybe) others would hear. Others would do something. He was just one person.

Of all things, this is what Dean thinks about as he parks and enters the visitors' wing of the county hospital. He sees that woman's face and her dirt-rimmed nails. He wonders what happened to her and what happened to those men. If they survived, if they have wives and children now, if they have little yellow houses, and if they have forgotten all about what they did in the fall of '44. He wonders, sometimes, if he does not deserve every suffering in the world to make up for that night. His inaction. And today, today, just as he was about to do something, this happens today. He is supposed to meet with Hal, supposed to be the one who speaks. Now, there is that paralysis in his stomach again. The do-nothing-run-and-hide feeling. Is this what sends Wilson into the shelter? This kind of dread?

Down the starched white hallway he goes, past pin-studded bulletin boards and coffee tables and buckets of blocks for children. Past an old woman using a walker.

To the front desk. A nurse sits in a wooden chair with glasses that consume her face. Her hair sticks out in tiny copper curls. She writes on a clipboard. Dean speaks and tries to steady his voice. "Where's my boy? Wilson Porter, roughly sixty, seventy pounds. Brown hair. He came from the school! He's ten, he fell."

The nurse says he must wait in the lobby. Still, the words gush from him.

"He's my son, can't I see him? God, I have to see him, please. Well—can you at least tell me—please, can you just check?"

The nurse seems to fold into herself. Dean's suddenly aware of his tone, his fist on the desk. Her white cap bobs as she says, "Sorry, sir, I don't know. They'll be right out. Please be patient, sir. They're doing all they can."

He moves to the lobby.

A blue chair. A basket of magazines. Bright travel posters in white frames. A lighthouse painting, all black-and-white stripes. A child— four, five?—sits on the floor. He has a runny nose and a popsicle stick, which he keeps licking though it's already stripped clean. A pregnant woman sips from a paper cup, her ankles swollen around tight white shoes. An elderly couple, one with a face mask looped behind her ears, flip through magazines.

Dean sits. He crosses his legs. He uncrosses them. He checks his watch. Forgets the time. Checks again.

Mrs. Jenkins was the one who called.

"We're so sorry to bother you at work, Mr. Porter—but, there's been an accident. He was knocked unconscious. We tried to stop him. I called the fire department immediately!"

He fought to slow the woman down. April stood beside him, shell-shocked and wide-eyed. Dean could almost feel the heat emanate off her body, their mutual embarrassment now eclipsed. She fiddled with her wedding ring. She tugged aggressively at her earlobe. Dean bit his lip and willed himself to bleed. Mrs. Jenkins spoke in such a frenzy that he found himself more panicked with every passing second.

He stared at the rotary dial on the black phone box.

"Now hold on right there, Mrs. Jenkins—he did what now?"

April placed her hand tentatively on his shoulder, but he shook her off. Jim and Sawyer Cunningham and the lab technicians all stared. He wanted to snap for them to vanish, leave him in peace. The silence was so loud, he could barely hear!

Lloyd burst through the doors with a bag of peanuts, paused, and then said, "What?"

Dean pressed the receiver closer to his ear.

"And, and what about Eddie? Eddie Pace, Bill's boy, he runs the pharmacy, they're friends? Thank God. Well, was anyone else hurt? I swear to God, that damn water tower is coming down. You hear me? Down. You better believe I'll be talking to the mayor about that, having a damn water tower on school property! You need to watch out for those children, Mrs. Jenkins. They're in your care. We leave them in your care in school, and you're telling me my boy could be *dying* because you weren't damn watching." The words ran hot and metallic like blood in his mouth. There was the distinct and muffled sound of a woman crying. He hung up the phone.

Time had turned to soup, hot and thick. He stared bloodshot around the lab. Everything made his brain fuzzy. Rain drummed on the roof and a grayish-blue light dusted the equipment. What he felt was only a hesitant shock. His feet were lead. Anger coursed through him—anger at April for witnessing this, at himself for being caught with April, at Jim for interrupting them, at Mrs. Jenkins, at himself for shouting, at Wilson for choosing today to be careless, today to get hurt. *Today* with his work and future on the line. He checked his watch. Ten till one. Five steps to his office. Quick, what did he need? Briefcase, keys, slip off the dosimeter. The report lay untouched on the desk—no time. He almost crashed into April, who hovered outside his office like a moth, expectant and confused. Down the hall past the caves and cubicles, past Sander who shouted, "What bloody happened to you?" Into the blinding sunlight, his car, the road—almost crashing into Campbell's van. The long drive through rain.

Dean knows that when he looks back, he will remember this with a distant feeling. There will be the facts of it, the numbers like data on a chart. Exactly twelve and a half miles from the Sterling Creek Laboratory to the Oakleigh County Hospital. Exactly twenty-eight minutes of driving time and exactly two protestors, pickets beside them, that he almost hit with his car. Four people in the lobby, five counting himself. There will be this: twenty-five feet. His boy fell twenty-five feet.

The lobby is small, stale but clean. Particles of dust catch the light shafts, illuminated like mosquitoes netting a streetlamp in the night. He makes out the smell of coffee and cleaning supplies and Vick's Vapo-Rub. There is the click of heels on tile. Those perfect little white uniforms as the nurses dart in and out of rooms, like bees on a mission. This is not real because boys do not just fall from water towers. Little boys are supposed to be safe at school. School is where you learn, not where you die.

The child with the popsicle stick licks it one last time. He then abandons it on the floor and picks up a toy car, shiny and green. He moves on hands and knees, running the car repeatedly into the sofa legs. He must be four, Dean thinks. He still has that doughiness.

Wilson at four: a small thing, all baby fat and deer legs. He whined when Nellie left the room, as though afraid she wouldn't come back. He climbed onto the kitchen counters, asked why the pasta was wiggling, asked why the kettle was whistling, asked why this bird was red but this one was brown—asked and asked until Dean, exhausted and reading, longed to shout, *Be quiet, son, be quiet.* He took spoons into the garden and dug. He buried toys, little green army men, and placed stones to mark the spots. He whispered in milk-laden baby breath, "They *died*," when Dean asked what he was doing. Later, he dug them up and hid them around the house. His soldiers all had television names like Beaver or Huckleberry or Tonto. Nellie would squeal upon finding muddy toys on the bookshelf or in her soup tureen. At the time, this was almost charming to Dean, the oddness of it. He wanted his son to play.

Dean leans over his knees, clasps his hands as though praying. He thinks he might vomit. They are working on his son back there, his baby. His miniature is in the emergency wing. There is a doctor examining his bones, his brain.

"I don't know why he went up there," Mrs. Jenkins said over and over. "He knows not to go up there. There are signs. There's a fence. I don't know why he'd do such a thing. There's a fence!"

Dean knew why.

When did the early signs manifest? When did he first sense that something was off?

They were only little things then, buried toys. He had a compulsion, sure, toward war games. He was afraid of the dark and needed a warm pool of light to fill his room. Then he started drawing black scribbles and jarring flames of orange and yellow. He never used the color red. That crayon always stayed in the little cardboard home, untouched and perfect. When did buried toys become binoculars, traipsing through the garden, crushing flowers beneath his rain boots?

Twenty-five feet, Mrs. Jenkins said. That's over three stories, and this is not a story Dean likes. He does not want the ending that follows this chapter.

What happens when a terrified child climbs a water tower where a water tower should never be? When he slips and falls? When the fire department is already there but too late, just seconds too late? When the decade-old body hits the ground at five meters a second? When brain collides with bone? Will it alter forever the balance of ions and chemicals, so delicate, so pristine, aligned like precious atoms? Did his child's brain slosh too hard against the skull? Was there something irreparably damaged in that beautiful mind?

The elderly couple speaks in low tones to each other. The little boy whimpers, having accidentally pushed his car too far under the couch. He wriggles to his belly, reaches one arm deep into the pit of dust bunnies under the faded lobby sofa.

Wilson at four: always playing stealth, a game Dean wished he'd never learned. It gave him chills, that being-watched feeling. The way he could sit in his office for a half hour before realizing that Wilson was crouched under the desk, shadowed. The way he would be shaving or combing his hair, turning into his work self, only to sense child-eyes peering from behind the shower curtain. Wilson would erupt in giggles upon being spotted like this was a game of hide-and-seek. Like he'd been taught to tuck himself away in secret. He'd press both hands to his cheeks, make his chubbiness cushion out like a pillow.

Dean wrings his hands. *Oh, my boy. My boy, my boy.*

And where is Nellie?

Mrs. Jenkins had said, "We can't reach her. We've called four times. I can keep trying. No one seems to know where she is."

He aches for her now—for all her storminess, she would know what to do, how to weather this. She would run her thick nails through his hair. She would say, "Everything is *fine*. Don't worry so much." Her voice would be sharp but reassuring.

There is a pay phone near the bulletin board. Dean rummages in his pocket for change, and in a second, he is at the phone. He waits for the lilt of the dial tone and the groggy slur of Nellie's voice, freshly awakened from a nap. "Come on!" he hisses, tapping his foot, "Come on, Nel, pick up!" but there is no answer. He hangs up. Waits. Calls again.

But there is no Nellie.

WHEN HIS MOTHER CALLED to say his father had died, Dean was at work. This was December of 1950. He had just published a series of articles in prestigious journals. In a few short months, he'd be officially invited to join the Sterling Creek staff. The town of Ellenton would vanish. His family farm would become a reactor or a seepage basin or maybe just a stretch of land between buildings. After a day of paperwork and hunching over experiments, Dean was coming in from the greenhouse. He wore white coveralls streaked with soil. One of his research assistants—a toothy and freckled grad student from West Virginia—handed him the phone, said, "Your mother." Dean was in a hurry. It was after five, dinner would be on the stove. His wife was waiting. "What?" he said, his voice clipped and urgent. She said his father had a heart attack and died on the kitchen floor, just like that. Dean was ashamed that his first feeling was annoyance. *Today?* his mind asked. He did not have time to bury his father, deal with a will, the land. It was the middle of the week. Death was inconvenient. But the instant he thought this, when he heard the crack of tears in his mother's voice, he felt such guilt. "It's like money you never get back," she was saying over the phone. He should have known by the very presence of a call that something was wrong. They did not own a phone. This means she drove into town and called from the post office or from a friend's house.

"That's what he said to me, the very last thing. Time with him is all I want back." He hung up and told the intern, "My father died," before packing and walking home in the cold. He left his coat at work. He wanted to feel the chill.

WHAT FOLLOWS IS A series of small actions that absorb the hour. Dean sits back down. He stands, paces, runs his hands through his hair. Kneels to the linoleum, reaches his hand under the sofa, retrieves the car for the whimpering boy. Pats the child's head before realizing what he's doing. The boy watches him warily. Dean paces again, ten steps to the front desk, ten steps back. Asks the nurse, "Any news yet?" Groans when she shakes her head. Replays Mrs. Jenkins over and over: "He was knocked unconscious—not much blood, but some. The fire department was already there—we'd already called. I don't know why he climbed up there, Mr. Porter. We tried to stop him." Moves through the hospital corridor in a stupor, returns to the front desk, asks if the nurse can break a twenty so he can call the house again, and she says no, they don't exchange money. Finally, he asks the elderly couple if they can spot him a few coins for the pay phone. He calls home again—nothing. He asks the operator for Jim and Lois Shepherd—nothing there either. He hangs up the receiver with a clatter. Paces again. Remembers April following him through the lab, "Dean, what's wrong? What happened, you can tell me!" Trailing him as though she'd forgotten what transpired, the way she'd leaned away from him as though repulsed just minutes before.

He sits back and stares at the magazine covers, memorizes the curve of John Glenn's face, the intricate array of gold on Liz Taylor's Cleopatra crown. All thought of Hal is buried, the report with it. There is only this: the lighthouse painting in a lobby, the walls so terribly, cheerfully white, the light a sickly blue from those bulbs overhead. He wants to smash them, send the glass down in a sea of shards. He wants to feel slivers of pain all through his fist, wants to watch the blood trickle over his knuckles, his fingers—wants to feel *anything* but this.

He finds himself praying, though he hates that. He does not want to believe in a God who lets bad things happen to children, to women who are war victims, who allows bombs to fall on cities. But he mouths the words. "Is this punishment? For everything? Punish me, not him. I'm trying to do better. Punish me."

That night was so dark. And his shoulders ached beyond pain. All he wanted was to sleep and escape the horror of what was happening to the French woman who was a maid for a German officer, because what else was she to do?

He has watched as nuclear waste settled into the earth, forgotten like corpses. He has kissed another woman. He has let his son descend into an underground playhouse—his son who may be dying right now behind a blue hospital curtain. But this is what he thinks of: this moment when he turned away.

"Not my son, not my son." His knuckles turn white. "Oh God, please, not my son."

Where is Nellie? He needs her, he needs her.

When his father died, when Dean arrived home shivering and numb and unable to cry, his new bride sat him down at the kitchen table. She poured him a drink. She listened and forgot about dinner on the stove, let it burn. He loved that then, how she let it burn, how she sat with his hand in hers while soup congealed and stuck to the pot until the apartment smelled of burnt garlic. He confessed, even, his feeling of resentment, his guilt, and she said, "You're a good man, Dean Porter. A good man." He smiled at her because he did not believe this about himself. Nellie was the one who drove them to Ellenton, though she hated driving. She was the one who ordered flowers for the church and coordinated a small reception, insisted they needed a "proper funeral." She gathered the family Bible and a few pictures, bought lemon bars and tea. Dean could only take up the shovel and love his father that way, bury him with his own two hands. Love was returning to the land. But Nellie wanted beauty and a certain order of things. She could snap life into place in the wake of loss. Later, when his mother died, Nellie would do the same thing, though Wilson was still cooking in her belly.

The entrance swings open. Dean looks up, hoping to see her. She would be tall and resplendent with raindrops freckling her coat, her

eyes wide with worry. Instead, Bill Pace enters, sweating profusely in a
sweater vest, dark crescents under his arms. Eddie is beside him with
a plastic bag of gum balls and licorice. A roll of comic books is under
his arm. Eddie's red hair is especially unruly, making him look like a
Lost Boy. Blood has crusted around his nostrils, as though from a latent nosebleed.

"I brought this," Eddie says. He passes the candy to Dean. He looks
sheepish and shy. "His favorites. He only likes the orange and green and
yellow and blue ones, so I only brought those, and black licorice. Also,
some comic books." Eddie looks around expectantly. "Where is he?"

"In the back." Dean tries to smile but cannot.

"Awful sorry about this, Porter," says Bill. He pockets his hands.
The two men do not know each other well, are tethered in life only by
their sons. But Dean meets his eyes with gratitude. "Eddie came home
shouting about it. I closed early. Have you seen him?"

"Not yet."

"They let our whole class go home," says Eddie. He reaches one
hand into the candy bag and plucks a licorice. He unbraids it strand
by strand. "He was being a big dummy, Mr. Porter. I told him that, too.
He'd kill me for telling you this, but he's not here so I'll tell you. He got
kissed today. Kissed, and I saw it, and he just stood there. Geez Louise.
It's like he went crazy or something, just spazzed. I wouldn't just stand
there, I'd've known what to do. But he just *stood* there."

"Kissed by who?"

"Now that's top secret information." Eddie's eyes twinkle. "Then he
takes off. Just like that." He snaps his licorice-free fingers. "He wanted
me to follow, but I said, *no siree.* He said I was a sissy, but I think he was
stupid for doing what he was doing. I followed, all screaming. It was
dumb. Geez Louise. I tried to stop him, Mr. Porter. I did, I tried. I told
him it was *stupid.* I told him it was *dumb* to do that."

"I believe you did, son," says Dean. He nods reassuringly. "I believe
you did."

Eddie's voice takes on a more serious tone. "He just went up and up.
Until he was only a speck." He raises his thumb in the air, as though
blocking out the sun on a bright day.

"Wait—how high did he go?" Dean asks.

"All the way up. He was a little Wilson speck up there. Like I said, it was stupid." And then: "I'll ride his bike home for him, since he left it at school. Is that good? I think he'd like that. He wouldn't want his bike left out like that."

"Yes, that's fine, anything. Thank you."

He sees it all now, how Wilson must have climbed the whole way. Why had he only pictured a short climb? Only twenty-five feet? What if the fall had been worse, higher than Mrs. Jenkins had estimated? A water tower is what, one hundred and sixty feet or so? What if they aren't letting him see Wilson because he is, in fact, already dead?

"We'll let you be," says Bill. He places both hands on Eddie's shoulders and steers him back toward the door. "You'll let us know when you hear anything?"

Dean nods. The words die in his throat. He watches Bill and Eddie leave, become father and son silhouettes in the light from the outside world.

This is when his name is called. He stands, but there is not a doctor waiting for him. Instead, there are two police officers and a fireman in the emergency wing door.

NELLIE

She saw her father once in Columbia. That was 1947. It must have been the weekend, she thinks now, for she was in town for a wedding. (A horrid wedding, all hot and buggy, outside in summer. Her cousin, a garden club socialite.) Nellie sat reading Auden in a Parisian-themed cafe. She was alone. At first, the shape in the glass across the street was so familiar it seemed almost dreamlike. That was not her father, that was a phantom of her father. The thought was absurd. A ghost man. She was seeing a ghost! She returned to reading. *We would rather be ruined than changed / We would rather die in our dread.* But when she looked again, she saw him distinctly. Saw the cut and curve of his jaw—so like hers! Saw that sway she knew from her own walk, the way the shoulders curved, the head bent forward. Mother was always saying, *walk like there's a string up your spine, walk straight like a queen*, but Nellie never did. Nellie walked like her father. She walked like there was a burden on her back. Now here he was, impossible! And he walked beside a woman, so young, almost waifish, her hair all rosebud curls pinned to the skull. This new woman held the hand of a child. The little girl wore white socks up to her knees. She wore braids and blue bows that blustered in the wind. They were going into a children's clothing store, Little Bert's Boutique.

Nellie spilled coffee on herself, on her book. The words blurred. *Than climb the cross of the moment / And let our illusions die.*

Later, she would have so many questions. Why would you leave me, forget me? Why marry someone my age? Were you a sympathizer, really? Why did you *do it*?

She cannot remember if she has been back to Columbia since. That was fourteen years ago.

Nellie places a gloved hand on the window of the bus as they arrive at the curb. The bus has been stuffy, warmed by bodies. She smelled rather than felt the sweat that gathered in the crooks of her sleeve. No, she has not been here in fourteen years. When she visits her mother (the rare occasion, only when truly necessary), Nellie takes the back roads to Lamming and refuses to drive through the city.

"Columbia town center," the bus driver announces.

There is a quick shuffle. A few passengers got off at the prior stop. Some remain onboard now. The mother with her little boy are just ahead. The child glances back at Nellie and catches her eye. He clutches his paper boat to his chest, as though it is a precious treasure.

"We'll need to get some wax," the mother says in hushed tones. "We'll paint it on. How's that? We'll pull out mommy's nice brushes, okay? Would you like that?"

Nellie is the last one off. Outside, the air has chilled even more. But there is no rain here, only smoggy gray clouds.

The town center sprawls before her in all its suburban glory. Skeletons of magnolia trees line the gray-green medians. Weeds sprout through the sidewalk cracks in concrete. She walks toward the storefronts. The wind cuts through her coat, and she grips her pocketbook. The two hundred dollars are still there, deliciously! She passes lines of cars, women with baby carriages, a toddler crying outside a 1958 Plymouth, furious as his father loads him into the back seat. Then the white script of Sears, that sign of promise. Then the glass doors, her reflection in the window. She looks older than she feels, Nellie realizes. Her shoes are out of date. She needs a haircut, she needs new clothes.

The ground floor opens into the home decor section. (Her favorite!) Here are various model rooms, household possibilities. YOU DESIGN IT, WE'LL MAKE IT HAPPEN reads a sign suspended from the ceiling beside a twinkling chandelier. Nellie walks through the rooms, little displays of life. She runs her fingers over pillow fringe and down the scalloped edge of sofa trim. The colors this season are all named after foods: red currant, olive, pistachio. Ginger, boysenberry, grape.

The sofas are tipped in rosewood and lined with embroidered green silk. The furniture is every shape and size. Pod chairs and tables of metal and PVC. Danish shelves built into the walls. And the art! This is what she loves the most. In the living room models, art is mounted over chaises or hung over mantles. Moroccan tapestries and bold-splashed canvases. Most are shapeless and odd, as though the painter simply poured a cup of liquid color and called it a day. One painting in particular catches her attention. It looks like two squares, one atop the other. The top is yellow, and the bottom is red. That is all. In her mother's house, all the art was hung in gilded frames: portraits of ancestors or Grecian oil scenes, pink nymphs at a feast. Nothing like this! Nellie stares, enraptured. She longs to reach out and touch the thick layers of paint knifed onto the canvas. What she sees in the squares are window-panes. This is a window of light. Inside, there may be a family around a table. There may be a little boy in the kitchen with a large glass of milk, and this little boy may like to read the newspaper, and his father may like to fix clocks.

Wilson will be getting home soon. He won't be able to find her this time.

She moves languidly through the models. She sits in the chairs and props her legs on the Turkish-style poufs. She pretends that this is where she'd place a bar cart. This is where she'd store her magazines. This is for the radio, the reading chair, that red-and-yellow painting.

In one room—with wood paneled walls and a long-haired white rug—Nellie passes a couple. The woman is pregnant, and her husband has his hand on the small of her back.

"I think this one for the nursery," the woman points at a polka-dot blanket.

Nellie veers left to the fabric department. Vast swaths of curtains hang from rods on the ceiling in a colorful palette. Velvet, brocade, patterned polyester. Fiberglass pleated buckram in sage green! Provincial florals on cotton! A blue astro pattern tagged, "Rocket age saga—for those with interest in missiles. Easy-care, washable all-cotton!" She reaches for a floral print named "Blyth." It reminds her of years ago when she'd picked out curtains. That fabric was white with birds. The birds were blue and gold. She and Dean lived in Clemson then in his old apartment, which was not a place meant for a family. It was dank and dark, ideal for cold winters of textbooks and reheated coffee. (The draft! Nellie remembers. Horrid!) But it was not a nest for baby and wife. She was simply trying to cheer up the place and make it hers.

This fabric has yellow lilies along the hem. How nice it would look in the clear morning sun. She can just picture it: she will sew them herself. She will hang them in the kitchen, and those little flowers will greet her over breakfast.

A saleswoman approaches her in dark plaid and mules.

"Can I help you?" she smiles.

"Yes, I love this." Nellie raises her chin.

"You have a nice eye," the woman says. She smiles through her teeth. "Shall I order some cuts for you?"

"How much?"

The woman names the price.

"I'll take twelve yards."

Nellie glides through the store, past the plumbing and electric supplies including state-of-the-art lawnmowers and portable grills—by the sign in block letters, OUR BEST QUALITY—START YOUR DREAM KITCHEN NOW, which hangs from the ceiling over a choice of two faucet styles: single stream or dual.

All around are other signs straight from the catalogue: *Get your stylishly slim portable TV—the 17-inch Silverstone Suburbanite. Even Mom can carry this one . . . it's just 31 pounds light! Looks smart in any room in its handsome plastic case.*

There are shoji room dividers, which remind her of Myra's house. Dec-A-Shelf units with woodgrain vinyl, and she can just picture the teacups and fake plants she'd line on the shelves.

This is her protest. A giddy joy curdles in her stomach.

In Sears, Nellie has the feeling that order and beauty are still attainable. Here is a world of promise, possibility. Hate that gray? Wash it away! You'll be a little lovelier each day with fabulous, pink Camay! Here is the boxed perfection of wicker chairs, the brushed chrome of bar stools. It's not that the world must be perfect. (It isn't—oh how she knows. This is a world of war, a world, as Myra put it, with the *threat of nuclear proliferation*!) But it's the hope that there's something to look forward to, beyond the sameness of routine and ritual, the loneliness that can expand to fill an empty house. Sears lets her do this. Sears, where America shops. She loves it all. The musk and jasmine of Yves Saint Laurent—the cedarwood, sandalwood, myrrh. The music lilting from somewhere. A live harpist, she surmises, the string sounds rising from Women's Wear.

Nellie wants to run her hands over everything and absorb the memory of fabric. It is sensual, the touch of silk. She is in Cosmetics now. After spritzing various bottles, she smells of competing scents and doesn't care. A clerk asks if she wants to be a Revlon Girl and try their new super-soft cheek brush? Does she ever! Wristwatches and earrings glint behind glass counters. She stops at jewelry, at the diamonds. Her own wedding ring catches the light. It is a pinprick of a stone.

(The memory comes in a bolt. Dean on one knee. This was after a date at the movie theater. How can she have forgotten which film, on such an important day? They walked to a pub he frequented and ordered hot sandwiches and tea with thick cubes of ice. He proposed there, in public with his knee pressed to the grease-streaked floor. And she was so stunned by the faces craning to look from their booths, so surprised that *this—this was where it was happening*, surprised that Dean was saying, "Whadda ya say, Nel? How about we get married? I love you, you know. I love you, and I want you to be my wife. Will you marry me?")

It was his mother's ring.

Before she knows what she's doing, she slips the ring off. Nellie slides it into her purse just as the store clerk—a tall and serious woman, her nose beakish—comes over.

"Are you shopping for a special someone?" she asks.

"For me."

"Are you a new bride?" The woman's eye drops to Nellie's hand.

"Yes—" she says slowly. Then again, with more confidence. "Yes. Yes, I am. I am a widow. I'm remarrying, and I just want to browse."

She is not just window shopping like Holly, not today.

Out comes the tray of diamond rings, pressed into velvet, like stars studded to the sky. Nellie slips them on her finger one by one, thrilled by the cold metal, by the impossible size and shape and color of the stones.

There is a solitaire. There is a yellow gold marquise. Her mother's ring, hidden away in that jewelry box, was European cut and platinum. The small diamonds sat inlaid around the center like a constellation.

"This one is from our fall catalog," the woman says as she adjusts the scarf around her neck. She looks, Nellie thinks, like a flight stewardess. Like some jet-setter from Western Europe. Oh how Nellie longs to fly somewhere, anywhere! "It's a keepsake diamond, square cut. And it comes with a matching stacked wedding band. Would you like to see that?"

Nellie shakes her head. She places her pocketbook on the glass counter. Somewhere in the distance, a baby cries.

"Do you have any styles from the '20s? Something classical, elegant. A big stone with all these little stones?" she asks.

"I may," says the woman. "Let me just check and see." She takes out a key and rummages in a hidden drawer.

Nellie stares at her naked hand. It was wrong, she thought as a child, for her mother's hand to be bare, for that ring to be buried in a box and forgotten.

"You never wanted it to work," she said to her mother once, a Christmas before she moved out for college. Her mother still scoffed at the idea of college for girls. "You wanted him to leave."

"Nothing I did could have made that man happy," her mother said then, her voice laced with threat as if to say, *Don't push me, Nellie. You don't know.* But she did know! She lived this, too!

The woman still searches behind the counter. She says things like, "We can also check our Palladium collection." And, "Have you considered any other stones, like sapphire? That's very vogue now."

"I'm sorry," Nellie says and steps away from the counter. "I'm feeling a little—a little lightheaded. Where is the powder room?"

NELLIE FOLLOWED THEM, her father and his family. She never told anyone this, not her mother, not Dean, not the interviewer ten years ago. She put that poetry book in her bag. She marched out of the cafe, into the blinding street, and she crossed without thinking. She could remember the honk of the cars and the quick-slowing tires on concrete. She walked into Little Bert's Boutique, lined with rows of expensive children's clothes, all ruffles and lace and oversized buttons. How did her father have money? Had he married a wealthy widow, was that child even his? She would never know. But she followed the sound of his voice, warm and low, still grizzled in the throat the way she remembered. *See me, see me!* she thought, but at the same time dreaded that possibility. (For years, she'd longed for him to rescue her from her mother. She'd imagined him in Venice, rowing a gondola under patches of starlight. She'd imagined him riding rails out West, sifting for gold in a river. She'd imagined him in New York City, in a glass-lined high-rise, back to accounting. She had never pictured him here, just miles away, with a new wife, a patched-up life, a replacement daughter.) He was the man who escaped. Now he stood beside a wall of children's shoes. The new wife, her voice all nasal and wet, held up a blush pink dress, said, "Do you think this will match the coat we already have? It has to match the coat."

He must have felt her staring because he turned and met her eye. The years were evident in his face. He seemed so old that Nellie doubted briefly if this was really him. But there was a small scar on his chin she recognized. From what? She could not remember. She was twenty-one years old, he'd been gone eleven years, and that little girl couldn't be younger than seven, maybe eight. Those were his sea-green eyes, the same shade as hers. That was his hairline arcing across his scalp. He looked away without recognition.

She did not attend his funeral a few short years later.

NELLIE IS IN THE powder room, pinching her cheeks to bring out color, when she remembers her dream. Two other women stand at the mirror, both in gray tweed. They are talking loudly about a play they just saw.

"I wasn't sure I understood why he dropped the plates," the first woman says. She is replacing a bobby pin in her front curl. "Was that clear to you?"

"He was angry. It was a sign of anger," says the second woman. "I think it was supposed to be symbolic or something."

Nellie sits in a rose armchair. She takes a deep breath. She clutches her pocketbook, considers putting on her wedding ring again.

The dream returns to her in panicky shapes. The light is wrinkled and thin. The roof shakes, and the harp music is drowned out by the air raid signal. The sound seems to gallop. Plaster dust rains on her head, and still the two women are talking about the actor who broke the plates on stage, about what a shame it is for a good plate to be destroyed for every matinee and evening show. What a waste! But Nellie watches as the chandelier above her rattles. The makeup counter is replaced by the lines of soup cans and water barrels. By the Geiger counter. She even sees Wilson's toys splayed on the ground, little green army men in dead poses. They will be trampled, she thinks. Their plastic arms will break off. Is Dean at work or driving home? Did he make it? Will she make it? Will she emerge from this place to reenter her world, to see if there is a hollow depression where the house used to be? Or will she stay in her private safe zone, buried here forever?

The dream dissipates. The two women have left, and she is alone blinking at her reflection.

A store clerk enters, says, "Ma'am, are you alright? Do you need something to drink?"

She says she does. But the woman returns with only water.

In the storefront again, she shops with a frenzy. She passes women with baby carriages, women in housewife clusters. She hears the sales-women. ("Yes, these cufflinks come in silver." "We can have these in by Christmas!" "Have you seen our new Spyder bike? It's a twenty-inch beauty.") A toddler ambles away from his mother and conducts a quick game of hide-and-seek in the toy department. Nellie overhears the commotion.

To the beauty parlor she goes, all gold and champagne! She requests a short cut, sleek and elegant.

"You look like Doris Day," says the stylist, who is thin and twiggy, suntanned.

She does not look like Doris Day, but she enjoys the feeling of the plastic around her neck. She relishes the nails on her scalp, someone else's hands on her skin.

After, a new woman, she waltzes through Evening Wear. She treads in patent leather through Women's Shoes. Her arms are full of beautiful things: combed cotton dresses and stretchy pants, a box coat in lavender.

The dressing rooms are vast and white. The floors are marble. An attendant hangs the clothes for her on brass handles. Alone, Nellie strips to her girdle. She looks disapprovingly in the mirror at all the folds and lumps and jiggles that come with being an aging woman. (And she is only thirty-five. Ha! So much of this damn life left.) The fabric pulls over her skin, softer than a kiss. This one is an evening gown with a boat neckline, the type suitable for the White House, for Jackie. Nellie spins in the mirror and laughs at herself. Where would she ever wear this while married to Dean?

Her stomach rumbles from hunger, but she keeps spinning. She relishes the taffeta next, the sound of crinkled fabric like paper. She could wear this for Christmas, for a holiday party at the Ramsey. Maybe Dean will take her somewhere nice, finally, and maybe things will be different. She will run a gloved hand down the banister. No unruly protests for this woman on strike, only silk. Only satin. Only the bright white beauty of opera pumps. And maybe, just maybe, she will get a job. She will walk into the *Oakleigh Gazette* tomorrow and say, "Hello, I'm Nellie Porter, and I'd like to work for a newspaper. Let me do anything. I'll do anything."

It's a wild and dangerous world for a woman with dreams like that.

No more scrubbing baking soda to remove a stain from a favorite sweater. No more counting coins into the palm of Dean's hand. *This* is her proof of change.

Yes, she will walk out of Sears a new woman today. She is not being reckless. She rarely spends money.

The checkout clerk does not question Nellie's purchases, or her right to the two hundred dollars, which she pulls out carefully. He wraps everything in tissue paper and hands the bag to Nellie.

ATOMIC ENERGY COMMISSION ANNOUNCES PLAN TO BUILD HYDROGEN BOMB PLANT IN SOUTH CAROLINA

By Wanda Gale

Builders broke ground on the hydrogen-bomb plant in Oakleigh County, after claiming thousands of acres by eminent domain. The Atomic Energy Commission (AEC) stresses that the new facility—currently unnamed and boundaries unannounced—will not be manufacturing nuclear weapons, but instead producing the necessary materials for building the bombs elsewhere.

The United States Congress has appropriated roughly $200,000,000 toward the construction of this site. President Truman has called it "one of the most pressing national security projects in our nation's short history."

Henry Dean Porter, a former resident of Ellenton, is one of the scientists currently onsite. Porter, a graduate of Ellenton High School, lived on a fruit farm that provided work to many local tenants before enlisting in the United States Army in 1942. After graduating from Clemson A&M for both undergraduate and graduate work, Porter has been the leading agronomist in an experimental lab.

"Our goal is to minimize any environmental impact," Porter told the Gazette, "It's important to have those goals in mind. Years from now, you won't know we were ever here."

Neither Porter nor his team—including a chemist from the Hanford site—could give any more details about the work being completed along the Savannah River.

Local officials say the public reaction has been mostly positive. Chamber of Commerce secretary, Lou Metcalf, told the Gazette, "This was not a political decision. It was a patriotic one." Mayor Brown estimates that the selection of Oakleigh County will bring tens of thousands of jobs to midcountry South Carolina: "We'll be the science city—like what Hollywood did to Los Angeles and what automobiles did to Detroit."

Oakleigh has long been considered a winter colony, a jewel of the South, known for its polo courses, riding trails, and luxurious gardens. Similar to Savannah, it has maintained a small-town charm—which is what concerns the deputy mayor of housing, Lionel Schaafsma. "We'll be reexamining the zoning in Oakleigh," said Schaafsma. "Right now, there's just not enough infrastructure to house and sustain all the new plant employees. We need new roads, schools, houses. And quickly. Our first priority is to avoid the shantytown situation that happened at Oak Ridge. We don't need any honky-tonks moving into our neighborhoods."

Some town conservatives are also concerned about what the influx of new residents will mean for preserving local culture. According to a source within the AEC, the plant will bring in northerners, Midwesterners, and academics from around the world.

"We may not all share the same beliefs on the economy or race relations or education," said Metcalf, when asked about the social impact. "But what we do share is a desire to preserve our country from the dangers of Communism."

Many questions are still unanswered, such as how the land will be appraised and acquired. Roughly 6,000 residents of the former Ellenton are currently being relocated to a new settlement roughly twenty miles away from their original homes, in what is being called New Ellenton. Ellenton is a predominantly poor and rural area. Most of the residents being relocated are tenants and African American sharecroppers.

"It's difficult," says Zadie Cato, an 86-year-old resident who has lived in Ellenton for all of her life. "This is my home. I wanted to die here. I wanted to be buried here." Cato told the Gazette that she and her family heard the announcement on the radio. "It was just an ordinary day," she said. "How is it that your life can change, your future can just die, while you're sitting at your table having coffee like any other morning?"

DEAN

I will go get my boy. Exactly ten years ago, to the day, Nellie placed their baby outside the apartment and shut the door. That was the first time he felt the panic of not being able to reach his son. The terror that his child might die and he—father, soldier, scientist—could do absolutely nothing.

Now there is a hospital. The sight of police officers and firemen seems impossible, almost ludicrous. Dean wants to laugh. These officers are speaking to him about his son. They ask unthinkable questions. They ask about life at home, about Nellie, about him.

Is this his first head injury?

Has he shown prior signs of erratic behavior?

Has he ever threatened to harm himself or others?

Is he ever left unattended?

They have pulled him into a long white corridor. Nurses rush by them. A pregnant woman is rolled by on a gurney. The head officer is pole-thin and keeps hitching up his pants in a nervous habit.

"I just want to see my boy," Dean says, pleading. "Please, I need to know if he's all right. If he's alive. No one is telling me anything."

He hears Nellie on that long-ago day. *I don't think I'm so good at this mother thing.* He thinks back to that 1951 Nellie, wishes he could tell her, *I don't think I'm so good at this father thing, either.*

"We'll leave the doctors to answer any medical questions, we just want to get our facts right."

The men exchange glances, as if trying to be discreet but failing.

The quiet one makes notes. For a moment there is just the waggle and scratch of his pen.

"I heard that he made it all the way up," Dean says. He can picture the squat turnip head of the water tower. His boy like a little bean on top. It's almost amazing, that thought. Such a tiny person with such strength of will. If he wasn't so terrified and so angry, he might even be proud.

The officer nods.

"Grant here was going up after him." He nods to the fireman, a burly man, his mustache blond and clipped too short. "Almost reached him."

"Thank you," Dean manages. "And I'm so sorry for your trouble. He's not usually like this. He's a good kid, he really is. He just gets these wild ideas sometimes, I guess. He takes his games too far."

"Honestly, sir." The mustached man speaks, his voice surprisingly soft. "We don't see any reason why he slipped at the last minute. That's what we wanted to tell you."

He raises his eyebrows, as if hoping that Dean understands his intimation. He doesn't.

"What is it?" Dean says. "What aren't you telling me?"

"It's just that it's unclear." The head officer licks his lips and hitches up his pants with a thumb around the belt. "Unclear if he fell or if he jumped."

After the data trip to Ellenton, when Dean carried his case up the flights of stairs, when he opened the door to the small apartment that smelled of books and lemon furniture polish, he expected to find chaos. To find Wilson sleeping in the sink or diapers stacked high in the refrigerator. Instead, there was an uneasy normalcy. Nellie was the sight of happiness. She wore a buttercup yellow dress, too light for her complexion, but cheery. There was no gin on her breath. She'd dressed Wilson in an infant sailor suit with buttons bigger than his eyes. All panic had been rinsed from her face, as though nothing wrong had happened.

"Did you bring me anything from Oakleigh or Augusta?" she asked, though she seemed to know already that he hadn't.

"I brought me," he said. And he hoped this would be enough.

He picked up Wilson, held him all that night until bed. Wilson gummed his fist, blew raspberries, did all the baby things, and Dean watched, rapt. "Father missed you," he whispered repeatedly, whenever Nellie was out of earshot. "I want you to know it subconsciously. I want you to know it in here." And he ran his hand along Wilson's chest, relished in the magical pulse—the work-on-its-own beauty of a heartbeat.

I will go get my boy.

"I need to see him," Dean says and excuses himself. The officers do not follow.

The hospital is a maze of white. The rain has stopped. He can tell by the deafening silence, the distinct lack of white noise on the roof. He follows a blue line on the ground back to the lobby, back to the horrible room of prints and magazines and coffee in styrofoam. The small boy is still on the floor, back to licking his popsicle stick, and Dean has half a mind to scream, "Where in God's name is your mother?"

But where in God's name is Nellie?

The doors to the visitors area swing open. Lois Shepherd enters with her two children in tow, looking panicked. She is dressed all in black, as though mourning.

"Dean!" she says, clearly relieved to see him. "I came as soon as I heard. We had to wait for Todd to—" Lois scans the lobby. "Where's Nellie?"

"I don't know. Have you seen her?" He wants to say this softly, but it comes out like an accusation.

"Not in several hours. She isn't home? I was with Myra all day. We were busy, and I got home to find Penny back early, crying, she said—"

But Dean does not hear what it was Penny said.

The hospital doors open. A nurse calls for him. "Porter!"

He moves as though swimming. He is swimming in the Savannah River, and the water is a murky dark. It is tannin-colored. It is silt and salt, and when he opens his eyes, he can make out only the shapes directly in front of him, an arms' length away. This is the water of his boyhood, the land of his life. He is swimming, and the water poisons him slowly. He can feel the pain in his feet, the tingle in his fingers, the burn behind his eyes.

Into the emergency ward. There are rows of blue curtains, all hiding bodies and sounds. There is coughing, the scrape of chairs on linoleum, the almost imperceptible click of a radio dial.

Then the nurse stops. She is young and plump—too young, Dean thinks, to be a nurse. She pulls back a curtain. And there is Wilson, so small on the bed. His eyes are open, but he does not meet Dean's gaze. He stares straight ahead. His gray lips move softly. His right arm is in a cast. Bandage strips encircle his head like a laurel wreath.

"What's wrong with him?" Dean says. He kneels beside the bed, takes one of Wilson's hands. The skin is cold but sweaty. Still, Wilson doesn't turn to him. Dean snaps back to the nurse: "What's *wrong* with him, why is he like this?"

"Sir, please remain—"

"Where's the doctor, I need to see the doctor, my boy is—what's wrong with him?" He's aware that he's shouting only when the nurse steps back, palms up.

The curtain rustles, and a doctor strides in. He wears a dark navy suit, and his oily hair is combed violently to the left. "Are you the father?" he asks. He has a Georgia drawl.

"Yes, yes, I'm Dean Porter. I'm the father."

He has not let go of Wilson's hand. He keeps it tight in his own.

"I'm Dr. Webb. I apologize about the wait. We wanted to give him some time first. He wasn't himself. He was confused."

"Confused, what do you mean, confused?"

"Step out with me, sir."

Dean lets go of Wilson's hand reluctantly. It falls on the bed like dead weight. Dr. Webb takes him only steps away from Wilson's curtain, but even those steps seem too far. Dean has to force himself to concentrate.

"This happens sometimes in head trauma cases," Dr. Webb is saying. "When he came to, he wasn't himself, Mr. Porter. He was kicking and screaming for over an hour. He was saying gibberish. Nothing we did would calm him. Every few minutes, he forgot what had happened. He asked where he was, what was going on. He wasn't making new memories." The doctor glances back at Wilson. "I have seen cases where that doesn't go away. They stop being able to make new memories altogether. We wanted to monitor that, make sure his continuous memory function would return."

"And will it?"

"I believe so. We administered morphine about half an hour ago. He's been calming down ever since. You didn't want to see him like that."

"Is he—" Dean's voice cracks. "Is he going to be okay?"

"He did sustain a severe hit to the head. But his fall is survivable, especially at his age. His vitals are stable, and we've set his fractured humerus. We want to keep him overnight to watch for any bleeding or other side effects, but right now, I do expect a full recovery."

When Wilson was a baby, after that disastrous research trip, Dean was afraid he would hurt him on accident. He would bump Wilson's head into the wall when carrying him. He would drop him, break that fragile skull. There was something terrifyingly delicate about a newborn, the softness in their bones, the complete and utter dependence on you, the adult, the parent. And Dean, like Nellie, was an only child. There had been no preparation for this—no textbook for him to study, no data explaining how not to lose your child. Those fears seem silly now, so uninformed. But Dean knew his love grew in that fear. Fear of losing something was proof of love, wasn't it? A sign that your life would not be whole without them?

Now he kneels by Wilson's bedside and sees his child like a baby bird. Like a plover curled over itself. Dr. Webb and the nurse have moved on. They will be back in a few minutes. The emergency room is a cascade of sounds, other people's illnesses. It is a small county hospital, and the curtains are thin, but Dean hears none of it. He hears nothing but Wilson's breath, sees only this beautiful skin. He takes in every detail, wants to sear this in his brain: the cowlick of hair around the bandages, the hooded eyelids, those gray-green eyes like the river before rain.

WILSON

Outside, the world is gunmetal gray. Everywhere, there is ash and a cold unlike anything he's felt before. His skin rises in bumps. He'd expected heat. He'd expected fire and seismic ebbs rippling through the city like a wrinkle in fabric. He'd seen and reseen the buildings collapse and the bomb plant cave in the inverted eruption of life. The color, where red meets orange and pink and lightning blue, would eat the world. But this is a great nothingness. This is a dull and smoky place. Fog smears the corpse town. Wilson walks and feels like he's moving through breath.

Your chances of surviving an atomic attack are better than you may have thought.

Wilson survived. He carries a canvas rucksack. He wears galoshes on his feet and goggles around his neck. He shivers in the chill. He has no jacket, only a thin cotton shirt and khaki shorts. His socks are plaid and knee-high.

To his right is the pharmacy, rubble now. The glass storefront is shattered, and the peppermint-striped awning lies in shreds, streamers floating in the breeze. Bicycles, warped and tangled, lie in heaps. There is a filminess to everything, like looking through a Coke bottle. The white light has gone, and in its place, there is a black rain. Fat drops fall from the sky like gasoline. Wilson dabs at his arms, trying in vain to rub the rain away.

He keeps walking. To his left is a pile of white, powdered cement and fiberglass that was once the water tower. The school flag lies in tatters. Street signs warped to paper-thin metal. Has no one else survived? There is the vague memory—as if from another life—of the plane, the climb. Didn't he sound the alarm? Did no one listen to his report?

He wracks his brain. Must remember the instructions. Must remember the facts about fallout.

In the city of Hiroshima, slightly over half the people who were a mile from the atomic explosion are still alive.

Surely there are others, perhaps some still bunkered and breathless, waiting for orders. They will have descended into their shelters and hibernated like bears.

By the street that should be Main Street, Wilson kneels. He slings his rucksack to the ground, sending a plume of dust into the air. This is no ordinary dust. He coughs. (Is he coughing the remains of buildings, people, incinerated animals?) He opens the bag and sees all his gear. In his field guide, the last entry simply says *Annie's ribunz*, and he remembers the red ribbons in class, that Soviet spy Annie Yuknavitch smirking in Room 3. Wilson jimmies through the bag, past his Swiss army knife and gauze roll, past the candy and flashlight, and takes out the transistor radio. Yes, the radio should still work, and that is the key instruction for any survivor. Tune in. He blows off dust and turns the dial to CONELRAD 640. Then he presses the radio to his ear. But there is nothing. Not even a wooly static. He tries CONELRAD 1240. Still nothing. Even the radio towers have gone silent.

He coughs again, then remembers—*lingering radioactivity.* The fallout may still be fresh. He may have survived, but there's radiation sickness to account for. His head throbs, like tiny hammers in his skull, and his teeth ache at the gums. The black rain continues to fall, bleeding on his skin.

The war may have changed their way of life, but they are not riddled with cancer. Their children are normal.

Wilson slings the backpack over his shoulder and keeps walking.

Now he sees the bodies in horrifying detail. Bodies strewn on the sidewalk, wrinkled like leather. Bodies frozen midmotion. They cradle their babies and hold dog leashes. Bodies midstride, calcified molds. Eyes bled out, thin ribbons of blood down their faces. (He will have nightmares about this for weeks!) Cars knuckled, half melted. He did not expect the stink of death. Everywhere, there is destruction.

Mr. Brubaker, a church deacon, lies limp in an alleyway; Mrs. Jenkins's shoes with the brass buckles are strewn near the storm drain. There are bags and singed clothes, whole bodies and vaporized bones. On the steps of the Baptist church, the bell tower collapsed, there is a nuclear shadow—an outline of a stooped woman and walker, her body gone.

Windows have melted. Buildings are crushed. There are craters in the ground. What's left: only the silken remains of ash, hardening now in the cold. Fear mushrooms into despair.

Should you happen to be one of the unlucky people right under the bomb, there is practically no hope of living through it.

He walks and wonders where Father and the rest of the plant staff are hiding. They must have survived. Wilson can imagine no future without Father. They'd have retreated into the bomb plant shelter, a great cement barricade underground. They'd have closed the hatch if they survived the epicenter shock and dialed Washington.

"Hello, Mr. President? Yes, we've made it, sir. Now what?"

And the president would say, "Us, too. Now we wait?"

No, that couldn't be right. This was the president. Wouldn't he have a plan? Maybe he'd say, "Now we fight back?"

Even as he thinks this, Wilson is unconvinced. How to fight back with a dead country? No army, no citizens. They'd be hiding out like rats in a hole, eating beans out of cans, spraying for vermin in the shelter corners just like everyone else. Wilson cannot imagine Mr. President pissing in a metal can, sleeping with military-grade blankets on a cold cement block. He cannot imagine Father doing this, either.

"We need to do something, sir," Father would say. He'd drum his fingers on the military table.

From one-half to one mile away, you have a 50-50 chance.

Yes, Father must be making plans. Father is drawing up blueprints. Father stands somewhere among a room of survivors and says, "This is not a game, not a drill. We've got to *do something*." Father will be strong when he says this. He'll roll up his white shirt, streaked with grease stains. He'll dab at the sweat on his forehead. He will not shout or sound hurried. He will be steady. He will be slow. There will be that cadence, almost musical, like he's about to tell a story. Thinking this, Wilson starts to cry. Because *that* is where he wants to be—where

Father is. In their house with the clocks and the yellow walls, with the ticking and the yelling and the silences he slips through. He is a ghost child, so stealthy. In the garage, hiding out behind the boxes he *observes* while Father tinkers on the car or realigns an offset clock weight. He wants to be in a normal family—whose father might possibly be a barber. Or a pharmacist. A Little League coach. He wants there to be no secrets. He wants them to have a dog. He wants there to be no such thing as a hydrogen bomb, ever. No such thing as death. Even though Wilson has known about death for a long time. He knows that scientists die, like Louis Slotin, who he heard about once when eavesdropping, heard about the demon core and scorched hands, heard Father say, "What a terrible, terrible way to die," and this is when Wilson first began to ponder death and what made some deaths terrible and some less terrible, because to Wilson the thought of any nothingness at all was unfathomable.

Yes, he would even be quite happy (he would!) to be in Father's arms, being carried up the shelter stairs.

From one to one and a half miles out, the odds that you will be killed are only 15 in 100.

He walks away from the bodies, away from the Main Street that is no longer Main Street. Where are the other survivors? And God, where is Eddie Pace? Because Wilson has to tell him the truth now. The ground is nuclear waste, really this time, and truth blooms in his brain like a flower. The worst way to die is not freezing or burning or drowning or blowing into pieces—the worst is this! Being witness to it all. The worst is being alone.

Naturally, your chances of being injured are far greater than your chances of being killed.

The sky looks gray—but really, it's a cloud covering the earth like a thick wool blanket. He can see this now. Dust rises in brumes like volcanic remains. Above, there is a faint twinkling, too fast for the moon. The light slips through the stratosphere of gray, a flicker, a blip. A satellite. Watching the world pass, that all-seeing Soviet eye.

Like Sputnik: and he remembers Sputnik. He was still kid-Wilson then. He'd craned his head up at the inked sky, waited and waited for the movement of light, so like a shooting star. The parents made a night of it. They fixed lemonade in glass pitchers. They had a barbecue. Mothers lounged in lawn chairs with their babies. The other kids played jacks and four corners, but Wilson lay on the grass and stared. He wouldn't miss it. He had to see this beautiful thing. "What's a satellite?" he'd asked Father, and Father had said, "Well, it's floating metal," so Wilson had imagined aluminum bobbing in an ocean of outer space.

"Is there water in space?" he'd asked. And Father had said, "We don't know. There may be seas on the moon." And so Wilson had pictured a beach in the sky, where children could lap at the moon-water and grasp the stars that twinkled by, like glitter, like fire. Only this year, he'd heard some of Father's friends echo the president: *Whoever owns space, owns the world.* (Did the Soviets own space? How could anyone own the sky, the planets, the moon?)

He spent so much time wondering what the bombs would be like. And what is it like? His body trembles. Impossible to say. Like it all ends here. There is nothing like the end of everything.

Vomiting and diarrhea are the first signs of radiation sickness. By the time you lost your hair, you would be good and sick.

His stomach aches, and he wonders if he will puke.

Some of the houses still stand. Others have roofs blown off. Cars are stopped in the streets, their drivers impaled by flying glass. The lawns are scorched. Everything has been abandoned. Around him, the sky rains oil and debris but also paper—bills, letters, magazines, Sterling Creek Plant ID cards, remnants of a once-lived life. One day someone will gather these, he thinks. Some future schoolkid will read this and study *The Nuclear Detonation of the United States, 1961.*

He knew this was coming. He'd seen all the signs, yessir. And he'd even written to the president many times but received no replies.

Dear Mr. Kennedy Sir,

Can you please tell me the names of all the Communists in the U.S.? I want to help.

Wilson P.

Dear Mr. Kennedy,

I'm writing to let you know that ten years old is too young to die. Please come up with a plan, thanks.

Wilson P.

Dear Mr. Kennedy,

I have memorized survival secrets. I know how to duck and cover. If you invite me to the White House, I can show you some ideas.

Wilson P.

Wilson turns into what should be his neighborhood. It's darker here, like stepping from dusk into night.

He imagines Father and Mr. Shepherd, all the other laboratory men with their glasses and briefcases and hats that smelled of cigar smoke. He hears Father saying, "Well, we got to consider the half-life of U-235. Seven hundred million years, folks. We're in for a long haul."

If only he could break into the plant's underground unit. But there'd be guards, probably. Maybe a password. The government will have thought of that. Besides, he'd have no idea where the hatch would be. The plant stretches for miles and miles, Wilson doesn't know how many. It runs along the Savannah River to Georgia, he thinks. How would he ever navigate his way through the thick pines and cypress swamps? He imagines the Savannah River floating with the dead and irradiated marine life: eel and river otter, mink and pickerel and large-mouthed bass.

Wilson watches his feet, tries not to step on bones or bicycle tires, avoids the occasional toy and stroller. When he looks up at last, he stops short. His breath catches in his throat.

There—at the end of the road at the end of the world—shrouded in fog and white ash, is the pharaoh-faced Commie. His tie glints ruby red. The Commie tips his hat at Wilson, and Wilson's heart skips a beat. He panics. He freaks. Where to run? Out of the dust cloud, other Commies join him. They wear black. They are silent, emerging from the tree skeletons.

Communism is like an octopus, Mrs. Jenkins used to say, stretching its tentacles around the world. Now here they are. They will suck the life from him. There're three, eight, twelve, all suited and hatted. They block the road that used to be road and that is now a graveyard. (He knows how tentacles are: how they stick and suckle. He's read things.)

This is a moment from a comic book. Only, nothing about this is comic, not one bit. The cold around him deepens, and the sun seems to have turned to metal or to snow.

Wilson runs down a side street, his street. Brunnell. His backpack bounces, bruising his hip. Must run faster! Must outrace the Commies! Oh, where is a father when you need him?

He is at once vindicated and victorious and very much in danger. His lungs ache. The dust, the ash! His legs burn. He cranes his head to see the Commies running behind him. They seem to know this road real good. (Is one of them Mr. Yuknavitch? Has he been the pharaoh-faced Commie this whole time?) Wilson runs past his own house but hesitates at the sight. His house still stands, seemingly untouched by the blast. Like a fake house inside a snow globe or an aquarium. A shadow crosses the window, the shape of a woman. Mama?

He races toward his house, up the brick steps, and throws open the door.

Instantly, he is home, as if none of this ever happened. The house smells of vegetable oil and sliced ham. Like spoiled fruit. Mama's slippered feet are propped on the ottoman. There are Watchdog items hidden around the living room. Rubber gloves under Father's chair. An egg carton (holding stones for his slingshot) behind the bookcase. The slingshot itself dangles from the coat hanger. And there she is, slouched on a sofa, dressed in a bathrobe and oil-stained slippers, her hair half in curlers. The television is on. Mama's face is cast in the screen-glow, a murky light. Behind her, the clocks are all in rhythm. She holds an empty bottle in one hand, a magazine in the other.

The Commies have reached the house. Heavy booted footsteps approach the door. He can hear them slowing, hear the muffled slur of the Russian tongue. He must not be taken prisoner, that would be worse than death. He's heard it's worse than an alien abduction (though that, of course, is fiction, kid stuff—he's not *dumb*). The Commies would perform tests. They'd examine him, unzip his brain. They'd hook him up to a scanner, turn his organs *red*, his brain *red*, strip his memories. He'd be clone-Wilson. A doppelganger double. No, no!

The front door rattles just as Wilson scampers down the hall.

Into the office! He burrows under Father's desk. On the ground is a patchwork of miscellaneous items: paper clips and hand-scrawled notes, the stray unsmoked cigarette. The desk is small, but the opening is Wilson-sized. He leans his head against the wood and listens to the discernible groan of the front door.

Then, the realization. Father keeps his hunting rifle in his office closet. Yes, the hunting rifle. What's a Watchdog without a weapon of defense?

The hallway groans with the weight of Commie steps.

He'd like to show those Commies what he's made of.

Once, when he was kid-Wilson, he had a bit of a bully situation at school. Only, he didn't like to think of it as a bully situation because that made him sound puny, like one of those wimp kids who can barely run across the playground without having an asthma attack. One of Todd's friends—a kid named Harris, whose father owned the La Pen golf course across town—teased Wilson relentlessly. Harris called him "goggle eyes" and "007," which Wilson thought was odd. This all happened because one day, Harris caught him hiding out in a tree, using his binoculars to track the other kids. Wilson had fight-back plans. He wanted to show fifth-grader Harris what he was made of. There was a tussle on the playground that sent Wilson home with a bloodied cheek—only, Father wasn't pleased. "I expected more," was all he said. And at first, Wilson thought he meant more fighting. *You shoulda beaten him, son*, is what Wilson heard. Only later did he sense the oddness of a Father who disavowed violence.

Now the Commies are coming.

I'm sorry Father, I'm trying to be brave, Father. We have a bit of a bully situation on the home front, Father.

Maybe he could get to the shelter: could lock the hatch and hide away. Wait out the black rain and the gray clouds hovering over the earth, hovering like the invisible God.

Armageddon has come. This is it. The world is dying. The Dooms-day Clock has moved from "seven minutes to midnight" to "end of life" in just one day.

Father says that fear comes from what you don't understand. But Wilson thinks that's chickenshit. He's known about the bombs, and he knows how radiation kills you from the inside. He's already been exposed to the black rain. That means his bones will rot. His body will decay. He'll vomit and cough blood, and eventually, his DNA will pull apart. (However that happens.)

The world slows when they take him. And as he thrashes, as they pin his arms against his back, he decides that later: He will not drink like Mama, not ever. He will not have a government job. There will be no security badge clipped to his jacket every morning. He will be a dentist or a pharmacist. But not a physicist—nothing dangerous. There will be no bombs in Wilson's world. He will throw birthday parties with marble cakes, with bright blue balloons. The only bottles in his fridge will be colas. There will be an endless supply of colas. And he will even mow the lawn and learn to barbecue because that's what fathers do. He will let his children play in shelters if they want—he will be a club-house father.

Wilson bites at the hand holding his shoulders. He wriggles like a fish—like the fat catfish he and Eddie sometimes catch in Sterling Creek. But his head hurts. Oh, how it pounds! (Have they drugged him already?)

Never lose your head! And don't rush outside after a bomb.

They strap him to a gurney. The light is gauzy. The sound of mu-sic drifts from somewhere, the crackle of a radio. Then, the whir and pulse of machines. A voice he recognizes, from some dream of a dream. Behind his fluttering eyelids, he sees only red. The skin of apples. The color of lipstick. Flag with the sickle of death.

Wilson stirs. He feels a shot of pain in his arm, his head. His foot is numb. Where is he?

There is music. A drumbeat, familiar.

There is a doctor: Hair stuck to his forehead, breath like scallions. White gloves, a suit. The doctor is pale with blond stubble and oversized glasses. Will this doctor interrogate him? Do they have biomedical tactics? Wilson will be ready. He's prepared for interrogations. He's rehearsed questionings. He knows how to defend himself, how to scream bloody murder. He will show them what a Watchdog is made of.

From the ceiling, there are spangles of light. Then Father's voice.

NELLIE

"I hated him," Nellie told Dean once, when they were not yet married. She was afraid, still, of what he would think. "I hated my father when he left us."

Dean lay his thick hands on hers. They were the hands of a man who's known the weight of work. "You had a right to," he said simply.

Outside, night is rapidly approaching. Storm clouds hover on the horizon, miles away but close enough to be seen. There are streaks of rain, a wash of gray. She can almost make out the strands, like hair or ribbed cloth. The Sears parking lot is spare now. A few women walk past in a wave of lilac and heat. They carry white bags to their cars, load them like children in the back seat. Nellie stands back by the doors, listens as they open and close with customers, listens for the sliver of harp music that escapes each time.

Did her father come here? Did he get off at this station and see these trees along the median?

The chill has deepened. The bus will be back soon. She sees that circular sign, the little booth where an elderly couple waits on a bench.

But Nellie hesitates. She stays by the light emanating from the Sears glass. She fingers the bag handles and relishes the weight of her purchases. Three dresses, a coat, two pairs of shoes, the fabric.

Was it cold when he left? Was it summer? Would he have seen the trees in bloom or were they bare, promising future beauty? She cannot remember anymore. What she does know: she placed a tiny gloved hand on the car window. She was crying, "Take me with you, take me with you." His trunk made an awful grate on the sidewalk, left a mark the whole mile to the bus stop. He refused to look at her. His arm muscles rippled with the strain of his belongings. Mother screamed through the patch of open glass, she screamed as she drove, almost hit two curbs and one car. The worst would still come; Nellie saw this then. (Cotillion, remarriage, the wrath of a love-grieved mother!)

She said she'd hated him.

But this was not true. She envied him. And some lies are love.

THE BRAIN OF A child upon impact with ground: it is soft like gelatin. It bounces against the skull. Back and forth—the dizzy haze of stars before the light leaves.

The brain rotates inside the calvarium. There is whiplash. There is torque. Contusions form inside the cranium. The brain, quite literally, bruises. The bruising is surface-level and atomic: synapses detach and tear.

Behind the temples, behind the architecture of ears, there is the temporal bone.

This is what cracks.

November 1, 1951

Bufford O'Connor: Are you aware, Mrs. Porter, of how your husband secured this job?

Porter: His university job? He had it when I met him — he was already working there.

O'Connor: No, with the AEC, ma'am.

Porter: Oh. Well, not exactly. I know there were meetings. He'd come home all frantic, he'd go through his books, leave messes, but that's all. I know he'd had some journal publications that gave him some recognition in his field. It strikes me as funny, saying it like that. His *field*. He's a soil scientist, after all, though I don't know what that even entails. I don't know what there is to study about soil besides which flowers to plant where.

O'Connor: Has your husband ever expressed to you any concerns about policies in the presidential administration?

Porter: Not that I heard of.

O'Connor: Now, in regards to the war years. He served in the military, is that correct?

Porter: Yes, army. I didn't know him then. I was a girl. I was still in school.

O'Connor: Did your husband ever mention any men he met from the Red army? Did he mention any crossovers, any friends?

Porter: I don't think so. Did that ever even happen? I never heard of that — I don't think so.

O'Connor: When your husband returned from the war, he finished school. And, to your knowledge, did he ever join an organization called the Independent Citizens Committee of the Arts, Sciences, and Professions?

Porter: I don't mean to offend you, sir, but these are questions for Mr. Porter. I'm telling you, I don't know the answers. He is a very private man, my husband. And that's good, right? That's what you must want.

O'Connor: Has he mentioned any names to you in passing? Stanislaw Ulam, Edward Teller?

Porter: I mean — Oppenheimer. He respects Oppenheimer. I think he's read many of his papers. My husband saw a lecture of his once. He was traveling on the East Coast.

O'Connor: Has he expressed anything besides respect for Mr. J. Robert Oppenheimer?

Porter: What does the *J* stand for, in his name?

O'Connor: Julius, I believe.

Porter: What a name. Julius, like Caesar. It makes sense for him, that name.

O'Connor: The question, Mrs. Porter.

Porter: Not that I know of, I just know he respects him, is all. I saved a clipping — he was on the cover of *TIME* magazine a few years ago. Handsome man.

O'Connor: Thank you, Mrs. Porter. I think that answers all my questions.

Porter: Is there any trouble? Like I said — my husband. If you cut him open, red, white, and stars. He loves this country.

DEAN

The afternoon has already crested, begun its descent to night when Wilson awakes.

Dean thinks this word—*awakes*—though really, Wilson never slept at all. He seemed to be drifting in a dream place, lulled back by morphine.

Now, he shakes a little on the bed. A yellow patch trickles around him, soiling the sheets. He blinks, dewy-eyed.

Then, his voice so small, almost babyish: "Where am I? What happened?"

"It's okay," says Dean. He sits in a cold metal chair by the hospital bed. He strokes Wilson's arm. "You fell at school, but you're okay. You're safe."

From across the emergency hall, a patient's radio trills. *Got the housewife headache? In menopause, transition without tears! Milprem promptly relieves emotional distress with lasting control of physical symptoms!*

"Father missed you," Dean says. He blinks furiously. "I want you to know that subconsciously."

"What's sub-cone-shoos-ly?" Wilson asks, turning.

"It means you know it in here." Dean taps a finger on Wilson's bandaged head, ever so lightly. "It means you never have to doubt that fact. It's always there."

Wilson chews his lip for a moment, as though considering this seriously.

The plump nurse bustles back. "Got a wetter," she says cheerfully, though Wilson blushes at this. "We'll get you cleaned right up!"

She strips the bed and cleans Wilson with a wet rag. Still, he seems so dazed, not quite here. The nurse talks as she works. "You hungry, sweet pea? Have you had any lunch? How 'bout I get you some food. You'd like that? And some chocolate milk. Do you like chocolate milk?" Wilson nods.

The doctor returns just as the nurse leaves to get some dinner. He uses words like *hypoxia* and *lesions*—says they'll monitor his *intracranial pressure*. Says Wilson may be sensitive to light or sound for a few days. "He shouldn't run around yet or go back to school, or even watch television. Let his brain have time to heal." Dean says that yes, yes, he'll make sure of it. When the doctor leaves again, Wilson looks around, as though seeing the hospital for the first time. As though scouting.

Finally, he blinks at Dean.

"I won't get my dollar," he says.

"Your what?"

"My dollar. What day is it today?"

"Wednesday."

Wilson grins. He smiles as if he is not here in a hospital bed: he is home with his binoculars. He is tramping through Nellie's garden. "Pay day. We get our dollars on Wednesdays, I don't know why. I didn't do my rounds today. People didn't get their medicine." He cocks his head, considers this. "Will people die if they don't get their medicine?"

"Mr. Pace will take care of it. Everyone will get what they need."

Did you fall or did you jump? Dean longs to ask—but not yet. He cannot ask yet, cannot bear to know. Perhaps he will never ask.

Wilson counts on his fingers. "That's enough for . . . I don't know how many comic books, but a lot. I need the new Green Lantern. Plus I have other dollars at home. They're hidden. I won't tell you where, but they're hidden good."

"You know what?" Dean stands with his hands on his hips. Wilson mimics him with his one good arm, props his hand on his hip. "I think Eddie brought you some things. He stopped by."

"He did?"

"I'll go get it."

By the time Dean returns to the lobby, the room has filled with people. How long has he been back there, he wonders? An hour? Lois has settled with a magazine, her children arguing over a puzzle. Myra

Sorenson stands looking at the bulletin board. There are faces from school, from church, from work.

The popsicle stick child—thankfully—is gone.

"Is he all right?" Mrs. Jenkins, the teacher. She discards the *TIME* magazine she was reading. She fiddles with the buttons on her purple cardigan. A red rim outlines her eyes. "God, I've been worried sick, I—"

Dean ignores her. He scans the small crowd for a tall woman, blond with a halo of frizz. *Nellie, Nellie, please be here.* She will step forward. She will shake off the fighting face, she will wear buttercup yellow—she will be clothed in warmth. She can be so unpredictable, this woman, but she is all he wants to see. *Please be here, Nel. He needs his mother. I need my wife.* The lobby windows are streaked with rain. There is a shatter of light, chased by thunder.

"How's Wilson?" Lois stands. Penny, at her feet, pauses with a puzzle piece in hand.

It angers him for a moment that Lois is here with her two children, waiting in a stiff lobby chair, waiting for over an hour, while he doesn't even know where his wife is.

"Good," says Dean. "He's lucid now. He's himself."

Relief ripples through the room.

"Thank God." Lois moves a gloved hand to her mouth. "Oh God, we've been worried sick. Jim just called for you. I didn't know what to say. He was all, *he was a wreck, Lois, a real wreck.*" She looks at her children, the half-completed picture of a gazebo and garden, the sky missing all its clouds.

"Mr. Porter." The nurse at the front desk. "Telephone call for you."

Dean bounds to the mounted wall receiver. *Please be Nellie,* he prays. *Please, damn it, please.*

It's April.

"Do you know how long it took me to figure out where you'd gone?" she says. He can picture her in the staff lounge, twirling the cord around her finger. Tugging on her free earlobe, biting her lower lip.

"Why are you calling?" He glances around, afraid someone will overhear. That someone will see the twitch in his shoulders, the sweat on his forehead, and *know.*

"I was worried. I wanted to know if you're all right. You left in such a rush—you—oh, I just . . . I don't know what to say."

"Is it Nellie?" Lois calls from across the lobby. Dean shakes his head at her, then cups the receiver closer to his mouth.

"Listen, that came out harsher than I meant. It's not you, it's this whole goddamn mess, and no one seems to know where my wife is, and I thought you were her on the phone and—sorry. Thank you for calling."

April speaks more urgently now. "Hal waited in the conference room for a while before coming to look for you."

"What did you tell him?"

"I was with Bette. We were stocking supplies. I found him in your office—I said, you'd gotten a call, left in a hurry. I said you looked upset. I said, maybe someone died. What did happen, Dean?"

He cringes at the intimate softness in her tone.

"My boy. He was in an accident."

"Christ. Do you think? I mean—should I, should I come by?"

Dean hesitates. He aches to say, *Yes, yes, come now, come quickly.* But Lois is almost within earshot and Jim already knows and Nellie should be here—hopefully—any minute, not to mention April is Mrs. Gardner; she is another man's wife, a man stationed eight thousand miles away. She is only twenty-four.

He leans against the hospital wall and breathes slowly to keep from crying. A nurse brushes past, bringing with her the smells of antiseptic, camphor, iodine.

"No, don't," he says slowly. "I'll see you tomorrow?"

"Okay."

"Thank you for calling, Mrs. Gardner."

At last, April says, "I think Hal may come by." Then she hangs up.

He is aware of someone staring at him. He turns to see Penny, a puzzle piece still gripped in her hand. One of her braids is loose and frazzled.

"Can I see him?" she says. "I think he'd want to see me."

Dean nods. He gathers the gifts from Eddie—the candy bag and comics—and returns to the emergency ward. Mrs. Jenkins tries to say something else, but he doesn't even glance her way, cannot look at her, though he's aware through the thickness of his anger that this is not her fault. It's his. He is the father.

Lois, Penny, and Todd trail him back to Wilson's curtained wing.

"Look who I found," Dean says. He places the pile of gifts beside Wilson's bed, then runs his thumb over Wilson's bony hand.

Penny steps forward, smiling shyly.

"You look funny," she says before darting forward and planting the softest of kisses on his cheek. Wilson reddens with a sheepish smile.

After blinking for a good minute, Wilson launches into story mode. He describes the playground, his scouting vantage points, the wind, the climb. His voice enters an explorer tone. He speaks deeper than usual. He purses his lips. He is looking at Penny only, Dean notices, though Todd listens, too, farther back and with his arms crossed. Wilson is sharing his little boy world with Penny who leans rapt against the hospital bed, her chin propped on her hands.

Dean nods toward Lois, who steps away from the curtain with him.

"You said she was getting on a bus?" He dips his voice to a near whisper. "My wife?"

"Yes, I think so." Lois bites her lip, shrugs. "It was chaotic, there were people everywhere. And this was hours ago, maybe one o'clock. We got separated."

"People? What people?"

"The protest. Women Strike for Peace."

His shoulders tense. As if he didn't need another problem today. He swallows hard. "Nellie marched with you?"

Lois nods. She is at once grimly proud and shy. This is when he notices the button on her lapel, a white circle with the letters WSP. He cannot imagine Nellie with the antinuclears, Nellie carrying a banner, Nellie shouting in the road.

Then there is the matter of—Nellie does not ride the bus. She does not go anywhere. She hates tight spaces, public transportation. Where could she possibly be going? Her life follows a clear orbit: from the house to the grocery to the church to the school.

Don't ask me what I want. This whole thing is not what I want.

"Lois." His voice waves. He struggles to speak straight. "You need to tell me everything she said."

Lois looks incredulous. "Nothing, she seemed fine. Herself, but fine. I mean, she was surprising. She wasn't planning to come with us until just this morning. I guess she seemed agitated."

Nellie's father left by bus. She rarely spoke of him. He once reeled the story out of her. They were in his apartment, which would soon become their apartment. She kept spinning her teaspoon around the base of the cup, a chilling scrape.

"My mother broke a window," she said. "She was throwing his books out onto the lawn. I remember the paper flying. Isn't that such a weird thing to remember? The books opened when they fell so they looked like shot birds."

"And your father?" he asked. "Was that the last time you saw him?"

"No. I saw him later." But she said nothing more about this, only: "After the books, he walked to the bus station. That was the last straw, I think. He dragged one trunk behind him. It was like he wanted to be seen, which was so strange for him, the show of it. He wanted the neighbors to see what he was doing, to make a public display." The scrape of the spoon, her eyes faraway. "We followed in the car. It was quite a scene, and everyone knew what was happening. I remember my friends watching from their porch steps. I remember being so upset by that, more than anything else. The being-watched feeling. Knowing that they would tease me in school about it. The thought of airing our dirty laundry, as Mother used to say. What didn't help was the car. She didn't know how to drive very well. The car kept stalling. She had me in the back seat. I think she wanted to guilt him that way, by saying, *Look what you're leaving, not just me, but our girl.* She wanted everyone to see, too. Wanted everyone to know what he was doing to us, that this wasn't her fault." She stopped swirling the spoon and licked it clean. When she looked up, there was a coldness in her eyes, like silver coins. "Do you think he always knew he would leave? Or do you think that one day, he just decided to give up on everything, start clean?"

"I don't know."

"I think he must have known," Nellie said, so softly he could barely

hear. "You don't just wake up one morning and say, that's it. I'm throwing in the towel. It's not a one-day, sudden decision. I think it's something you know for a long time but resist. You delay it as long as you
can. Because you like the life you've pretended to love." She smiled ruefully. "But I understand, I think. My mother could be dreadful." Then
she finished her tea and refused to speak of her father again.

From the hospital bed, Wilson laughs. Penny has settled herself tentatively beside him. Todd works on a hangnail until a sliver of blood
appears.

There has long been the latent, barely voiced fear that Nellie would
simply leave. He saw it in the way she sat on the porch during rain-
storms, a cigarette in her mouth, tipsy and staring at nothing. He saw
it in the way she was always trying to perfect the house, asking if he
noticed anything different? (A new plate hung on the wall, the armchair moved half a foot.) He never noticed these small troubles, and
this vexed her to no end.

Lois's voice brings him back to the hospital.

"Is everything all right?" she's saying.

"I hate to ask this," he says. "But I don't know who else. Can you
do something for me? Can you go to our house, see if she's there? I
haven't been able to reach her." He looks back to the hospital bed. Wilson's skin is near translucent in the bleached hospital light. "I can't leave
him."

HERE'S WHAT THE WAR was like for other men: it was looking over
your shoulder, back to a prior life. It was missing the birth of a child,
a first anniversary. It was missing the death of a sister. It was worrying
whether a girlfriend would write a "Dear John" letter and sleep with the
neighbor. Dean was a lonely, bookish, country farm boy. All he had to
look back to was a classroom and lab reports and a farm always on the
brink of ruin. What he stood to lose felt small—so small that he felt
guilt when burying men who were already husbands and fathers. They
all were sons, but some were more. Dean wore the watch. Others kissed
sepia pictures. Others cried when lockets of hair were misplaced, buried

in rubble. Others couldn't sleep at night, missed the warmth of another body, soft curves beside them. One man kept a baby bootie tied around his neck. The thing was, the life they remembered from before the war would never be what they discovered upon returning home. This new life was like a shadow version. Even Dean, who fell asleep dreaming of the farmhouse by the river, remembered it as warm days running barefoot, as peach juice on his fingers. He would be surprised upon returning home to see the broken beams on the porch from termites, to taste the chalky residue in the water.

THE LOBBY HAS THINNED. Dean followed Lois, Penny, and Todd back through the hospital wing. He watched as Lois opened a wide black umbrella and clutched her children close to her as they entered the rain. Mrs. Jenkins had already left, and most of the other visitors with her.

Dean steps outside for some air. Under the roof's covering, he watches the rain. Dean loves the town at night. In the haze, the streetlamps offer a homey gold. Beams of light leave pools on the asphalt. The county hospital sits just a few blocks away from Main Street. A car drives past, and its headlights briefly illuminate the side of a warehouse behind the bike shop. The light catches the yellow of the fallout shelter sign. The stamp of the CDA.

"Your wife is a surprising woman."

He starts, turns, and sees Myra sitting cross-legged on a bench, hidden mostly in shadow. A plaque on the wood gleams behind her: *In memory of Nancy, 1957*. Like Lois, Myra is dressed all in black. A sleek umbrella is propped beside her.

"Out for some fresh air?" she says.

"I think I'm waiting for your husband. Someone called, said he may come by."

"Ah." Myra lights a cigarette and brings it delicately to her lips.

"What did you mean about my wife? That she's surprising?"

He did not think Myra knew Nellie very well. In fact, he suspected that few people knew Nellie very well. They'd had one dinner party at the Sorensons' when he and Nellie first moved to town. The evening

had started with chaos. He arrived home from work, breathless after a good day. And what was it that happened? He tries to remember. Didn't he find the babysitter waiting on the front porch, the door
locked? Hadn't he run through the house shouting for Nellie? Wasn't
Wilson sitting alone with a pile of blocks, he not even two? He found
Nellie asleep in the laundry room, her legs tucked between the washer
and dryer, as though lulled by the warmth and vibration of the machines. He shook her awake, angry, afraid of being late, shouting things
like, *What the hell are you doing, sleeping like that? What if Wilson hurt
himself, what if he broke something, hit his head?* All through dinner, she
sent her silent anger at him in radio waves across the table. He tried to
cover for her, said things like, "Nellie's had a rough day. Got some bad
news from her mother." *Anything* to account for the way she poured
generously from the decanter, the way she barely ate.

So yes, Nellie could be surprising in her own way.

"What I mean is, I was not expecting her to join the march," says Myra.

"That makes two of us."

"Did you know that some of the strongest antisuffragists were
women? Sometimes women want to hurt other women, want to keep
them from growing."

"Nellie's mother was like that, I think," says Dean.

"Mine, too. It's a generational thing, perhaps. Or perhaps not. So
what I'm saying is that I was proud of Nellie. She was brave today—she
showed up."

"Well, you've been filling her head with things she can't understand."
Dean fights the desire to shout at this woman. But this is Myra Sorenson. This is Hal's wife.

Myra sits up a little straighter. She flicks the cigarette so a spray of
ash falls, searing when it hits the rain-wet ground.

"You know that was the worst part about the Manhattan Project,"
she says, smoke escaping through her open mouth. "People at Los
Alamos—even people here—they were so trapped by the goal. They
were so focused on these big issues that they lost sight of things they
could control. The bomb means nothing if we can't keep our own children safe."

This feels like a slice to the gut.

"Why are you here, Mrs. Sorenson?"

"Because there's nowhere better to be."

"I mean why are you still here." He checks his watch. It's after seven. "You must've been here for hours."

She stands with heft, but with grace. She is almost his height.

"I'm here because I saw the ambulance arrive at the school," she says. Her nails drum the handle of her umbrella. "Because your wife was with us today. Because I have the sincere feeling that what we marched about—the very thing we're protesting—has a lot to do with what happened."

"This has nothing to do with your protest," he says. "This is my son being afraid."

"Children's fear doesn't come from nothing."

She looks at him then, as though seeing right through to his brain, as though his mind is a file cabinet, and she is April thumbing through records, plucking the right report. As though she can pull out the transcript from last night's fight with Nellie, from his dream of yellow soil and his skin in shreds, as though she can see—like he does—his boy falling through the air on repeat.

Finally, she says, "Nellie will be back."

Myra smiles, then nods to the parking lot as twin lights pull in. "That looks like Hal's car," she says. She unfolds her umbrella like a tent and strides into the drizzle, pausing at Hal's door. They exchange a few words through an open window before she continues on in the night.

DEAN'S DREAM LAST NIGHT did not end with the farmland and the red Carolina clay. After walking through his father's fields, after feeling his skin bleed and burn away, there was this: four bodies. The first two: his parents, skeletal, worms through their eye sockets. They were lifted by crane. Dream-Dean watched, stricken. Their bodies were loose in the ground in this dream, though he buried them himself. He buried them in Batesville metal coffins. But in the febrile dream version, there were no caskets, only parental skeletons, only this moving away from their land to miles south. He tried to run after them and shout, "This is their home! Let them stay!" He was afraid they would wake up somehow, in a heaven that looked like home, only to find that home had moved. They would recognize nothing. The dream melted past. The two remaining bodies: one, his. He saw himself as though from a distance. He was all blood and mucus and black pores. He was the walking nightmare of a nuclear meltdown, as though he swam in waste. In the dream, he ran through Oakleigh, dropping chunks of flesh like mummy bandages. He ran toward home, the shelter, feverishly fast. The hatch was locked when he got there, and in his dream-logic he worried that someone had hijacked his spot, that someone would shoot him if he opened the door. No one shot him. The last body was Nellie. She opened the hatch, she pulled him in. He saw her clearly in the single-bulb light. A gingham fabric, like picnic-table print, was ironed into her cheek and neck. Her arms were popcorned from heat. He tried to speak but found his voice was gone. And he was suddenly so cold, so hungry, longed only for the sweetness of a peach, the softness of his wife.

THEN THERE IS HAL. He strolls toward the hospital, slow and meandering, hands in his pockets. He moves as though unaware of the rain that fills the brim of his hat or the puddles that slosh his shoes. When he reaches Dean under the awning, there is a grim handshake, a mutual lighting of cigarettes. There is a silence heavier than words.

NELLIE

The bus is less crowded heading back to Oakleigh. Besides Nellie, there is an elderly man with a graying beard and cane; a teenaged couple, perhaps sixteen; a mother with a baby and two children; three men with briefcases, likely returning home from work; a woman with wide black glasses, who, Nellie notes, wears a WOMEN STRIKE FOR PEACE pin.

As they leave Columbia, the road becomes bare. More trees, fewer houses. The rich green of a county highway. The kudzu climbs over fences and telephone poles.

The bus rattles and jolts. Nellie clutches her purchases close, the beauties.

With every passing mile, she feels a certain twist of dread knot tighter in her stomach. She will arrive home soon. What will she find? Dean making dinner? (The thought!) Wilson crying, looking for her—but no, he's too old for that. Wilson crying as Dean nails the shelter shut? It was bound to happen eventually. There will be coldness from Dean, she can sense this now. He will not shout at her, not raise his hand. He will see the Sears bags and say, "Where'd you go, Nel? I worried. Why didn't you leave a note? Didn't you think I'd worry? And where'd you get the money?" And sometimes—she thinks this as they turn onto the smaller highway that leads to Oakleigh—sometimes she wants him to shout at her so she can shout back.

They will pass the bomb plant on the way to town.

The woman with the baby and two small children sits just in front of Nellie. The kids are playing some sort of game with folded paper while the woman coos at her baby.

"One, two, three, four," the oldest, a girl, says. "You got four."

"What's that mean?"

"Let's open it. We'll see your fortune." The crinkle of paper. "L-O-V-E. That means you'll find *love* soon. Maybe Danny Ducantis!"

"Yuck," says the youngest.

Nellie leans her head against the bus window. The night is darkening rapidly, and they have entered the rain. One minute: still silence. The next: fat drops fall in a steady drizzle. She watches the wet streak across the glass blur the world. Still, she stares—waits for any sight of the bomb plant, with its barbed wire circumference, its checkpoint, like a tiny war zone in her town. Its chain-metal fence like necklaces roped back and forth.

Because here is what Nellie fears: tomorrow, everything will slide back into the normal. (Isn't that how life is? One minute a desperate show, the next like nothing ever happened.) Tomorrow, there will be the same ordered leaving. There will be coffee and breakfast. There will be Wilson at the table with the newspaper. The work-Dean, so ordered and starched! He will peck her cheek, maybe. He will call her "My Nellie, my own," and he will disappear into that world she cannot follow. He will leave her in a house so lonely, so quiet, filled only by the ticking clocks—reminding her of the many hours she will spend alone. She will watch the morning moon vanish.

Ahead, the little girl pushes the paper contraption in her sister's face. "Circle, circle, dot, dot, now I've got my cootie shot!"

"Hush girls, we're in public," the mother whispers.

The woman says this just as there is the smell of exhaust fumes and that horrid jolt forward, then back. The bus lurches to a stop. Nellie feels herself rise out of her seat. She hovers for just a moment (almost wonderful, that off-the-ground feeling) before the fall.

The bus driver stands. He takes off his cap, a black visor, and runs his hands through his graying hair. He is dark and old, his face whipped with wrinkles.

"Sorry, folks," he says. "Looks like engine trouble."

Of course. Nellie sighs deeply. Because of course this would happen in the rain, at night, when she's already so late heading home.

Everyone files off the bus. Umbrellas flutter and open in unison. The mother complains loudly that she'll be late, she needs to make dinner, the baby needs his bath. The teenaged couple stand holding hands, and the girl nestles her head in the crook of his shoulder.

Nellie has no umbrella. But she doesn't mind. The rain (so soft, like a brushing finger) drifts over her face. She closes her eyes, feels the water on her eyelids, running down the rim of her nose.

"Sorry, folks, so sorry, folks," the driver says. He is halfway under the bus by now.

The road is dark. There are no streetlamps here. Only the moonlight that shines in patches through the storm clouds. The pine and oak sway, all shadowed.

There is a metallic smell in the air, she thinks. Is it from the bomb plant? Is it sulfur? Is it iron? Suddenly, her Sears bags, getting heavier and rain-soaked, seem so foolish. Humiliating! Why would she think that this would help her marriage, her life?

The bags are heavy. Her feet and shoulders ache. Near the bus, sitting half on the steps, half off, the two children are back with their paper fortune teller. The oldest girl holds it carefully out of the rain. "One, two, three, four, five, six! You got a six this time!"

"Girls!" the mother shouts.

It is in the way this mother shouts this, with all the exasperated tenderness of an overtired woman. She holds the baby on her hip, an umbrella with her free hand. Her blond hair is getting wet and frizzed, but the baby stays dry. The baby sleeps with his face against her collarbone. The mother collects herself and walks to her daughters. "Are you warm enough, girls? Button your coats up, stay warm. Violet, help your sister."

Nellie wants to cry.

Ahead, a light appears on the road. Like a star—like a comet. It is so impossibly warm, this spotlight in the inked dark. The shuffle of shoes: everyone moves to the curb, stands in the grass, waiting. The old man sniffles, rubs his nose repeatedly with his sleeve. The teenaged couple moves into the shadows. They kiss as if no one can see them. But Nellie doesn't move. She cannot. She watches the light approach. *Don't try to patch it up, tear it up, tear it up*—this is what she hears in her brain. That damn song! She stands there, the Sears bags clutched in her fists, and she thinks of the party in all its colors, aluminum covers on spooky dishes, the howl of children. Her husband was late. Well today, she will be late. (She'll show him! Ha ha!) Today, she is striking for something.

This light is closer now, so beautiful—confectionary like marzipan. There are two now, she can distinguish them, like twin glowing starlights.

We would rather be ruined than changed, Auden wrote.

Someone calls to her, but she doesn't register the words. There is no sound, only this: a light in the darkness—at last, finally.

DEAN

Enshrouded in blankets, Wilson looks mealy. He could go for a haircut and a bath. But he has also never seemed more beautiful, this person stitched from Dean and Nellie, a perfect combination of slender bones and teeth and dirt-rimmed nails. His pensive brown eyes study the comics as though they are homework to be memorized. He holds up a page to show Dean.

"Look here," Wilson explains. "This is Cimota Mouse. Cimota is atomic spelled backwards, obviously. He's really an ordinary mouse, but he's been shrunk to the size of an atom, see?"

Dean nods. "I see."

Dean runs his hands through Wilson's hair. He'll take him to the barber tomorrow, he decides, and fix him up with a nice crew cut. Then they'll get ice cream cones or floats, whatever Wilson wants. They can walk to one of the rivulets and fish; they can go to the theater, maybe see *West Side Story*. Wilson can show him the best bike paths through town, and they can visit Eddie at the pharmacy. Dean will even, maybe, let him go rabbit hunting like Campbell and Marcel. He will see the world through Wilson's eyes tomorrow.

"And while he's an atom, all this tiny—" Wilson squashes his pointer finger to his thumb, "—there's this professor character who gives him pills of what's called U-235, which is—"

"I know what that is," says Dean.

"Oh. So, it gives him superpowers, and in this issue, he's having a face-off with Count Gatto."

"That's nice," says Dean.

Someone moans from across the emergency ward. The voice is old, the cry is deep.

"We'll do whatever you want tomorrow," Dean whispers, leaning forward. "You and me, okay? I'm not going in to work. I'm going to take the day off. It'll be me and you all day. And we'll do whatever you want, all right, Wilson? You name it."

Wilson stares at him, then shrugs. "Okay."

"Is there something you want to do?"

"I don't know." Wilson turns a page of the comic book.

Dean blinks furiously to stop the tears, but he cannot. They keep falling. He runs his fingers gently across the cast.

HAL SPOKE FIRST.

"I saw your report, Porter."

Dean suddenly felt exhaustion come over him like a heavy coat. It was thick and warm. It was soft with goose feathers, and he had the urge to sleep.

"Let's step out of the rain, sir," he said. The chill seeped through his clothes to the bone. "And I need to get back to my boy soon."

Hal followed him through the visitors lobby door. The lobby had filled again with an array of ragtag patients. Another woman, very pregnant. A child with a cough, sitting blueish in his father's lap. An older man sat near them, picking at his whiskers as though plucking paint from brush bristles.

"I went looking for you," Hal said. This is when Dean noticed the gray under Hal's eyes. "Got concerned when you didn't show."

"Someone should have told you." Dean felt a flicker of annoyance at his lab techs, at April. Did no one think to tell Hal that an emergency had come up? He pictured Hal and the Atomic Energy Commission representatives, all waiting, checking their watches. "I'm sorry you waited around."

"Don't give it a second thought. Your boy, is he—"

"He's going to be fine."

"Let's walk," Dean said, aware of their voices amid the quiet shuffling of shoes and murmurings.

They walked the halls. The hospital was a small one, thirty beds, and the corridors made perpendicular shapes, past patient wards and operating rooms. Small panes of glass were inlaid in the doors.

"BEING A WATCHDOG IS kind of like being a superhero," Wilson says.

"Being a what?" Dean asks.

Wilson's eyes glimmer with secret knowledge. He turns a page in his comic book. "That's what I am, you know. And all superheroes have secret powers. They know things. Right? They have an extra sense. Or they have magic. But magic isn't real." He pauses, sticks his tongue through the gap in his teeth as if thinking, then continues: "Today, you know what we did? We did math. And we did other things. But we had to walk into the gym like this." Wilson drops the book, puts his free hand behind his head. "We had to walk like that. But I knew it was Code Orange. I knew because of the tag, obviously."

This is when Wilson spazzes. He twitches his arm. He looks around the hospital bed with frantic energy. His clothes are in a pile on the side table. His boots, his backpack.

"Where is it?" His voice is loud and shrill.

"Where's what?" Dean asks. He places a hand on Wilson's chest and tries to calm him.

"My tag, where is it?" Wilson claws at his neck. His casted arm shifts on the bed, and he winces. "I need it—where'd it go? My things—where is it? I need it. I *need it.*" The tears come in spurts.

"Hey, be calm now, you'll hurt yourself. We'll find it."

"It could be at school. I could have lost it. What if it fell? What if it's in the grass? I need it!" He writhes now, and Dean finds himself stepping back in panic.

One of the nurses runs in and slides back Wilson's curtain with a *shhhh.* In a fluid motion, she injects a shot in his free arm.

"More morphine," she explains.

After a moment, Wilson relaxes into the bed again. He is limp against the white pillow. His hair bunches around the bandages like feathers. A green trickle runs from his nose, and he sniffles every few seconds.

"I need it." His voice is thick with sleep. "I need it, I need it."

Dean sits again. He stares at his child on the hospital bed. He can't help it: he pictures Wilson on the water tower as he climbs, slips, flies. The fall couldn't have lasted long, just a few seconds. He can't stop imagining it, a hundred times over, each with different endings. He sees the descent. Wilson, arms spread wide. Wilson, mangled on the ground. Now Wilson, broken in the hospital bed.

The nurse appears again, looking tired. "Call for you at the front desk," she says. "It's a Mrs. Shepherd. She says there's no one home."

THEY STOPPED OUTSIDE THE door to the neonatal wing. Through the glass, Dean saw rows and rows of cribs, all curved brass. A stocky nurse—graying and matronly—held a wriggly pink baby in the crook of her elbow. Dean stood in a hospital just like this one ten years ago. He stood and paced the hallways and waited to hear if they'd had a boy or girl, waited for that beautiful infant howl.

"So my report," he said at last. "You read it?"

"I did. You start to sound goddamn poetic there by the end, Porter." Hal reached into his jacket pocket and retrieved the document, halved and folded.

The immediate environmental consequences of unmanaged nuclear waste may prove to be catastrophic. The high quota and demand for materials at our facilities have led to years of ecologically destructive behavior which threatens to contaminate water resources in the area. Our goal at the Sterling Creek Laboratory should be total containment—and this means thinking not only of the problems we already have, but the problems we will have in the future. We need to continually monitor the groundwater, vegetation, fauna, seepage basins, soil, and assess how to secure a more permanent storage method. Otherwise, we condemn future generations to a cleanup of unthinkable proportions, with radioisotopes of unthinkable life spans.

A nurse passed by, pushing a cart with rattling glass bottles. She raised her eyebrows at them but said nothing, then steered through the door of the ward. The bottles, Dean realized, were full of infant formula.

"We shouldn't be talking about this now, but I can't help it." Hal's voice dropped to a near whisper. "Is this the only copy?"

Dean nodded, said nothing.

"Good. I want you to shred it."

"Sir?"

"Do you really think the suits from D.C. will take kindly to this? The accusation that bleeds across these pages that they've been negligent?"

"But they have—"

"Making them angry won't get you anything. We have to find ways to fix our problems quietly. This is an example where we should solve the problem, then inform them. We ask forgiveness, not permission."

Dean shook his head, so exhausted he could hardly think straight.

"Sir, I wish I'd had the chance to explain myself more thoroughly. Maybe tomorrow we can discuss this in depth."

"We will not. You're going to shred this."

"And if I don't?"

"Well, the AEC will care less about someone who's not the head of his department, won't they?"

Dean steeled at this.

"What about all that talk of *I've done things I can't live with*? Don't you remember that? Your father, the lawyer. The arson case. And you said, I remember this, you said it was so ironic that you'd chosen science as your career. You wanted to help people. I want to help people."

"So why do you think I stayed?" Dean had never seen Hal angry, and the grim husk to his voice made him start. "Sometimes you stay to fix the problems from the inside. Like family, like when your marriage is a mess, you don't just leave. You stay and fix it—you try to stop the worst from happening, because you love the thing that hurts you. Yes, by God, I have done things I cannot live with. I have done worse than you. In Nagasaki, the worst thing I saw as we went through the rubble was a newborn baby boy still attached to his mother by the umbilical cord. They'd both been dead for days. So don't you lecture me, Porter, about wanting to help people. Don't you dare lecture me. I stay because I want, never, for that to happen again—never. I dream of them every night. I dream and know, *I helped my country kill you.* But guess what? Oppie would've been wise to be like me, to fix things quietly from the inside. At least, from the inside, you have power, you have sway."

Hal sighed and paused for so long that Dean wondered if he'd speak more. At last, he added, "Listen, Porter. I don't need to tell you what can happen. You know very well what the AEC is capable of. They can ruin you. This country is not ready for people to critique it. Maybe we never will be. But there are more important things in life than being on the right side of history."

He handed Dean the report, marked up with red.

"I know that," Dean said softly.

Hal smiled then, as if nothing of any importance had transpired between them.

"I take it you and Mrs. Sorenson don't agree on some of this, do you?" Dean ventured. "I mean on the staying."

"Oh hell, Myra always wants to be a revolutionary," Hal said. "She wanted me to be like Oppie, I think. A martyr. But it's all intellectual for her, all abstract. That's the difference between those who know about something and those of us who have to make real choices."

Dean nodded slowly.

There was so much he wanted to tell Hal in that moment. He wanted to confide about April—to tell him about Nellie. He wanted to say, "She's always been volatile, so deeply, deeply sad. A sad woman, always angry. Her father killed himself years ago. Did you know that? She only heard when she saw an obit in the papers. I never met the man. She didn't know him well—left the family years ago. First, he left. Then remarried. Then killed himself." Nellie was haunted by this, he always knew. And so was he. Dean wanted to tell Hal about the shelter, about Wilson, the reason for the fall—everything. The way Hal looked at him, with knowing, with exhaustion. This was a man who understood. This was a man who'd lived it, too.

"Where is Mrs. Porter?" Hal ventured, sipping his coffee.

"I don't know."

They said nothing for a few minutes. There was only the grate of cart wheels and doors closing. The sound of hinges. Awareness lengthened between them like shadows.

"You know what I bet?" said Hal. He placed a hand on Dean's shoulder, led him back toward the lobby. "I bet she just forgot to tell you she had plans. She's at the cinema. Catching a show. She'll be back."

"It's more than that," Dean said, believing it.

WILSON RETURNS TO READING the comic, though he now holds it close to his face. Dean reaches for Wilson's wrist. He feels his pulse, gentle, undulating, for no other reason than to be reassured that he is really, truly alive.

Stillness settles in the hospital corridor. Dean feels himself succumb to exhaustion, the weight of the day settling on his shoulders. His eyelids flutter.

Then: "My head hurts," says Wilson. The comic book drops, and he stares blankly at the blue curtain.

This is when Dean sees Wilson's eyes, dilated black discs like eclipsed moons.

Oakleigh Gazette, NOVEMBER 1, 1961

WOMEN AS PEACE WARRIORS:
THE ANTI-NUCLEAR MOVEMENT
HITS OAKLEIGH

By Olive Montgomery

Today, dozens of women marched through the Oakleigh town center to protest the atmospheric testing of nuclear weapons. The protestors, calling themselves Women Strike for Peace, marched through Main Street to the county courthouse, where leaders proceeded to meet with town officials, before delivering handwritten letters to the post office. These letters, according to eyewitness accounts, were made out to Mrs. Jacqueline Kennedy and Mrs. Nina Krushchev.

Women Strike for Peace is a grassroots organization, launched by Dagmar Wilson, a children's book illustrator and activist based in Washington, D.C.

"We've got to do something," participator Cornelia (Nellie) Porter told the Gazette. "If you want change, you have to do something. You have to make it known. You have to be seen."

Oakleigh's protest was organized by Myra Sorenson, wife to the current laboratory manager at the Sterling Creek Plant. Sorenson—who holds a degree from UCLA and a Master's from Columbia—says that today's protest is grounded in the history of women's activist movements: "Women need to recognize that they have powerful political capital. But the beauty in our movement is that anyone can march. Housewife or maid, professor or illiterate, anyone and everyone is affected by nuclear war. Just as the vote should not be withheld from anyone, so protesting should not be."

When asked to give a statement, Mayor Peterson called the protest "precious," saying they were "women who simply wanted to get out of the house."

But Sorenson insists this dependence on motherhood is exactly what makes WSP successful: "We are not protesting for ourselves. We are protesting for those we love."

The scope of this movement is still being felt. But reports are surfacing of similar protests around the country, in major cities and also in small towns affected by nuclear weapons.

This is a developing story.

A TEN-YEAR-OLD BODY AND ten-year-old brain. A small piece of bone breaks, a splinter. There is the quick slice of an artery. There is a red ribbon of blood. He vomits. He screams. A surge of electricity bolts through his brain. His body spasms on the hospital cot. Messages are sent back and forth from damaged cells.

Nurses rush past the curtain. They feel his skin, see the mound rising through the flesh on his temples. The brain expands.

Dean follows, screaming, as they wheel his cot to an operating room. The doctor calls for a surgical drill.

NELLIE

Here is Oakleigh at night. The houses are dark, lit by little patches of liquid gold through the windows. Jack-o'-lanterns grin from porch steps like ominous watchers. But there are no candles in them—they are only shadowed things, gourds with gaping teeth.

Brunnell Street. Nellie turns. She walks faster. Her shoes rub on her heels from where her pantyhose got wet. The bags tore two blocks back. She has carried the Sears purchases loose in her arms since then. (Like a child held to her breast!)

Their house is close, she can see it now. Their russet roof, the driveway. Empty—is no one home? Maybe the car is in the shop.

Outside the front door, she hesitates. Even from here, she can hear the hum of clocks in sync. She considers knocking and pictures Wilson running to open the door in his footed pajamas, welcoming back the mother. Then she thinks that's absurd; this is her house, too. She turns the knob, enters.

It was the cry from that baby, getting wet as the mother dropped her umbrella in panic. It was the cry that woke Nellie up. Someone's hands were on her shoulders—the teenager, away from his girlfriend to help a crazy woman. He was shouting, "Get out of the road!" Nellie shrieked as the car honked and skidded past them. The light left. But it was the cry from the baby more than the hands on her shoulders; she was sure of it. She turned in the rain to see the bus still in need of repair, passengers waiting in the rain like vagabonds. The baby was crying, his voice birdish and shrill. He sounded like Wilson when he cried. He sounded like Wilson when she put him in the apartment hallway and bolted the lock, shaking and crying herself as she collapsed in exhaustion, leaning her head against the door. "I'm sorry, I'm sorry," she murmured. "I can't do it. I'm sorry." Like Wilson when she hid from him in the laundry room.

But she did do it. (However poorly, she tried, she tried!) Love meant a life of atonement, and she tried. Wasn't it enough to try? To not die in her dread but to try? She opened the door and picked up Wilson, so purple from screaming. He fisted the air, desperate baby flailing. She would not be like her father and abandon her family. Nellie kissed his wrinkled infant face, hushed, "My sweet baby, my sweet perfect baby." She used childish words, so soft in her mouth, and tried to steady herself.

The bus was broken down for over an hour. They waited out the rain, and Nellie stood against the cool metal of the bus door as far from the road as she could be. The others kept eyeing her tentatively, as though she might jump in front of the rare car. Whenever headlights appeared, she felt their eyes on her, felt the weight of their worry.

Now the house is empty. Now there is pregnant quiet.

"Wilson? Dean?"

She drops the Sears bundle by the door.

The television is off. There are no lit lights. The clocks tick off the seconds. Nellie walks forward, palms the air until she reaches the standing lamp and turns it on to coat the room in soft yellow. "Wilson? Dean?" The kitchen table is empty—no sign of dinner. There is Wilson's cereal bowl, his half-drunk cup. She swims through the dark kitchen but sees no sign of them. Nothing! To the bedroom hallway. Where are the clothes Wilson usually discards at bath time, one after the other, as he strips while walking, abandons everything on the hardwood? Where is Dean's briefcase, his work badge with the little black-and-white snapshot? Instead, she steps on party plates she never picked up. She knocks over someone's beer but ignores the pool that forms on the rug. Maybe, she thinks, throwing open the bedroom door to see only the matted sheets from this morning. Maybe they came home, saw she was gone, and left, too. Maybe they're in a hotel? But no, she decides, fumbling open the bathroom, then the shower curtain, no, Dean wouldn't waste money that way. Into his office, untouched still—the cigar box there on his desk. Maybe there was a call from her mother? Maybe her mother was ill, and they left?

But without her? They wouldn't leave without her.

Back in the kitchen, Nellie slumps at the table. She pours herself a sip of gin from her hidden pantry stash, then another.

Perhaps there was an emergency at the plant. A crack somewhere, a fission. Maybe Dean had to stay late. Wilson could be with Eddie Pace. Yes, a sleepover with Eddie.

This is what makes her call Bill Pace, at his house behind the pharmacy. This is how she learns.

DEAN

Wilson couldn't have been more than eight when he first asked what half-life was. Nellie was boiling potatoes, in one of her moods, on her third glass of something or other. Dean was reading in his chair.

Suddenly, Wilson was at Dean's side, staring. He smelled like sweat and lemons and grass.

"What is half-life?" he asked.

Dean lowered the newspaper, sighed.

"It's how we measure decay," he said slowly. "It's a fixed rate."

"So, what's my half-life?"

"What?"

"Four, I guess. But I can hardly remember that far back."

"You don't have a half-life because you're not a decaying radioactive isotope."

He can remember so vividly the irritation that caught in his muscles. How much he longed for Wilson to disappear into his room, let him rest. The day had been difficult, but he forgets now what went wrong. (Miscalculations? Lost data?) Perhaps this was why Nellie let him play in the shelter.

But Wilson sat at Dean's feet, mimicked his crossed leg. When Dean tapped his knee, Wilson tapped his knee. When Dean *hmm*ed, Wilson *hmm*ed—until finally, Dean retreated to his office and turned the lock.

What he wouldn't give now to go back and open that door!

Now Dean sits in the lobby, bent over his knees. His white shirt is streaked with blood and speckled with vomit. Around him is a haze of hospital sounds, hacking coughs and clattering bed trays and heels on linoleum. He plays the scene over and over in his mind: Wilson's wide black pupils, the way his body went stiff, then his little arms—so pale!—jerked uncontrollably on the cot. His lips puckered, he retched on himself, still shaking. Dean screamed. What to do? How to help?

A nurse approaches now, hands clasped in front. Dean knows.

IN ONE ROOM: A baby has just been stillborn. In another, an elderly man has breathed his last. In a surgical theater lies a boy with a drill hole in his skull, a puddle of blood on his pillow. His belongings lie forgotten in the emergency ward, his comic book open to a colorful war. There is a child in Southwest Japan whose grandmother lived through the bombings, skin forever ridged with keloid scars. A boy in Vietnam is, even now, being trained to monkey-crawl through the jungle, silent enough to slit a sleeping throat. A child in Iowa sits on his bed, practices turning the radio dial to CONELRAD 640—just in case. A military wife arrives home to an empty house and starts a letter to her husband, so far away across the sea. A lanky teen downstream of the Savannah River wades into the water for a late-night swim. He will dive deep, his feet will trail the fish. He will swallow some water. And at the bomb plant near this river, in a clean white laboratory, techs are working late on this Wednesday night, grinding children's teeth into a fine dust. They will scan this tooth dust with a large Geiger counter, hewn from the hull of a retired battleship. There are children whose fathers died in Pearl Harbor, Stalingrad, Normandy, children who did nothing, who were born with the wounds of war, the seen and unseen scars. There is a man, an agronomist, in a small county hospital with only thirty beds, who sits in the lobby and grieves his son—his life.

NELLIE

ow she enters the hospital slowly. She is wet. She is wind-swept.

She has been in this hospital a few times—when Wilson sprained his ankle falling from a tree, or when one of his toys punctured his foot, right between the bones. When Wilson was ill, she always seemed to know what to do. He couldn't have been more than three when he had chicken pox, still thin then but with a tubby belly, a button that stuck out. She bathed him in oatmeal. She rubbed his skin with calamine. She played mother. He sat dabbling in the bathtub, with toys he loved to sink, with little green army men he pretended were drowning, and she knelt beside him. She got her knees wet. (Didn't she? Weren't there bubbles rising from the hot water, catching the mirror light? Didn't she lift up each perfect, tender toe, wiggle it, watch him squirm with delight? Didn't she scoop water in a cup and pour it over his head, careful to shield his eyes with her hand, to scrub behind his ears? Yes, weren't there moments—so beautiful, so warmed by water and the smell of Ivory soap—when she knew how to love him, knew what to do?)

Nellie hears Dean before she sees him, that chest-racking sound of his sobs. He is bent over himself in a lobby chair.

Her hand moves to her mouth and trembles visibly.

"My God," she says. "My God, my God."

DEAN

There she is in her brass-buttoned coat, bedraggled and beautiful. Her hair is haywire from the rain.

Dean stands, flooded with relief. She is here, she is back. Only her grief can match his own. She rushes to him, and he takes her roughly, desperately, into his arms. The hospital sounds have hushed with nightfall. For a moment there is only the feel of the most familiar person. He buries his nose in Nellie's hair and takes in her smell: perfume and sweat and petrichor. "Nellie, Nellie," he murmurs, his voice breaking. There is nothing else. What do you say to your spouse, to your bride, when life itself has imploded? When your only child has died? For a long while, there are no words. She clutches him, her grasp tight on his spine, and they sway as though dancing.

And then, Nellie pulls away. Without warning, she doubles over and vomits yellow bile on the floor. Dean steps back and a nurse takes his place. Nellie screams that she has to see him. And she does—the nurse takes her back.

Dean returns to his seat in the lobby. He knows what death looks like. He does not want to see the body that is no longer his son. He wants to remember him alive and rosy: Wilson with his first steps, Wilson at Christmas, pounding on their door at first light. He wants to remember clipping baby toenails over the sink, careful not to slice that tender skin. He wants to remember every little thing before the satellites and shelters.

WHEN THE STERLING CREEK Plant offered him a position in their new Health Physics Laboratory, Dean felt as though every thread of his life

was braided perfectly together. He was back from the war, a new spouse
and father, a new man. He could go home. Back to the land. On that
scouting trip in '51 as he waded through the silty river, he was warmed
with a sense of purpose. Around him, the crew took samples of any
flora they could gather. They had vials of moss and bark and the tea-
colored water. It was midsummer, and the sun was hot and the air thick
as sorghum. There was that rich dirt smell he loved, like honeysuckles
and sunbaked clay. As they waded near where Ellenton used to be, he
saw the wreckage from the decimated town. Bricks lay in heaps from
crumbled chimneys. Abandoned banana crates lay on the ground. And
near a small, sloped bank, perfect for fishing, Dean saw a tiny pair of
children's shoes, forgotten on the sand.

He would always wonder if these had belonged to the girl he saw
wandering through the ghost town. She must have been one of the last
to be evacuated before the bulldozers came through. Goodbye, curb.
Goodbye, pond.

She saw him looking. She caught his gaze, and hers was hard, defiant.
She was the first victim of the Cold War he saw with his own eyes.

"HOW WILL WE EVER talk about anything but this again?" says Nellie.

They are in the car. He has started the engine, but the thought of
driving home to their eternally empty house makes him want to drive
off a bridge. He cannot move.

"Maybe we won't," he says.

"I don't remember the last thing I said to him. Do you?"

"I don't even know if we spoke this morning. My head was up there."
He gestures to the sky.

"Was it, tie your shoes? Was it, you'll be late if you don't hurry? Probably something like that. It was just a morning. I just let him walk out
the front door to the end of his life."

Her lip quavers like it does when she wants a drink, a smoke.

"You couldn't have known," he says.

But they could have. Couldn't they? How many times had Dean
worried about Wilson's obsession? It grew like mold, silent and poisonous. It was in every toy, every game, every show, every lesson. *If a*

bomb falls five miles north of Town A and eight miles east of Town B, how far is Town A from Town B? Already, everything from the day feels so small in the wake of Wilson. The report, his job, the kiss. It's like he's interred under layers of loamy soil. Perhaps he will always feel like this, buried alive.

Nellie leans against the passenger window.

"I used to wake up in the middle of the night when he was still a baby and check that he was breathing."

Dean looks at her. He didn't know this.

"I'd have these awful dreams of, oh, I don't know, anything bad I could conjure up. Our house in an earthquake, him drowning in the tub, and I'd wake up in a panic. Why does love feel like that so much, like panic? I'd run to his room and put my hand to his nose and just wait for that little breath. I was always so afraid something would happen to him." She pauses. "Or that I would do something to him."

Nellie does not return Dean's gaze. She keeps her forehead on the glass and stares, listless, out the window.

Here is his wife in the night, a mother who will soon bury a child, and Dean wonders if they've ever had such a pure and honest moment.

Then she says: "If we hadn't put in the shelter." And something in him snaps.

"Don't. Don't you dare do that."

"It's true, you know it's true. He began to think he'd die. He was practicing for it. If we hadn't put in the shelter, then maybe—"

"Goddamn it, Nellie. If his mother wasn't a drunk. If I didn't work where I worked. If he wasn't the way he was."

"He was a boy. He was just a little boy!"

Dean hits the steering wheel. The smack of his palm jars them both. He does it again, then again, *smack smack smack*. The sound, the pain, is a release, and he can't stop. Nellie screams and her breath is sour, still, from bile, and she cough-cries into her coat sleeve. She makes sounds Dean has never heard from her before and never will again—she screams like the French woman, like someone who has lost the will to live. He joins her. He screams for Wilson, for his beautiful boy.

There they sit in the hospital lot, crying together until the rain lets up, until stars appear in the dark sky at last.

NIGHT: IMPOSSIBLY DARK. STORM clouds cover the moon. In the distance: thunder, the smell of rain that, in the early hours of twilight, might just start to freeze.

The house is scattered with the last of Wilson. Green army men are poised around the living room. His Tommy Mattel gun lies abandoned under the ottoman.

The clocks are ticking, a cacophony of time.

There is only one thing to do, it seems. They leave their coats on the rack. They both walk, knowing. They move through the satin dark, into the kitchen still cluttered with the aftermath of party. They open the back door, kick off their shoes and walk barefoot through the chilled grass. The shelter hatch squeals when Dean heaves it open, and there is that smell of boyhood and grass, the memory of latex and cigarettes.

Nellie has not been down here in ages, and when she sees the evidence of Wilson's clubhouse—the map of Oakleigh, the toys tucked behind cans—she cries again. Dean runs a hand along the drawing of their house with the words YOU ARE HERE.

Later, they will take the drawings down. They will burn the CDA posters: DISASTER MAY OCCUR HERE. GIVE ME SHELTER. They will store his bicycle, unpack his bag that was saved at the hospital. They will cry at the sight of his things: his secondhand goggles and CDA guide and inventory of shelter items, his first aid kit and "field guide." They will order a child-shaped coffin, begin the unthinkable task of planning a boy's funeral. They will donate his toys to the Salvation Army and board up the shelter forever. Dean will not shred his report— he will send it, in full, to the *Oakleigh Gazette*. He will quit his job. There will be more protests.

But for now, tonight, there is this. One cot, two people. They will not face this alone, they know. That is the only miracle of this night. There is the sound of another's breath. There is the weight and warmth of someone else's grief.

And Nellie dreams, though fitfully, of that papery light. A cord and bulb, tile floors, silk and fur in her arms. Then: the air raid siren. Store clerks pull blackout curtains over the windows, then return to the perfume counters, spray fragrant clouds into the air. But through the dream, there is that sense of searching for something. Nellie moves through home decor, through women's clothes. At the end of every corridor, she swears, there is a rustling. The faintest giggle and shuffle of shoes, a tousle of hair and binoculars peeking through the racks.

ACKNOWLEDGMENTS

I AM GRATEFUL TO so many people who have championed this project over the years! Many thanks to Brenda Peynado and Jamie Poissant, my teachers and mentors at the University of Central Florida MFA program. Thank you to my dear writing friends Rebecca Fox and Heather Orlando for encouraging me and reading countless drafts. You believed when I did not. Thank you for helping me continue. I want to thank Donovan Swift, Justin Brozanski, Kara Delemeester, Katherine Ervin, Adam Byko, and all others from the UCF MFA program who read this novel in an early (messy) form and provided invaluable feedback.

Thank you to Rachel Ekstrom and Jamie Chambliss at Folio. You fought relentlessly for this book, and I could not ask for a better team. And a sincere thank you to Maggie Auffarth—I know I owe you a great deal, and I'm eternally grateful that you helped my novel get seen.

Thank you to Robin Miura, Lynn York, and the entire team at Blair for selecting this novel. You have made my lifelong dream come true!

Thank you to Jake Wolff and Gina Ochsner for reviewing the manuscript before we embarked on the submission process.

My sincere gratitude to Nicole Mazzarella, who witnessed the birth of this project and encouraged the story in its infancy, when I was only nineteen at Wheaton College.

And as I am not a nuclear scientist, I have a great many sources to thank. *Atomic Family* is a work of fiction, and both the town of Oakleigh and the nuclear plant are fictive representations inspired by real places. Many texts were foundational for the research in this book: *Women Strike for Peace: Traditional Motherhood and Radical Politics in the 1960s* by Amy Swerdlow and *In the Shadow of the Bomb* by Silvan S. Schweber; *History of DuPont at the Savannah River Plant* by W. P. Bebbington; *The Savannah River Site at 50* by Mary Beth Reed, Mark

Swanson, Steve Gaither, Dr. J. W. Joseph, William Henry, Tracey Fe-
dor, and Barbara Smith Strack; "Deadly Legacy: Savannah River Site
Near Aiken One of the Most Contaminated Places on Earth" by Doug
Pardue (*Charleston Post and Courier*, May 21, 2017 [updated June 28,
2021]); "The Golden Age of Pharmacy" by Truman Lastinger (*Drug
Topics*, May 30, 2016); "That Others May Live: The Cold War Sacrifice
of Ellenton, South Carolina" by Samuel Ritchie (Master's thesis, Clemson University, 2009); *American Prometheus: The Triumph and Tragedy
of J. Robert Oppenheimer* by Kai Bird and Martin J. Sherwin; *Women
of the 1960s* by Sheila Hardy; *Cold War Comforts* by Tarah Brookfield;
*Haunted Plantations: Ghosts of Slavery and Legends of the Cotton King-
doms* by Geordie Buxton; *Uprooted*, directed by Sonja Curry-Johnson;
The Bomb Plant — 3 AM Nightmare from DC Bureau, by Bobbye Pyke;
and original declassified reports from the Health Physics department
of the Savannah River Plant, written by my grandfather James Henry
Horton, whose life and work inspired this book. Thank you to Wal-
ter Joseph for the in-depth interview, and thank you to Jon Coburn
for supplying original documents from the Women Strike for Peace
movement, including "Eleanor Garst—Draft of Letter to Accompany
Leaflet, 22 September 1961" from the Swarthmore College Peace Collection and "Halloween 1961—An Open Letter to the World's Women,
Eleanor Garst, 31 October 1961" from the archives at the State Historical Society of Wisconsin.

This novel does, of course, quote directly from original newspaper
articles, propaganda videos, and Civil Defense materials from the 1950s
and 1960s, such as "Survival under Atomic Attack," "Are Our Children in Danger?" "The Ground Observers' Guide," and "How to Spot
a Communist," among others. I am indebted to the Atomic Heritage
Foundation for their records, interview transcripts, and historical pres-
ervation. Thank you to Haley Horton for the science read. I have done
my best to demonstrate the atmosphere and mood of the Cold War in
this novel—any factual errors are my own.

Finally, thank you to John and Leia Horton for reading every teenaged project. You watched me try to write novels in high school, and
you supported me in this strange and wonderful literary pursuit. Dad,

thank you for telling me all those stories about life in Aiken and the Savannah River Plant. This novel would not exist without you and your story—and without Henry and his.

And to my husband, Mitchell: thank you for never doubting me. For making coffee on those long writing nights. For celebrating every small win and every big one. I love you more than words can say.